1

Two years had passed since the world as he knew it had become a vast and treacherous wasteland … two very long and lonely years. The survivors were sparse, almost nonexistent, and scattered throughout the world. Over time, a group of seven had assembled in the Houston area. Their goal was to travel east in search of any others who might have discovered a way to survive in the new wilderness, the new wastelands.

Drake Munroe was a forty-three-year-old mechanic who loved his life. He recalled coming home and turning the news on that fateful New Year's Day in 2026. He could still see the sweaty foreheads and resigned faces of the panicked news anchors telling their audience of the impending destruction. They announced that a large meteor had broken into more than fifty separate pieces and were all heading into the earth's atmosphere. They pinpointed the major locations that would suffer the greatest impact.

Drake looked outside his apartment window and saw a hysterical world racing around in search of a place to escape, but there was nowhere to escape to. Ten meteors were set to hit the continent of Asia, four would impact the center of Europe, seven each would slam both Africa and South

America. Another ten were aimed straight for the Pacific Ocean, seven for the Atlantic Ocean and three for the Indian Ocean. He saw that the final eight or nine would critically impact North and Central America.

His body began to tremble violently. In a subconscious effort to calm himself, he closed his eyes, took deep several breaths and then exhaled slowly while he pushed his dark brown, wavy hair back with his hands.

Drake began to realize that everything was he'd ever known was about to change in just a few hours. The earth would see the birth of new mountain ranges, new gorges, new bodies of water, along with extreme cold and punishing darkness. He didn't know how substantial the impact would be, or that those chain of events would bring about a new mini ice age. He did know that his life was hanging in the balance.

For days, Drake watched and listened as the meteor impacts killed millions and the violent earthquakes created a chain of events that killed millions more. Then, the tsunamis came and swept away entire coastal regions, urban and rural alike. He felt like he was staring into some bizarre science-fiction movie. The power grids shut down and Drake became isolated from any news of the outside world.

Soon, temperatures plummeted drastically and the sky became clouded both day and night with dust, smoke and acid rain. The nights were black and cold, freezing, subzero. The good days were dim and shadowy with temperatures rising only to near twenty degrees.

Drake felt the shifting of his isolated world and he barely escaped his apartment building as the walls around him collapsed fiercely into the streets below. Kicking for miles through rubble and debris, he eventually found a small brick house outside the city that had managed to remain intact despite the elements. Drake knew that staying there would most likely be the safest choice for his survival until others showed up to rescue him … but no one came to rescue him.

He spent his days bundling up in layers of clothing and searching for canned goods, bottled water, warm blankets and firewood, creating an arsenal of sustenance and protection. At night, he remained indoors. The darkness brought about the unknown and in this new brutal world, Drake, didn't want to come face to face with a hungry wild animal or a desperate survivor with a loaded gun. He watched as surviving zoo animals, once held in captivity, roamed freely. Some of the animals were able to withstand the frigid temperatures and some perished.

He attempted to get cars started with his mechanical knowhow but it proved hopeless. Even if the cars started, the debris from fallen buildings and cratered streets made them impossible to move. He even had an idea that he could somehow make the electrical grids work again. But now, he realized it would take an army of men with more knowledge of electronics than he did. Drake resigned himself to the fact he was now living in a hostile wasteland and had to treat it as such. It wasn't about living anymore. It was about his own survival and it seemed he adapted to the idea quickly. He had no other choice.

Drake spent his evenings writing in a journal, explaining what happened each day, from the dramatic to the mundane. He'd close his eyes and recall the blood-curdling screams of the dying masses, still fresh in his mind. He could still see the bodies scattered in the streets everywhere in this open graveyard.

Days, weeks and months had passed as Drake concentrated on doing what was necessary to sustain his life. Always self-reliant, he adapted and honed his survival skills.

After the first year, most of the human remains were eaten by the wild animals that were able to adapt to the temperatures. Bears, wolves, coyotes, lions and other notorious predators also found a way to survive in their surroundings and they flourished.

Drake came up with the idea to move east towards Florida and then further and further south or perhaps to head down through Mexico and into Central America. Without any real evidence, he believed moving closer to the equator would provide more favorable weather conditions. The tentative plan was put on hold since Drake was afraid to travel hundreds of miles in the snow by himself. He didn't know what hidden dangers might lie ahead.

In his spare time, he built a ham-radio from old parts he'd found from other broken radios. He decided it was time to see if anyone else was out there. The radio was small and only seemed to work some of the time. He always carried it with him, waiting to hear another human voice, wanting to know he wasn't the last man on earth, but all he heard was static and buzzing sounds.

After two long and lonely years of moving to the outskirts of Houston, he accidentally came upon a twenty-two-year-old girl named Porsha Miller, who had once been a young and beautiful, vibrant bartender in one of Houston's busiest nightclubs. She was barely alive when he found her lying there. She too was alone, living on canned foods and remaining inside unless absolutely necessary.

One day, when she had to trudge to the grocery store to stock up on bottled water, she accidentally slipped on the icy sidewalk and hit her head. By the time she woke up it was pitch dark and freezing. She managed to get up and attempted to make it back to her shelter but found herself too weak and confused to continue.

Hours later she tried to walk again but still felt muddled and frail. She wasn't able to locate the building she called home.

For several days, she sought shelter in any structure that would keep her warm and out of danger, eating and drinking what very little she could scrape together.

Drake found her sleeping on a bench inside a bus terminal, wrapped in several blankets and old newspapers. He could see she was suffering from malnutrition, dehydration and possible hypothermia. He asked, "Do you need help, miss?"

She mumbled softly, "I think I hit my head."

Drake leaned down and checked her head for injuries. He found some bruised swelling on the crown of her head. "I think you could use a little medical attention."

"I couldn't find my way back and it's so

cold in here."

"I have a safe place that you can go. I'll get you home."

Porsha whispered, "Thank you. It's so cold today. I didn't know how much longer I'd last in this cold."

He lifted her up and carried her back to his little brick house, slipping and sliding as he walked. It was there that he took care of her.

Eventually, months later, Porsha regained her strength and good health. She and Drake became good friends, almost like a father and daughter. They'd go about their daily routines happy to know they had someone else to talk to. But still, Drake wondered if there could be anyone else out there or were Porsha and himself all that was left. He speculated at the possibility that there could be someone like them, trying to connect with other survivors.

On a particularly brisk morning, Porsha left the house on her own to retrieve some store-bought logs. Drake remained in the house tinkering with his radio and other mechanical devices he'd been fooling with. While he was playing around with the radio, he received a strange transmission. It was from a faraway voice. The voice was interrupted often with static but he could tell it was a female voice telling him she was alone and scared. "Hello, is there anyone out there?"

Drake responded, "Yes, I'm here."

The voice stated, "I'm in Crystal River, in Florida. I'm scared and …"

Hers was the only voice he heard on that receiver. The transmission came through in February of that year. It was a short conversation, only revealing her whereabouts and nothing more. After two or three minutes her curious voice disappeared and a buzzing noise came across the radio waves. That's when he knew for certain there were others out there.

When Porsha returned to the house, he told her about the woman in Florida. She questioned it at first. She didn't know if he'd actually heard another voice or whether he'd wanted to hear one so badly that his mind created it. She asked, "What exactly did this woman say to you, Drake?"

"There was a lot of static but I'm sure she said she was in Florida, a town called Crystal River. I think that's on the west coast of the state. She told me she was alone and scared."

She inquired, "Is that all she said? Wasn't there anything else?"

"No, that's all. We lost communication after a few minutes."

Porsha pulled her dark hair into a ponytail as

she stated, "All that proves is that there's three people left alive on earth."

Drake sat silently. It was an uncomfortable silence. She could see he was thinking of a plan to fix the problem. She realized what he was about to say and before he could say it, she asserted, "No way, Drake. That's just crazy. I'm not risking my life and travelling all the way across the country to save one person from being alone."

"Why not?"

"That's crazy. It's only twenty degrees during the days, if we're lucky. There's bears and wolves and lions roaming everywhere. We'll die out there!"

Drake presented his argument. "I thought about this carefully. It can't be done alone but if two of us go ..."

"No! Not in a million years, Drake! I'm fine right here where I am."

Continuing to plan as if Porsha had agreed to go, Drake proposed, "We'll take supplies with us, plenty of supplies. I'm sure we can camp in old houses and buildings at night and travel only by day. I have plenty of guns and ammo to protect us from the animals."

Porsha leaned in and looked him in the eye. "Why? Why are you so dead set on going there to save one woman?"

"I also have a theory that the weather might get a little warmer if we move closer to the equator. It just seems like a logical thing to do."

She continued to stare him down and try to reason. "Why should we move on when we're doing just fine here?"

"We're not fine here. We're only surviving, Porsha."

"And if traveling around the country was so easy, why am I the only other person you've seen in two years?"

Drake thought for a minute and then said, "I guess I haven't found anyone else because I really haven't been looking."

Porsha's eyes welled up with tears. She said softly, "I can't do it, Drake. I love you to death but I won't go out there and kill myself in that wasteland. I survived all these years for a reason and I don't believe the reason was for me to go out in the cold and get killed."

Drake didn't know what else he could say to persuade Porsha to change her mind. She shook her head and walked away, signaling to Drake that the conversation was over. Porsha remained silent for the rest of the day.

Drake resigned himself to the fact he'd never be able to save the woman in Florida. For hours every day, he'd listened to his radio. He waited to hear her voice but it was always the buzzing and static. He figured he and the woman could no longer connect or perhaps she'd already passed away.

When April rolled around and he finally heard from her again. This time, the broadcast lasted almost ten minutes. She revealed that she was still alone and scared of what was waiting out there for her. She told him her name was Carolyn King and she used to be a high school teacher. Before the devastation, she was married to a wonderful man and they had three young daughters. Drake could hear the sorrow in her voice when she told him that she watched her husband and children die violently. He asked, "How are you keeping yourself safe? Where are you living?"

She responded, "I've been getting by in an old Speedy Mart convenience store. I have lots of food and water stored up."

"What're the temperatures in Florida? Is it warmer there than here?"

"Usually it climbs to around forty to forty-five degrees during the day. One day it even made it all the way up to fifty-five. At night it falls quickly to about ten below."

Drake mentioned, "It's a lot warmer than the conditions we've been living in." He asked, "Are you sure there's no one else out there? Have you even checked?"

"I haven't wandered too far from this place. I don't know what's out there and I'm afraid to find out."

"Oh Carolyn, I wish I could come to get to you but we're almost a thousand miles away from you. Cars don't work anymore and, even if they did, there's no gas left to make them run. It just seems impossible."

Porsha entered the room, stunned to hear the woman's voice coming over the airwaves. "She's a real person?"

Drake stated, "Of course she's a real person. You didn't believe me?"

Carolyn's voice announced, "I have to go now. I hear a banging on the wall outside. I don't know what it is."

Concerned, Drake asked, "Carolyn, do you have any weapons with you?"

"No, I don't. Well, just some small branches and logs I collected."

"I suggest you get out and find a few guns and bullets. You have to learn to protect yourself from whatever's out there."

The static got louder until it turned into one continuous buzzing again. Still stunned by Porsha's reaction to hearing Carolyn's voice, Drake turned to her and questioned, "You didn't believe she was real? You think I'm crazy?"

Porsha calmly explained, "I never said you were crazy. I just thought you were so desperate to hear another person that your mind might have invented her voice somehow. I'm sorry for doubting you, Drake."

Drake put the radio in his pocket and left for the store to pick up some bottled water. He didn't utter another word to Porsha for the rest of the day and the next day. He was disappointed to find out she didn't think he was of sound mind after all the time they'd spent together.

The days continued with the same routine as every other day, opening a can of food, drinking a bottle of water, keeping warm and avoiding contact with any unknown hazards outside the safety of their walls.

July brought about another earthquake. This one measured higher than the usual. Porsha and Drake took shelter and prayed their structure would remain intact. The ground shook for several minutes before it all became still. They checked the area for any damage. There was none. Then, the aftershocks followed for several weeks.

After a long period of silence, Drake received a third transmission from Carolyn in

September. This discussion lasted two and a half minutes, just long enough for her trembling voice to tell him, "I was attacked. I went out at night and I shouldn't have. It all happened a little over two months ago."

"Are you alright, Carolyn?"

"I'm doing much better now. At first, I thought I was going to die. It took time and a lot of prayers but I pulled through."

Drake asked, "Do you know what attacked you? How did you get away?"

"It was very dark but I believe it might have been a bobcat or a cougar …"

Suddenly, the static came through and Carolyn was gone again. He never had time to find out if she'd acquired a gun to protect herself from the dangers.

Drake informed Porsha of the third call but she didn't want to hear about it. She was determined to stay in one place, one safe place.

Drake and Porsha lived there in Houston for nearly a year and a half before they came upon any other survivors.

2

Drake and Porsha kept a calendar on the kitchen wall to keep aware of the days and the seasons, even though every season had become the same … winter.

In July of 2029, they woke to the sound of another human voice in the distance outside their home.

From about three-hundred yards away, the echo of a female voice hollered, "Hello! Is there anyone around?"

Drake leapt out of his bed and looked out the window. He saw a woman dressed in heavily layered clothing and a stocking mask over her face. Porsha began bundling up when she heard the friendly voice calling out, "Hello! Is there anyone around? I see smoke coming out of your chimney. I know you're in there."

After they hurried to the front porch, Drake waved his arm in the air and shouted, "Over here! We're over here!"

The woman spotted them, jumped up and down and waved back. She started moving toward them, lugging two large sacks behind her. As she got closer, she began running until she reached the front yard. She questioned, "Are you friendly? Is it alright if I come inside?"

Porsha smiled and welcomed the woman with open arms. "Oh my God, of course you can come inside. You must be freezing."

Drake went into the living room and put

more logs in the fireplace. The woman took off her many layers of clothing as the room warmed up. Drake could see she was a beautiful dark-haired woman in her early thirties who had been battling the elements for God knows how long. Porsha made her a hot cup of coffee and sat with her.

She introduced herself, "My name is Katie Bradshaw. I was a great nurse but now I'm not. Not much need for great nurses these days." Katie laughed at herself.

Porsha responded, "Well, I'm Porsha and this is Drake. I've been living here with him for a year and a half."

Drake asked, "Where the hell did you even come from?"

Katie took a quick sip of her coffee before answering. "Texas City. I was in Texas City when the impact happened. I was on duty at the hospital when we got the word. I still can't believe I got out of there alive."

Drake questioned, "Texas City? Isn't Texas City on Galveston Bay?"

"It used to be but not anymore. Not after all of the floods happened. Now, Galveston Bay is covering most of Texas City. The water kept rising, so I had to move as far west of the city as I could and it's still beachfront property." Katie laughed at herself again.

Porsha got up and refilled Katie's coffee mug before asking, "Have you ever seen any other people out there?"

"No, not a soul but I did spend nearly a year traveling to the south. I was hoping and searching to find a warmer climate."

Drake glanced over at Katie and questioned, "You were alone?"

"All by myself."

Drake was curious. "And what did you find there? Why did you come back?"

"The weather was slightly, only slightly milder, I'd say about ten degrees warmer as I moved further south from Corpus Christi and into Mexico but then I had to turn back. I didn't have a choice."

Porsha asked, "Why? If it was warmer, why would you turn back?"

Katie took a sip and then set her cup on the table before she delivered her disturbing news. She bowed her head for a moment and took a breath before she said, "I had to turn back because, by the time I got to the mountains in Monterrey, I saw that there was no more Mexico and probably no more Central America."

Drake probed, "What do you mean, there was no more Mexico?"

"I mean the Atlantic and Pacific Oceans

came together as one large body of water. All the land between North and South America is under water. I saw it with my own eyes. After Monterrey there's nothing but ocean waters for as far as the eye can see."

Drake stood up and paced the floor. "I knew the landscape would change but I never dreamed it would change so drastically."

Katie shrugged and said, "Well, thanks to me, now you know."

Porsha muttered, "Scary."

Drake said, "I hope you know you can stay here with us for as long as you want. Our home is your home, Katie."

Katie smiled and said, "Thank you. Thank both of you. I'd love to stay here with you until my next trip."

Drake stopped pacing the floor and queried, "Next trip? What next trip?"

"Oh, I'm still going to move farther south. I just have to change my route. I'm going to find out if Florida's still on the map."

Drake blurted, "It is still there. I know it is."

"How do you know for sure?"

"We've been in contact with a woman there. Her name is Carolyn King and she lives in Crystal River, Florida."

Katie was shocked. "You've been able to

talk to a woman in Florida? How?"

Proudly, Drake said, "I built a small radio, a transmitter, and we somehow connected three times now, but the calls have been months apart from each other."

Katie smiled. She appeared excited. "That means I can get to Florida. I don't have to worry if it's there or not."

Porsha stopped their conversation with her hand slamming down on the coffee table. "What's wrong with the two of you?"

Katie asked, "I don't understand. Why do you seem so angry?"

"I'm angry because you're both insane. You don't know what's between us and Florida. Why would you risk your lives trudging over a thousand miles of ice and snow to find a climate that's only a few degrees warmer than this one?"

Drake attempted to explain his position to Porsha. "It could be better for us. If the weather is warm enough, we could possibly grow some of our own food, maybe even try to domesticate some of the animals that made it through. You know, the canned goods won't last forever."

Katie looked at Porsha and said, "He has a good point."

Porsha angrily shook her head, crossed her arms and walked away from the conversation and into the kitchen. Drake and Katie looked at each other. They both knew the other one had the same burning desire to move toward Florida, but neither one had a clue on how to convince Porsha it was a good thing.

As the days moved forward, Katie became the third member of the household, helping with every detail of their daily lives and becoming very close to Drake.

One night in August of 2029, Katie retired early. Drake and Porsha sat in the living room close to the fire.

Porsha decided to speak her mind. "I see the way you look at her."

Drake lowered his brows and asked, "What are you talking about, Porsha?"

She continued, "I see the way you look at Katie and the way she looks back at you. I know you're in love with her, Drake."

He stood up and corrected her. "I'm not in love with Katie. She's a friend, a good friend, and the family dynamics have changed in the world, just in case you haven't noticed."

Porsha stated, "Oh, I don't have a problem with it if you are in love with her, I just wish you'd admit it to yourself."

Drake pondered what she said. He didn't

respond. He stared into the fire as Porsha got up and retired for the evening. Drake sat on the sofa for several hours, writing in his journal, before he too got up and went to bed.

Almost a year after the last, in September, a transmission came through on Drake's radio. It was Carolyn's voice again. Porsha and Katie gathered around to hear what new information she had to report.

She muttered, "Hello, Drake, it's Carolyn. Are you there?"

"I'm here. I'm here."

Carolyn explained, "I've been trying to get through to you for a year but I've had no luck at all. I'm glad I finally got you."

Drake responded, "I'm glad too. It's always good to hear your voice. Since the last time we talked another woman has joined us. Her name's Katie and she was a nurse."

With a hint of sadness in her voice, Carolyn replied, "I'm happy to know there's more survivors out there. Sadly, I'm still here alone. I'm so very alone."

Drake bowed his head when he sensed her loneliness. He recalled how lonely and frightening his life was before Porsha and Katie came along. His heart was heavy.

She announced, "I finally moved out of the

convenience store and into a new place. I'm living in the old firehouse now. It's nice. I feel secure and protected here."

He responded, "That's a good thing. You have to keep yourself safe."

She asked, "Why?"

Drake was surprised with her response. He wasn't sure what to say. Instead, Carolyn continued. "Why do I need to stay safe? I'm here and alone. There's no one else. I'm probably going to die here alone. So, what's the difference if I die tonight or ten years from now. No one will be here to mourn my passing."

Katie looked at Porsha and Porsha looked at Drake with a glimmer of sadness in her eyes. He stated, "Maybe you won't be alone forever. Look at what happened to me."

There was a silence. Then, they could hear the woman crying. "I guess you just got very lucky, Drake."

The sorrow filled voice became static and buzzing again. Katie, Drake and Porsha looked at each other but didn't speak. They didn't know what to say. No words could help the poor soul trapped in Crystal River.

Later Porsha sat next to Katie on the living room sofa. She appeared sad and preoccupied. Katie asked, "Still thinking about Carolyn?"

Porsha confessed, "I can't stop thinking about her situation. She's out there with no one. She was crying. The tone of her voice was so defeated. I feel so helpless."

Katie put her arm on Porsha's shoulder and comforted her. "We're a long way from Carolyn, a thousand miles and, like you mentioned, we don't know what lies between us and Florida. It could be more ocean like what happened with me in Mexico or it could be something even worse. For all we know, the state of Florida could be an island right now. I respect the fact that you don't want to do this. Fear of the unknown is the greatest fear there is. I don't want you to be afraid."

Porsha smiled at Katie, "Thanks. I needed to hear that."

"Put it out of your head. There's no use worrying about something you can't control. It'll just give you gray hair like it did with me." Katie laughed at herself.

Porsha grinned at Katie's joke and agreed, "You're right, Katie. I can't control it. None of us have control anymore."

Drake sat in the dining room eavesdropping in on the conversation, contemplating if his feelings for Katie were real. He took a sip on his coffee and opened his journal. He flipped through his last few entries and scanned through them carefully. Then he pulled out a pen and began writing his daily events and thoughts.

3

In November 2029, Drake, Porsha and Katie were at the grocery store gathering the last of the canned goods and bottled water. The store was now officially cleaned out. They knew they'd have to start traveling to the other grocery store that was five blocks further away.

It was a blustery day. The cold winds were blowing and temperatures were around zero. Katie grabbed her sack of goods and started out the front door when she spotted an silver-haired woman, who looked much older than her actual years, walking down the street with a teenage boy alongside her. She watched as they spoke to each other and slowly sauntered along, almost seeming nomadic. Katie called out to Drake and Porsha, "Guys! Get out here! Hurry up!"

Drake and Porsha ran to the front of the store and saw the strangers. They observed them for a moment before Drake called out, "Hey! Where are you going?"

The woman and boy, startled at first, turned and smiled. They saw the threesome standing in front of the store and walked toward them. Drake walked cautiously into the parking lot and greeted them. "I'm Drake Munroe." He pointed. "That's Porsha Miller."

Porsha lifted her hand, smiled and waved. Drake pointed again and said, "And over there is Katie Bradshaw."

He looked over and saw Katie waving and smiling too. The woman approached closer. "I'm Naomi Zappa, and this young man is Granger Thomas. We left Austin a long time ago. We've been drifting … well, it seems like it's been forever and a day."

Katie walked up to Naomi and stated, "Why don't you two help us get these supplies back to the house. You can get warm there and I'll make dinner tonight for everyone."

Naomi appreciatively responded, "Oh, that would be nice but we don't want to eat what little food you may have."

Drake laughed. "We have plenty of food. It's just good to see two other people who survived the devastation."

A curious smile appeared on Naomi's face. "Survived? Did we really survive the meteors or are we just prolonging the fact that we're all going to be casualties too?" Then, the woman bowed her head in sorrow.

Granger took the woman by the hand and

said, "Come on, Naomi. Everything's going to be better now. We found other living people, a warm place and a meal. That's a whole lot more than we had twenty minutes ago. Maybe things are about to change for us."

Naomi grinned and stared at the boy. "I love your positive attitude, Granger. It's the only thing that's kept this fifty-two-year-old body going for all these years."

Granger smiled before he grabbed some sacks from the store. Naomi felt weak and tired. She only grabbed one sack. She wasn't sure how much more weight she could handle. They followed the others to the brick house.

When they arrived at the house, Drake built a fire and the house warmed up quickly. Katie and Porsha went into the kitchen and started opening cans of food. Naomi wanted to help prepare the meal but she was much too exhausted. She removed her layered jackets and gloves before she collapsed on the sofa. Drake and Granger sat on the sofa on the opposite side of the room and watched Naomi doze off into a deep sleep.

Granger commented, "She's been so tired lately. I don't think I've actually seen her sleep a full night in a year."

Drake asked, "She said you came from the Austin area. That's quite a few miles from here, a hundred and fifty miles. How long have you two been wandering?"

"We left there a year ago. We had to get out of there. The earthquakes kept opening the roads up and swallowing buildings. Naomi said it just wasn't safe anymore. There were a lot of animals that got out when the zoo collapsed. But I think that the cold killed some of them."

Drake questioned, "How did you survive out there for all that time? So many things that could have happened to you."

Granger stated, "You have no idea. We were chased by bears, hyenas and wolves. Luckily, I'm a pretty good shot with a gun. I'm only fourteen but I'm a crack shot."

"You ran into a lot of wild animals?"

Granger added, "Oh yeah. Like I said, the zoo animals and the animals that were already out there are doing well and they multiplying fast. We also had to find cover every time the acid rain came. That stuff burns your skin."

Drake looked over again at Naomi, sleeping as if she hadn't slept in years. He smiled at Granger and whispered, "I think we should let her sleep and we'll save some dinner for her for when she wakes up later on."

Granger whispered back, "Good idea. She needs the sleep more than she needs the food right now. She's a good woman, Drake."

Drake grinned and rubbed his hand on the top of Granger's head. "I know she is. I just met her and I already know that."

By December of that year, Naomi recouped a lot of her strength and she and Granger had settled into the red brick house with the others. It was tight quarters in the fifteen hundred square feet they had to work with.

Porsha and Naomi shared one bedroom, Drake and Granger shared a second bedroom and Katie took a small room off the kitchen and turned it into a third bedroom. The group of five found they were beginning to act as a family unit instead of total strangers.

Right around December 24th, Drake received a transmission from Carolyn. Elated to know that she was still alive, he gathered the others around to listen in. He remembered the day because the first thing he said to her when they spoke was, "Merry Christmas Carolyn."

She hadn't been keeping track of the days like Drake so she was completely caught off guard when he gave his greeting. She asked, "Christmas? It's Christmas?"

"It will be tomorrow."

There was a brief silence. Then, they could

hear Carolyn sobbing. Katie questioned, "What's the matter, Carolyn? It sounds like you're crying. Why are you so sad?"

"I'm still alone. I'm still alone. I have no one here to share anything with."

Katie looked at Drake. Drake turned and gave the others a glance. Everyone had a deeply concerned look on their face. Katie asked, "And you haven't seen anyone?"

Carolyn responded, "I try not to go out very often. I only go out when I need supplies. I'll get enough for a month and then I'll stay inside until it's time to go again. I've was attacked by two Florida panthers in the past and I don't want to experience that again."

Katie tried to explain, "If you don't go out each day and you just stay locked in that firehouse all the time, how will you know if anyone else is out there looking for you? We're all together by chance. Our meetings were all by chance."

Carolyn replied, "You're right Katie. I know you're right. I just have to get myself motivated and get out there every day."

Drake stepped forward and stated, "That sounds like a good idea. Just make sure you have some kind of protection. Did you get any guns like I asked you too?"

"Yes, I emptied an old pawn shop that was

just a block away. I have four or five handguns and boxes and boxes of bullets."

Drake then added, "Good. If you see the panthers or any other wildlife that could be a possible threat, shoot to kill. Eventually, you'll find other survivors. I'm believing more and more each day that there's more people out there, all scattered around, waiting to find someone or maybe even to be found."

Carolyn's tone didn't sound so sad anymore. "You're a good man, Drake. I don't know how I would have gotten through these past two years without your voice to guide me. You're like the voice of an angel."

The transmission ended with the usual abruptness of static and buzzing. After the call, everyone appeared a bit melancholy.

Katie tried to lighten the mood by putting up some old Christmas decorations she had found. She and Granger decorated the house to give it a warmer feel.

Drake poured each person a glass of wine to make a toast at midnight. They sat around the living room with their beverages, watching the fire. Drake stood up and made a toast, "To family. We may not be a traditional family but we are family. And to all missing friends who aren't as lucky as we are … to Carolyn King."

Everyone raised their glasses and repeated the toast, "To Carolyn King."

4

The following February brought about a great deal of change to the five survivors' daily lives. It was a cold morning when Drake and Granger decided to head out and chop down a few trees, pulling a homemade sled behind them. The firewood was getting low and the temperatures had plunged even colder than usual.

They walked about a mile to an old farm where the house was only partially standing. Drake handed Granger the axe and suggested, "Why don't you cut the first one down?"

Granger took the axe and hit the base of the fifteen-foot tree with all his might. Drake saw that Granger was getting the hang of it quickly. He said, "I'm going to check the farmhouse to see if there's anything inside that we could use." Drake walked to the farmhouse.

Granger continued taking whacks at the tree until it fell over, making a thunderous noise. He then chopped the tree into smaller pieces. Suddenly, when Granger turned around, he saw a pack of five wolves standing about forty feet away.

He stopped. He froze. He wasn't sure if he

should run or if he should scream for help or if he should start swinging the axe at them. He was confused.

He looked toward the farmhouse but didn't see Drake anywhere. The wolves moved a few feet closer. Granger's breathing became more rapid and noticeable. He felt as if his beating heart was going to burst out of his chest.

He backed up a few feet and the wolves stepped forward a few feet, growling and snarling at him. Granger looked at the farmhouse again, over two hundred feet away, contemplating if he could outrun the wolves. Abruptly, he turned and ran. The wolves did the same. He dropped the axe and let out a desperate scream, "Drake! Drake! Please! Help me! Help me!"

Drake heard the distressed screams and came to the front of the house where he saw the wolves jump onto Granger and knock him over. He was surrounded as the first one jumped on top of him.

Drake was too far away to get to Granger in time. He became frantic. A second wolf, bearing its fangs, jumped on Granger. He fought and struggled to protect his face with his hands. He screamed but that didn't seem to make much of a difference to the hungry animals.

Suddenly, gunshots rang out! A bullet hit

one of the wolves and it fell over. Another bullet hit a second wolf. It too fell next to Granger. The rest of the pack scattered and ran from the sound. Drake continued to race towards the boy as he heard a loud shout, "Woohoo!"

They saw a tall man on the other side of the field holding a rifle and dancing around in circles. It was his victory dance.

Thanks to the new stranger, Granger was unharmed, except for a few scratches on his hands. He stood up as Drake approached. They watched the man in the distance waving his rifle as he kept dancing in a circle. Granger commented, "He looks like he's going to be high maintenance." Drake nodded in agreement.

The man came running to them, dressed like a cowboy with a bandana tied around the lower half of his face. "Hello there, gentlemen, I'm Zack, Zack Strickland. Boy, I sure am pleased to see the two of you!"

Not as enthusiastically, "I'm Drake and this is Granger."

Granger walked up to the stranger and shook his hand. "That was amazing! You're amazing! You saved my life."

Zack removed the bandana from his face and said, "All in a day's work, young man. I saw you were in trouble, so I shot."

Drake interrupted, "Anyway, are you here alone?"

"Why yes, I am."

"We live in a small house about a mile from here. There's five of us living. If you want, we can provide you with some food and shelter and good conversation."

Zack was humbled. "That would be really nice. Why, you're the first people that I've seen in years."

Drake asked, "Could you help us load up the firewood, Zack?"

Zack looked around and pointed at the two dead wolves. "What about them?"

"What about them?"

"What are you going to do with them?"

Drake appeared perplexed, "Do with them? I'm not sure I know what you mean."

Zack stated, "Let's load them up on the sled. That's a lot of meat."

Granger and Zack stared at each other. Zack, asked, "Don't tell me you don't hunt for food. You live out of cans?"

Drake grinned, sort of embarrassed. "That's what we do and it's all worked out pretty well so far, Zack."

Zack wouldn't hear of it. He helped them load the wolves onto the sled. When they returned to the brick house, the women were introduced to him. He took the wolves' carcasses behind the house in a small shed where he skinned them and cut them up. That night, everyone realized how much they'd missed the taste of fresh meat cooked on an open flame.

It didn't take long until Zack, who called himself the Gunslinger, was sitting around telling his story to everyone. Porsha, who loved what she saw in Zack, started the conversation. "So, where did you come from?"

"San Antonio! Best city in the world. Well it was the best city in the world. Just isn't the same anymore. Since the blast San Antonio's lost some of its appeal."

Katie questioned, "Have you been traveling very long?"

"Why, I left San Antonio a couple months after it happened. I've been traveling due east since then. I didn't want to go west, like in the saying. The Rockies are a bitch and I didn't want to go it alone. So, I came this way and, lucky for me I did, 'cos I found all of you."

Drake and Naomi were a little put off by his "living on the prairie" expressions as he continued with his story. "I left San Antonio and came down Interstate 10. I figured that would be the easiest route east since it goes all the way to Jacksonville,

Florida. I stopped in a little town called Harwood. I found a barn and I moved in there for almost two years. That's when I started hunting for my own food. I killed deer, bear and coyote. I dug my own well, so I had plenty of water, but I was alone the whole time."

Porsha asked, "If it was so good there, why did you leave Harwood?"

"The well finally dried up and the food was getting scarce. I knew it was time to move on. So, I headed down the interstate again and found another town named Glidden. I pretty much did the same thing there."

Drake asked, "And you never saw anyone else in all that time?"

"Not a single soul."

Katie bowed her head. "Nobody."

"I'll tell you what. If there are survivors out there in the world, they're keeping hidden pretty well."

Naomi interjected, "I'm just happy you were there when Granger was attacked. I couldn't imagine losing my little man."

"I know one thing for sure," Granger said. "I'll never go anywhere without a gun again."

Zack gave Granger a reassuring gaze before he continued. "Naomi, I just did what any decent man would do. Heck, I'm nobody special. I'm just an ordinary guy."

Naomi giving a maternal grin, gently putting her hand on top of his hand, and whispering, "Well thank you, Zack."

Porsha asked, "What happened in Glidden? Why did you pick and leave there?"

"Same thing, food ran out, water ran out. So I hoofed it down the highway again. I was on the road for almost six months. That's when I found Drake and Granger."

As the next month passed, Drake and the others observed that Porsha and Zack were getting closer. At first, they noticed harmless flirting back and forth. Then, they were holding hands and sneaking kissing. Zack and Porsha had become a couple. Drake was happy to see that Porsha had finally connected with someone.

The cramped quarters were becoming even tighter. Drake thought it might be time to move on to a bigger place.

By April, another transmission had come through. Drake heard static but then, he heard Carolyn's voice coming through loud and clear. He checked around the house and saw no one else was there. He turned his attention back to the radio and his distant friend.

"Drake, are you there?"

"Yes Carolyn, I'm here. I can hear you."

She giggled a little and said, "Do you realize we've been talking to each other for more than two years and I don't even know what you look like and vice-versa?"

Drake realized she was right. He grinned. "Well, I'm about five eleven. I weigh about one-eighty, I have dark brown hair, with a little gray coming in, and dark brown eyes. I guess my golden tan has faded over the years." He laughed. "What about you?"

"I'm five seven, thirty-five years old. I have long red hair and hazel eyes. I weigh a lot less than I used to and I'm afraid my amazing tan has also seen better days."

Drake could see she was in a very good mood, very positive and motivated to joke around. He'd never heard this side of her. He asked, "Where are you now?"

She replied, "I'm sitting at the window in the third floor of my fire station staring at what used to be the Gulf of Mexico."

"What do you mean by used to be the Gulf of Mexico?"

"I guess that the meteor's impact and the earthquakes somehow created a mountain range right down the middle of it, high mountains, very high mountains."

Drake confided, "This new world we're living in, it barely resembles the one we lived in a few years ago. So many things have changed. So much destruction."

She agreed. "Nothing here will ever be the same. We just have to continue to find new ways to adapt and cope."

He commented, "I'd say, considering the unbelievable circumstances, we've done a pretty good job of adapting so far."

"Agreed. Just look at you. You've actually created a family out of what wasn't there before. By the way, how are your friends? Is everyone getting along?"

"Everyone's doing well. We had a new man join us. His name is Zack. He saved Granger's life from a pack of hungry wolves."

Carolyn gasped, "Oh, my lord! Is Granger alright?"

"Granger's just fine and becoming quite the hardworking and responsible young man. I only wish you could meet him. I wish you could meet all of them."

Carolyn became sad again. "I do too. I hear your voices and imagine what you all look like. I think of you when I have to find supplies. I pretend you're all with me and I'm safe. It's how I manage with this reality I've been thrown into."

Drake watched as the others filtered into the house while he was communicating with Carolyn. He kept looking at them as they whispered quietly to each other and grinned and chuckled. He was unaware of what was going on. "Carolyn, could you hold on for one tiny second."

"Of course, Drake."

Suspiciously, Drake turned his attention toward his housemates and asked, "Okay, what's going on around here. Why does everyone look like they're guilty of something that they're not telling me? What's all the whispering under your breath and giggling about?"

Katie, still with a big grin on her face, stepped up to the radio and said, "Hi, Carolyn, it's Katie. We just had a meeting outside. A meeting without Drake. We understand our biggest problem is that our house isn't large enough to accommodate all six people anymore."

Carolyn questioned, "Does that mean you're going to leave the little brick house I've pictured in my mind over and over?"

"It looks like we have to."

"Where will you go? You've been living in there for such a long time."

Katie, smiling and staring at Drake, said, "I'm moving. I don't know about anyone else but I decided I'm moving east to a place called Crystal River, Florida."

She watched Drake's stunned reaction and heard Carolyn gasp and then begin to weep. Zack stepped up and said, "Hello Carolyn. My name is Zack Strickland. I just joined this little family two months ago, and I do believe I'm in love with our sweet Porsha."

Carolyn's gentle voice came through, "Oh, that's wonderful Zack. I'm so happy and excited for the two of you."

Zack continued, "I just wanted to let you know that, after a little bit of arm-twisting, Porsha and I decided we'll be joining Katie on that trip. Yee-haw!"

Drake was astounded to find out Porsha and Zack wanted to go to Florida with Katie. He thought back to the endless arguments he and Porsha had over the subject. Next, Granger stepped up and said, "Hi Carolyn, it's Granger."

Carolyn's heart felt like it was melting when she heard the young man's voice. She responded, "Hello Granger. Drake told me about those wolves. I'm so glad to know you're doing alright."

He continued, "I do believe Naomi and I are moving to Crystal River with the other, if it's okay with you."

"What do you think, Granger? I better get to

see you and Naomi. I can't believe this is really happening."

Granger mentioned, "That only leaves one other person to make this unanimous." He turned and glanced at Drake.

Carolyn waited to hear Drake's voice. He put his mouth closer to the radio and shouted, "Hell yeah!"

Before the call ended Drake and Katie received directions to Carolyn's exact location once they got to Crystal River. Getting to Crystal River, Florida, was going to be the challenge.

Drake asked her to keep in closer contact with them if at all possible. He told her it would take a very long time before they got to her. He figured the transmissions would get a little clearer and more frequent as the journeyed farther east and closer to her.

During the following few weeks, the gang of six packed supplies, tents, firewood, first aid kits, tools and weapons. Drake and Granger built two large sleds to pull everything they were taking. It would be Drake's last transmission from the Houston area in May 2030 when he told Carolyn they were pulling out and on their way.

Katie, Naomi and Granger pulled the lighter sled over the slick and icy roads. Zack, Porsha and

Drake pulled the heavier one. Each person was confident they could make it to Florida but each one was also afraid of the unknown that lie ahead and the new landscape they'd have to face for almost a thousand miles. Drake laughed when Zack made an announcement as they were pulling out. "Goodbye forever, Houston, Texas. Hello again, Interstate 10! Woohoo!"

5

It was a slow-moving caravan over the ice- and snow-covered interstate. The roads themselves proved to be their greatest obstacles. It took them considerably extra time maneuvering around useless vehicles and old cars pileups, splits in the pavement and large boulders created from the blast.

They seemed to be getting closer to Carolyn by an average of three miles each day. They would basically get on the road as soon as the darkness became dimness with gray skies. By the time night rolled around, they'd find shelter in old structures or even pitch tents and camp when there was no other choice.

Camping was tricky because they had to build fires large enough to keep everyone warm throughout the night. The fire also served as a means to keep the nocturnal predators away from their camp. Zack, Katie or Drake would take turns keeping watch.

After the first week on the road, they came upon a small town. The tiny wooden sign that was posted on the road read "Welcome to Cove, Pop. 610". They didn't see 610 people. It was simply another desolate ghost town. Drake managed to find a small farmhouse with a well and a barn that was withering but still intact.

Katie and Drake went to the nearest grocery store to pick up some supplies. As they walked through the store, they noticed that many of the shelves were almost empty. Katie said, "This isn't right. There should be more canned goods in a town with no people." Katie glanced around the store but saw no one.

Drake agreed, "Someone else took the food. There's someone else in this town. There's another survivor here somewhere."

Drake and Katie took small handguns from their coat pockets and crept quietly around the store, checking each aisle carefully. Drake turned a corner near what was once the butcher's counter and heard Katie gasp, "Drake."

He walked across the store towards her voice. When he got to the dairy aisle, he jumped when he saw Katie standing there with a terrified look on her face. Her revolver was on the ground and a man was standing behind her holding a knife to her throat.

The man pressed the knife against her neck and warned, "You better drop the gun, mister, or I'm going to have to use this."

Katie whispered, "Don't do it, Drake. Don't listen to him."

Drake was petrified and confused. He bent down slowly and laid his gun on the floor. Katie lowered her head in disappointment. The man said, "Now kick the gun toward me, and I don't want any funny moves."

Drake did as the man asked. Just then, he heard a transmission coming through on the radio is his pocket. Carolyn's voice said, "Hello, Drake. Are you there?"

The stranger became progressively angrier. "What do you have in your pocket and whose voice is that?"

Drake cautiously pulled the radio out of his pocket and showed it to the stranger. "It's a radio I built a few years ago. We've been in contact with a woman in Florida. We're traveling there to find her and help her. Can I answer her?"

The man kept the knife steady at Katie's neck. She said nothing. He told Drake, "Go ahead. I want to hear what she has to say."

Drake held the radio to his face and said,

"Carolyn, it's Drake. I'm here."

Carolyn responded, "Where have you been? I haven't heard from you in weeks."

"We're still in Texas. Like I told you before, it's going to be a long time before we get to you. It may take a year or more."

She added, "Drake, I'm scared. I heard so many animals outside the other day, more than I ever heard before."

"We're moving as fast as we can. You have to understand we're trudging through ice and snow on foot."

"I know, Drake. I'm sorry I sound this way, so insistent, but now that I know you're coming, the days seem to be moving even slower that they did before."

Drake responded, "That's understandable, Carolyn."

Suddenly Carolyn's voice was drowned out by the hissing static. Drake knew, as always, that was the end of their conversation. He put the radio back in his pocket as the stranger watched carefully. Katie asked the man, "Why are you doing this to us? We're not a threat to you."

The man commented, "If you're here to take the supplies I need to live on, then you are a threat to me."

She turned and faced the man, who only

appeared to be in his mid-twenties. "But there's lots of supplies. We even have another man with us that hunts wolves and deer."

"You mean there's more people than just the two of you?"

Drake mentioned, "There's four more. We left Houston together, and, like I said, we're moving to Florida."

The stranger was perplexed, "You're going all that way for one woman? That doesn't make a whole lot of sense to me."

Katie blurted, "The climate is better there. The temperatures are ten to fifteen degrees warmer than they are here."

The man lowered his blade and bowed his head. "I'm really sorry, folks. I was only doing what I thought I needed to do."

Katie asked, "Why would you think we were a danger to you?"

The man made a staggering statement to Drake and Katie. "Well, because you're not the first people to come through here. There were others who came in a took a lot of my canned goods. I got a good look at them. I think they were crazy and almost ravenous."

Drake asked for clarification. "There were others? You saw other survivors? How many of them were there?"

"I saw three. A man and two women. I call them the rain people."

Katie tilted her head and questioned, "Why would you call them that?"

"On account of their skin. I saw their skin. They must have been caught in a real bad acid rain storm. Their skin was red and blistered. It looked mighty painful."

Drake inquired, "How long ago was it that they came through here?"

"Couple months ago. They had a couple rifles and big knives. I stayed hidden until I knew they were gone. I just figured they turned around and came back for more."

Drake glanced around at the store for a moment. Then he said, "I'm Drake Munroe and this is Katie Bradshaw." He extended his hand to the man to shake.

The stranger replied, "Good to know you. I'm Tony Morales and Cove is my hometown. It was my hometown, anyway."

Drake asked, "Would you like to come with us to Florida?"

Tony thought it over. He looked around the store as if he was about to say his final goodbye. "If you don't think the others would mind. I'd like to leave this place behind me."

Katie smiled and said, "I don't think they'd

mind a bit."

The three walked out of the grocery store and back to the farmhouse. As they walked, Tony asked, "You said you have another guy that hunts for fresh meat?"

Drake answered, "His name is Zack. He calls himself the Gunslinger ... and he takes a little getting used to."

Katie asked, "What did you used to do for a living, Tony?"

"I was a police officer, fourth year, very small police force, only three of us. But I liked my job because I used to believe in justice. I watched six-hundred and nine people die in this town. I saw them die violently when the impact hit. Now, what kind of justice is that?"

The three returned to the farmhouse and introduced Tony. Drake also told the others that Carolyn called while they were away. Zack took a few hours with Granger to set some traps and catch a few rabbits to cook for dinner. Tony enjoyed the first actual meal he'd had in years. As everyone enjoyed dinner, Tony stated, "Well, this is all just great! I'm eating a good hearty meal with some real fine people."

Drake and Katie saw that everyone was getting along well. They asked Tony to tell his story about the rain people. He told it and watched the faces of the others as they realized there were even more unexpected dangers in the world.

Two days later, the sleds were loaded with supplies and they were on the road again, always anticipating what problems might lie ahead.

Naomi appreciated Tony's presence. He'd help pull the sled most of the time which gave her weakened body more time to rest. Naomi realized she wasn't built for a trip like the one she was now a part of. She had constant bouts with depression and many physical problems that usually slowed the team down. But still, in spite of everything, she believed she was a fighter and continued on, no matter the circumstance. Granger continued to keep a close eye on her.

6

Almost a month had passed before the seven survivors made their way into Beaumont, where they planned to stay and rest for a few days. Zack and Porsha found a small neighborhood with some small homes still standing. They moved into one house with Granger and Naomi. Drake, Katie and Tony moved into the house next door.

The temperatures during that week, for some unknown reason, were warmer than usual. Drake watched the thermometer rise to thirty-six degrees at one point.

Everyone fell into their usual roles. Zack and Granger would hunt or trap for dinner. Drake, Katie and Tony went to convenience and grocery stores to pick up supplies. Porsha and Naomi stayed at the houses to clean and prepare everyone's meals and beds for the night.

As they walked through the old nostalgic downtown, Katie began looking in the different storefronts. Drake and Tony walked ahead of Katie when they spotted a Speedy Mart. Katie continued to meander and gaze at the signage in the windows. She smiled when she imagined what a quaint town it must have been, walking by the Curiosity Store, the Mayflower Antique Shop, Enders Bakery and Parker's Pet Store.

Katie continued to stroll down the sidewalk when she heard a loud bark. Abruptly, she stopped, turned around and looked back at the pet store. She saw nothing. She began walking away again. Bark! Then, another Bark! She walked to the window of the pet store and knocked on the window. Nothing. She knocked harder and spotted a woman walking through the store and unlocking the front door as if it was a normal business day. The door opened and the woman greeted Katie. "Hi, welcome to Parker's Pet Shop."

Katie looked down the street to see if Drake

and Tony were still in the convenience store. She didn't see them, so she cautiously entered the pet store. The woman introduced herself. "I'm Shireen Parker and this is my pet store."

As Katie walked into the store, she looked around. Shireen led her to the back of the store where she saw dogs, lots of dogs, dozens of dogs. "I haven't seen a dog in years! How did they survive the devastation?"

"I made sure they were protected. I took care of them, every one of them. After all, they all think I'm their mother."

Katie saw big dogs, small dogs and every size in between. There must have been at least thirty dogs running around. They were excited to see a new friend. Shireen commanded, "Everybody sit down. Sit."

Immediately, every dog sat and became silent. Shireen laughed, "All of my babies will do anything I ask them to do. We've been here together a long time."

"Aren't there any other people left in this town?"

Shireen, thirty-three, with shoulder-length red hair, confided in a low tone, "I saw a few people a couple months ago. Strange looking people, but they went through town and never even noticed us in here."

Katie had an inkling of who Shireen was talking about. "Did these people have red skin and big blisters?"

"Yes! That's them. I think there was a man with two women."

The dogs remained in a sitting position and waited for Shireen to give them the okay to run and play again. Katie questioned, "How can you keep all these dogs fed?"

"Well, when I take food from the store, or even those weird looking people did, no one takes the dog food. These guys are very lucky to be dogs. They eat pretty well."

Katie grinned when Shireen gave the word, "Okay, babies, you can play."

The dogs started walking around and playing with their squeaky toys. The tiniest of the group, a five-pound Yorkie hopped up into Katie's arms. She cuddled him and rubbed his belly. The little guy occasionally brought his head up and licked Katie's chin. Shireen was delighted to see this. "I like to trust their instincts. If Snickers likes you, then I like you."

Katie continued to hold Snickers as they spoke. "I'm with a group of six other people. We've been together since Houston."

"Where are you going?"

"Florida. We have quite a few good reasons

to get there."

Shireen smiled but appeared sad as she said, "That sounds so nice. I only wish I could go along with you."

Katie questioned, "Why couldn't you come along with us? I don't see why you'd want to stay here alone in Beaumont."

Shireen looked at her dogs and said, "But I'm not alone, Katie. I have thirty-two wonderful companions by my side."

Just then, Katie noticed Drake and Tony, from the corner of her eye, as they walked past the storefront. She rushed to the door and called them to come back, still holding Snickers in her arms.

She introduced them to Shireen and her dog pound and then, the four of them talked for nearly an hour.

Shireen showed how her canine companions obeyed her every command to the letter. Eventually, Drake had little Chynna, the blonde Pomeranian, in his arms, and Tony was sitting on the floor, petting Abby, the Chocolate Lab. As he stroked her head, an idea came to mind and he became excited. He stood up. Abby stood up too. He said, "I know how Shireen can go with us!"

Everyone turned their attention to Tony as he continued, "I counted. Twenty of these dogs are large enough to pull a sled. These animals are powerhouses."

Shireen questioned, "Pull sleds? What are you talking about?"

Drake realized what Tony had in mind and said, "We have two large sleds that we've been manually pulling for the last eighty miles. If we let the dogs pull the sleds, we can ride inside with the smaller dogs, and move much faster than we would on foot. I know the dogs can handle it. I can even build a third sled if we need to."

Katie, hopeful that Shireen would go along with the idea, said, "That's a great idea! Then you could go with us to Florida and all your four-legged friends will go too."

Shireen stared down at the dogs, walking around them, petting them. Snickers let out a bark. Shireen stated, "Well, if Snickers says yes, then so do I."

Drake looked at the dogs that would be doing the work. There were two Otterhounds, two Huskies, a Malamute, three German Shepherds, two Rottweilers and several other breeds that he knew would be able to endure the trip.

They left the pet shop and returned to the little neighborhood. Drake watched as every dog followed Shireen and listened to each one of her commands. He respected Shireen for how much time and energy she must have put into training and caring for them.

The others were surprised and happy to see the many dogs entering their world. Naomi found a little French Bulldog named Pierre. She and the dog soon became inseparable. Katie and Porsha noticed Pierre was helping to comfort Naomi with her poor health and depression.

Drake began work on a third sled for their journey. Tony and Granger helped to complete the project in less than two days. He presented the sled to the others with Snickers, Chynna and Pierre sitting in the driver's seat. Everyone laughed and applauded. Finally, there was a joyous time for the survivors. They'd forgotten how much comfort their companions could bring into their lives and how much easier the trip would be.

That evening Drake took the radio out of his pocket and stared at it. He wondered why he hadn't heard from Carolyn in a while. Katie sat next to him and, as if she was reading his mind, said, "You know how it goes with that radio. She'll call you when she can get through."

Drake smiled and turned to Katie. "I know she will. I think she'll be surprised to hear we'll be there a lot sooner than originally planned."

"I'm sure she'll be elated."

Shireen came into the house through the garage entrance. She sat at the table and Tony sat down next to her. She said, "All the babies are safe and warm for the night."

She looked at the corner of the room where Snickers and Chynna were curled up next to the fireplace. Like any overprotective mother would say, Shireen advised, "I don't want them pushed beyond their limit. Remember, only five or six of these dogs are actual sled dogs. The other big dogs won't be as fast or as agile. We're going to take our time and make sure all of my babies are well taken care of. We've been through a lot together and I don't plan to lose any of them."

Drake assured her, "Of course we're going to take care of them. They're part of our family too."

Shireen let out a breath of relief. She was happy and to hear this. Tony asked, "Do you know anything about sled dogs? Do you have any idea how fast they can go?"

"I know a little bit. The usual sled can move up to about twenty-five miles an hour. Our sleds will safely move between fifteen and twenty miles an hour."

Thankful, Tony commented, "That's going to cut down our travel time by months."

Shireen added, "It seems that way. I know they'll get us there as fast as they can."

Katie stated, "Talk about being in the right

place at the right time. In some strange way, we all saved each other."

Shireen agreed, "Yeah, I guess we did. I love my babies but it's actually nice to have other humans to have a conversation with."

Drake pulled out a piece of paper and tried to figure out the math. He scribbled, crossed it out and scribbled again. Tony watched and waited before he asked, "Well, Drake, what did you come up with?"

"It looks like travel time would be about seventy-five days. If we add in our stops for sleep and supplies, I think we could make it there within six months, maybe sooner. It all depends on what we find between here and there."

Katie added, "Well, I'm feeling a lot more positive about this trip now that we have Shireen and her four-legged clan."

Shireen glanced down at the floor one more time, looking at Snickers and Chynna sound asleep and warm. She asked, "Has anyone seen Pierre? He wasn't in the garage with the others and he's not in here with us."

In the house next door, Zack and Porsha had already gone to be. A crackling fire in the fireplace had the entire house toasty warm.

Granger was getting prepared to go do the same. He would always check on Naomi before he went to bed. He opened her bedroom door and peered into the room. He observed Naomi sleeping peacefully with Pierre curled up next to her. Pierre opened his eyes for a brief moment and looked at Granger, as if he was telling Granger, "Relax. She's alright, I'm with her now."

Granger smiled, backed out of the room and quietly closed the door behind him. Pierre stared at the door as it closed. Then, he put his head down and went to sleep.

7

The eight survivors were forced to make an emergency stop in Pinehurst, only twenty-five miles on the other side of Beaumont. This would be their last stop in Texas. Several boards had come off one of the sleds and needed to be repaired.

They pulled into the town and found many of the structures were still sound and available for them to stay in for a day or two. Many of the small stores were still filled with canned goods and other supplies. They found a small bed and breakfast and unpacked their belongings.

Drake explained, "These sleds weren't built for the speed they're traveling at. When I originally put them together, we thought we'd be pulling them for nine-hundred miles. It's a lot different when you switch from three miles an hour to fifteen miles an hour."

Tony asked, "But there's a way that we can make them sturdier? Right?"

Drake nodded and asked Granger and Tony to help him search for new planks to replace the broken ones. The three left and the others waited at the bed and breakfast. Zack grabbed his rifle and a few traps and he said, "It looks like we're going to be here a while. I think I'll go out and get us some dinner for tonight."

Shireen stood up and asked, "Can I go with you? I've always wanted to learn how to properly shoot a gun."

Zack replied, "Why, of course you can, little lady. I'd love to teach you."

Porsha wasn't happy with the fact that Zack was taking the new girl hunting. Abruptly, she said, "I'll go too."

Zack replied sternly, "Now, everyone can't go. I can't have that many distractions while I'm trying to hunt, Porsha. You need to stay here and help the others."

"Distraction? Is that what I am to you, a distraction?"

Zack could see that Porsha was getting angry at how he phrased his words. "I didn't say you were a distraction, Porsha. It's just that too many people aren't good when you're trying to be quiet out there."

Porsha flopped down on one of the billowy sofas, crossed her arms and pouted. Shireen felt embarrassed and uncomfortable that she was in the middle of their lover's quarrel. Trying to steer clear of a confrontation, she suggested, "I can stay here and you two can go. I'll just learn how to shoot a gun some other time."

Zack flat out refused to let Porsha's self-centeredness and jealousy ruin a good day with his new friend. "No, Shireen, you're going with me and Porsha's staying here."

They packed up the traps and the guns and were ready to leave when Zack leaned over Porsha and whispered, "We'll only be a few hours, baby. You have to let go of this thing where you think you own me." When he attempted to kiss her on the forehead, she flinched away. Zack could see that Porsha wasn't going to let it go of her anger. He left with Shireen.

Katie and Naomi entered the living room after overhearing most of the quarrel. Katie asked, "Are you okay, Porsha?"

At that point, Porsha was mad at the world and everyone in it. She wouldn't speak to Katie or Naomi, but they tried anyway.

After a long and uncomfortable silence,

Naomi, holding Pierre in her arms and trying to change the subject, stated, "This bed and breakfast has several rooms that we can use. I found an end room for me and Pierre."

Katie asked, "Would anyone like to join me at the convenience store down the street? I have to get some supplies."

Naomi shook her head. She was too worn out and wanted to rest. Porsha sat there with her arms crossed and a frozen pouty expression on her face. Katie scowled at Porsha and abruptly blurted, "Fine then! I'll go out and get the shit myself. You just stay here and wallow like a little brat." Katie stormed out.

Naomi went to the room she had picked out and tried to make it more comfortable. She grabbed a few smaller logs from one of the sleds and started a fire in the fireplace.

In a field, Zack was showing Shireen how to set traps to catch rabbits and squirrels. He saw she was a quick study. As they were crawled around the open field on their hands and knees, she asked, "Are you alright, Zack? You and Porsha said some pretty harsh words to each other back there."

Zack corrected her, "No, Porsha always has pretty harsh words for me. I don't get it. At first, it was great. But now, she seems to be jealous of everyone I talk to and everything I do. She even screamed at me once about spending too much time around Naomi."

"Naomi? You're kidding."

Zack replied, "I'm not kidding. Don't get me wrong. I like Porsha. I love Porsha but she's driving me crazy. She driving me away. That's what she's doing."

Shireen asked, "Are you sure you're not doing something to set her off? Maybe you don't even know what you're doing?"

Zack thought it over and said, "No, I don't think so. It's just like what happened a few minutes ago. There was no reason for her to get like she did. I think the girl has more issues than we know about, big issues."

Shireen stated, "You two need to sit down and talk it over. You should come to some type of understanding or an agreement."

Zack said, "I'll try to talk with her tonight but I don't think it's going to help. She is who she is and I can't change her."

Shireen smiled and suggested, "Just give it a try anyway. I mean, what have you got to lose? You may be very surprised by her reaction."

"Well, you sound a lot more positive about that prospect than I do."

Shireen stood up after the last trap was set. She said, "So, the two of you can talk tonight and by tomorrow it'll all be better."

Zack grinned and gave Shireen a warm hug, a hug that perhaps lasted a minute longer than it should have. "Thank you, Shireen. You've become such a good friend to me."

Shireen laughed as she changed the subject. "Well, the traps are all set. So, when are you going to teach me to shoot a rifle, Mr. Gunslinger?" Zack laughed with her.

Later than evening, Zack and Shireen brought back four rabbits to cook for dinner. Katie and Naomi prepared the meal. At dinner, Drake said, "We have enough lumber to fix the sleds so they'll be safer for travel. The repairs can all be done in a day."

Everyone at the table noticed Porsha wasn't speaking to Zack. They noticed she wasn't speaking to anyone. Zack didn't let her mood spoil his mood. He enjoyed his meal and then pulled Porsha to the side afterward. She followed but wouldn't do much talking. Instead, she acted as if his presence was annoying her. "What do you want, Zack? What the hell do you want?"

"I want to talk to you. I want to resolve this little fight we're having."

She chuckled, "Little?"

Zack tried to explain, "I can't keep doing this with you, Porsha. I can't be in a relationship with someone who doesn't trust me, who thinks she has some kind of ownership over me."

She shook her head and stared across the room, avoiding any eye contact. "You give me lots of reasons not to trust you."

Now, Zack was getting angry. He snapped, "That's not true. I haven't done anything but become a friend to these other people who survived this damned destruction."

She crossed her arms and started pouting again. Zack took his hands and moved her face forward so she had to look him in the eye. He asked, "Do you want to continue this relationship or would you feel better if we just called it quits right now? Your choice."

Porsha suddenly fabricated, in her mind, what she thought was happening. "Oh, I see. You want it over so you can move onto that slut with all the dogs."

Zack shook his head, "I don't understand you, Porsha. Where do you come up with this stuff? Sometimes, I think you're delusional."

"Delusional? It wasn't a delusion when you chose the dog lady over me. Why don't you just say that you want to be with her and not me? Why don't you admit it?"

"I don't want to be with Shireen. She's just a friend, like Drake or Katie. She makes me laugh and I can talk to her. That's something I can't seem to do with you anymore."

Porsha was felt threatened. In a desperate move, she stood up and put her arms around Zack. She put her head on his shoulder and whispered, "Alright, I'm sorry I attacked you like that, Zack. But, sometimes, it seems that you like to be with her more than you like to be with me."

"When you act out like you did today, I like being with anyone better than I like being with you, Porsha."

Nuzzling up to him even closer, she asked, "So, what do we do?"

Zack smiled and said, "We stay together and we work out our problems. I don't ever want to lose you, baby."

8

The sleds pulled into the Lake Charles area and down the city streets. Unfortunately, it appeared the earthquakes and aftershocks had flattened the entire city. The waters from the Gulf of Mexico had crept miles and miles north. Lake Charles had become a beachfront city and its eighty-thousand residents were gone.

Shireen called out to the canines and the sleds came to an abrupt stop. Drake and Zack hopped out and glanced around at the ruins. Drake stated, "I don't think we can stay in this city, Zack. There's nothing left, no buildings and no stores for supplies, nothing."

Zack added, "This is the worst ruin I've seen yet." He stopped for a moment and peered around. "It just doesn't feel safe here. Sometimes, I get a weird funny feeling in my bones and I'm getting that feeling right. We should keep moving east and look for the next small town."

Drake commented, "It's going to be getting dark soon. I don't think we should travel at night. We can't risk it."

"What if we head north for a little while to see if there's some small town on the other side of the interstate?"

Katie eavesdropped on the conversation and stepped out of the sled with a map in her hand. "There's a city about ten miles north of here. It's called Moss Bluff. If we hurry, we could be there in thirty minutes."

Drake looked at Zack and nodded his head. "Okay, let's go for it. Besides, we don't have a lot of choices right now."

Naomi, still seated in a sled with Pierre in her arms, questioned, "What's going on? Is there a problem, Drake?"

Drake replied, "No problem, Naomi. We

just decided to head north for a few miles. This city doesn't feel right."

She mentioned, "It is disturbing to look out at a city that used to have thousands of people and now it's empty and silent and vacant."

Shireen asked, "How much longer? The pack needs to rest and eat. Remember what you promised me, guys."

Katie guaranteed her it would only take a half hour to get to Moss Bluff."

Shireen questioned, "And what if that city looks like this city? Do we just keep riding around until the night predators find us?"

Katie said, "We'll be just fine, Shireen. The dogs will be fine."

Shireen wasn't feeling as positive as Katie, but she eventually saw it was there only choice and agreed to traveling the extra miles.

Unexpectedly, the ground started to quake. Another aftershock had begun. The sled dogs were barking and getting tangled in their homemade harnesses. Shireen quickly hopped out of her sled and helped Drake and Katie calm the dogs and untangle their lines. The tremor continued for thirty seconds.

When it stopped, Shireen helped to get the dogs focused again. They got back into the sleds and pulled away before the shaking started again.

Shireen headed the first sled north and the other two
followed closely behind. Katie grabbed hold of
Snickers as they rode along. Drake saw that little
Chynna was still trembling after the incident. He
picked her up and put her in his lap.

The ground began to shake again, but this
time Shireen shouted out commands and the team
remained attentive and on point. Porsha shifted
herself closer to Zack. He put his arm around her
and kissed the top of her head. "Don't fret, Porsha.
Nothing's ever going to happen to you, not as long
as I'm alive."

Naomi held Pierre close until the juddering
ended again. In only a few minutes, the sleds had
run past the welcome sign for Moss Bluff. They
pulled into the city and saw a few buildings that
were still structurally sound. They pulled in front of
a large estate that seemed to be unblemished by the
elements. The three-story manor appeared large
enough to house many people, many more than just
these eight.

Zack and Tony went inside the house first
and had a look around to see if the inside was as
welcoming as the outside. They eventually came out
and Zack told Drake, "This place has ten bedrooms
and a lot of fireplaces. The kitchen is even stocked
with canned goods and the sinks and bathrooms are
working fine. They must have had a well and septic

system."

Naomi looked at Granger and said, "Finally, a real house."

Granger laughed and held Pierre while Naomi stepped out of the sled. He joked, "I can't believe I finally get my own bedroom! It only took fourteen years."

Shireen began to unharness each of the dogs and take them into the house, one by one. Zack volunteered to help her with them. Shireen accepted his offer.

As they walked each dog into the house, talking and joking with each other, Porsha remained in the sled. Once again, she was becoming jealous of the friendship Zack had established with Shireen. She noticed they were getting friendlier with each passing day.

Shireen and Zack made sure the dogs were taken into the house and fed and boarded in one of the many large bedrooms. Tony, Drake and Granger unpacked the sleds while Katie walked behind the house to find firewood.

They settled into the house and found it quite accommodating, so accommodating they decided to remain there for a week. Drake said it would give them time to rest and regroup and just take it easy for a while.

On their second night in Moss Bluff, a

transmission came through from Florida. It was Carolyn. "Hello Drake, are you there?"

Drake responded immediately, "Carolyn, it's been a while. It's good to hear your voice. How have you been?"

"I've been fair. How are you? How far have you gotten?" She was expecting to hear they were still in Texas.

He announced, "We had something happen to us in Beaumont."

With a hint of concern in her tone, she asked, "What was that?"

"We found another survivor, a woman. Her name is Shireen Parker. Katie discovered her in a pet store."

Carolyn giggled, "In a pet store? What an odd place to live."

"She was living in the pet store because she owned the store. She was caring for her dogs, thirty-two dogs in all."

Carolyn's giggling stopped. "Thirty-two dogs?"

"Yes, thirty-two dogs and, believe it or not, over half of the dogs were large enough to pull our sleds behind them. They're going to get us to you even faster."

Carolyn was elated by the news. "Drake, that's wonderful."

"We just left Lake Charles and pulled into a town called Moss Bluff. We plan to stay here a few more days before we head out again."

"So, it's not going to take you a year to get here?"

Drake announced, "My guess is that we'll be there around Christmas, hopefully sooner. And that means you won't have to spend Christmas alone ever again."

Carolyn began to weep. "That's great. That's great news, Drake."

"And, when we get there, I have another surprise. I have little guy I want you to meet. He's a miniature Schnauzer and his name is Maximillian. Max for short."

Carolyn's mood seemed positive and upbeat. "I can't wait for my little Christmas present and all of you to arrive."

Drake was glad his news was able to help and motivate Carolyn. He told her about Tony and the earthquakes in Lake Charles. Then he alerted her to the story Tony and Shireen had told them about the rain people. Carolyn responded, "Well, I don't have to worry about that. Here in Florida there are no people."

The rest of the conversation went well before the static took over again. Soon, Drake set the radio down and checked on Snickers and

Chynna who were sleeping in the corner of the room. Katie came into the room and joined him. Drake sat on the sofa and stared into the fire. He put his arm around Katie and they both seemed almost hypnotized by the flame. He pondered, "What do you suppose is still waiting for us down the road? What else is out there?"

"Who knows? It could be anything. It could be a lot of things, or it could just be nothing, like we saw in Lake Charles."

Drake nodded. "Yeah, sometimes nothing is better."

Katie mentioned, "We still have over seven hundred miles to go. Who the hell knows what the future has in store for us?"

Drake stated, "But we're with a great bunch of people."

"The best. Finding Shireen is like a blessing from God, and Zack going out there, hunting for our food every day. Granger looking out for Naomi, and Tony and Porsha are always willing to help above and beyond what they're asked to do."

Drake scowled. Katie wondered what she said to make him do this. "What did I say? Why are you frowning?"

He smiled and remarked, "You forgot to mention Snickers and Chynna and Max and Pierre and Abby and ..."

"I get it. I get it. Those dogs are the true blessing."

Drake said, "Carolyn is very excited at the news. I told her, if nothing else happens, we'd be to her by Christmas."

Katie thought about Carolyn for a moment as she stared into the flame. "I can't imagine what that poor woman is going through. What it must be like to be so completely alone except for a voice over the radio every so often."

"We've all been through it, and then we found each other and solved the problem. She'll be better once we get there."

"I'm sure she will. I just hate to think she's going through it all by herself."

Drake stated, "When we were alone, we didn't know if there was anyone else out there. At least she knows we're here and risking our safety to be with her. That thought must help her during the solitary times."

Katie posed the question, "Once we get to this Crystal River and find Carolyn, what then? Is there a plan?"

Drake looked into Katie's eyes. "Funny, I never thought about it. I suppose we'll get Carolyn and move inland, to the center of the state, away from the water. I suppose, we can start to build a community."

"Or perhaps we can move even further south down the state."

Drake interjected, "Providing that southern Florida is still there. The rest of the state could be underwater for all we know."

Katie agreed, "That's a possibility. We'll just have to wait and see."

Drake gazed at the fire. Then, he turned his attention to Katie. He put his hand on top of her hand and they locked fingers. He leaned in to kiss her. She backed her head up an inch to stop him. She asked, "Are you sure you want to do this? It's a big step."

He responded with a whisper, "Yes. Why would you think I didn't?"

"I hear the way you speak to Carolyn when she calls. I see your face when the two of you are talking. I notice your mood when the call ends. Are you sure you're not in love with this voice on your radio?"

Drake bowed his head and let her words sink in. Then, he lifted his head, leaned in and kissed her. When the long and gentle kiss was finished, he whispered, "I'm sure. It's not about Carolyn at all. It's only about Katie."

She chuckled and blushed. Then, her facial expression got serious again. "Drake Munroe, I'm only going to tell you this one time. Don't you dare break my heart."

He leaned in and kissed her again. She wrapped her arms around his neck while he slowly wedged himself on top of her. The kissing went on for hours before they retired to the same bedroom for the evening.

A few days later, Zack travelled several miles from the house with Granger. They were planning to trap rabbit or squirrel. The temperature had dropped below zero. Porsha decided to follow them. She felt she needed to talk to Zack about his friendship with Shireen again.

Granger was setting traps when Zack spotted a deer. He signaled to Granger to remain completely still as he took aim.

Suddenly, Porsha stomped up from behind and shouted, "Zack! We need to have a talk now! Right now!"

The deer heard her voice and darted across the field. The deer was gone. Zack lowered his rifle and turned to Porsha. He was angry. She said, "We need to talk!"

He set his gun down on the ground and asked, "What do we have to talk about Porsha? You just ruined my perfect shot."

Granger continued setting traps and tried not to eavesdrop on the argument. He observed Porsha throwing her hands in the air as she shouted, "I'm at the end of my rope! I need to know what you plan to do with her!"

Zack questioned, "With who? Who are you talking about this time?"

"Shireen, who else? I noticed the way you look at her and flirt with her every chance you get, Mr. Gunslinger!"

"Girl, that's crazy. You're crazy. Shireen is just a friend."

Porsha crossed her arms and stomped her foot. "That's not what it looks like to me. I think you're more than just friends!"

Granger continued to wander further away as the dispute got even louder. Zack began to shout back. "There's nothing going on between me and Shireen, or me and anyone! You have to stop with this jealousy and wild accusations!"

"I don't believe you, Zack! I know there's something going on between the two of you and I want to know what it is!"

Zack turned away from Porsha and stared at the ground. Then he turned back around and stated, "You're the only woman that I love, Porsha. I'm not in love with Shireen. I'm not in love with Katie or Naomi … just you … only you. Get that through your thick skull, woman."

Porsha began to cry. Zack could see the

confrontation wasn't going to be over for a while. He put his hand on her cheek and asked, "Why are you crying, sweetie?"

She slapped his hand away, looked into his eyes and said, "I don't believe you, Zack. And don't call me sweetie ever again!"

Porsha turned and began to stomp out of the field. Granger had almost disappeared out of sight. Zack leaned down and picked up his rifle again. He looked out and saw Granger jumping and shouting but he couldn't hear what he was shouting about. He heard Porsha scream.

As he spun around, he saw a black bear run out from between the trees and lung at Porsha. Granger ran frantically toward them. Zack picked up his rifle and aimed it at the bear. He fired once and hit the bear in the back but it continued to maul Porsha. She screamed a horrifying screech. Zack fired another shot and hit the bear again. This time the bullet tore through the back of its head. The bear stood up and howled before it clumsily retreated to the woods.

Zack and Granger ran to be near Porsha, slipping on the icy ground a few times before they got to her. Zack looked down and what he saw made his head spin. He saw that the bear had torn Porsha's neck completely open. She laid there in the cold field, lifeless, with her still eyes open and a look of terror still painted on her face. Blood soaked her jacket and her face. Granger began to cry out hysterically. Zack fell to his knees and looked up at the sky. He bellowed, "Why? Why did you do this to her?"

He laid down next to her and put his head on her shoulder. Her blood seeped onto his shirt and his cheek. Time passed before Granger went back to the manor alone to tell everyone what happened. Zack remained in the field lying next to Porsha's cold body.

Granger brought the others to the field. He was hoping someone could talk Zack into leaving the field before nightfall. Shireen approached Zack. "Zack, it was an accident. It was a bear. This could have been anyone of us."

Zack, with tears in his eyes, replied, "No, it wasn't an accident. She came out because she was jealous of our friendship, Shireen. None of this was an accident."

"I don't understand. Why would she be so upset over our friendship?"

He got loud. "Because she thought it was more than a friendship! She thought she was being pushed to the side!"

Shireen was flabbergasted. "I hope you told her she was wrong."

"I did. I told her she was the only woman I

loved but she didn't believe me. You should have seen the look in her eyes when she spoke to me. She was so damn angry."

Shireen put her hand on Zack's shoulder. He jerked it away. "Leave me alone. I think you've done enough for one day, Shireen."

She gasped when she realized Zack was somehow blaming her for Porsha's death. Her face went blank and emotionless as she quietly stood up and walked out of the field. She didn't say another word. Naomi followed her.

Drake approached Zack and stated, "Zack, we're going to have to go back to the house soon. It'll be dark before you know it."

"I don't want to go back to the house. I want to stay here with Porsha. It's so damned cold here. I want to keep her warm."

Drake countered, "You know, Zack, in the beginning, it was just me and her. She was one of the best friends I ever had the pleasure of knowing. We were so different, complete opposites, as a matter of fact. I never, in a million years, thought I could get along with her. We went through so many highs and lows together, but we cured each other's loneliness."

Zack whispered, "I already know all this stuff, Drake. What's your point?"

Drake responded, "You're not the only one

hurting. Everyone in this house loved her. Each one loved her in their own way. Some like a sister, others like a daughter and I know you loved her most of all."

Zack wept as he spoke, "I did, Drake. I did love her. I never loved anyone as hard as I loved Porsha."

"So, why don't we take Porsha back to the house? She'll be warm there. Then, we can arrange a funeral for her tomorrow.

Zack didn't respond. He began to cry more. Granger added, "That's a good idea, Zack. Porsha wouldn't like being left here in this cold field. We can carry her back to the house together. You're not alone."

Still, Zack made no response. Granger looked at Drake but Drake had nothing else to say. Granger walked out of the field and back to the house.

An hour had passed and the skies were black. Night had come while Drake, Katie and Tony stood in the field waiting for Zack to make a choice. Katie knelt down next to Zack, rubbed his back and whispered, "If you decide to stay here, I'm going to stay here with you all night."

Zack said, "No Katie, that wouldn't be wise. Remember, there's bears and other animals waiting to pounce."

She bargained, "I'll go home if you go with me. Otherwise, I'm not going anywhere. It's your decision."

He knew what he had to do. He sat up, hugged Katie and whispered. "Thank you, Katie. You're one tough bitch."

Katie burst out in laughter. "And don't you ever forget that, Zack."

Soon, Zack started laughing too. He picked Porsha up and carried her in his arms all the way back to the house.

The following day, Drake found a place on the grounds to bury Porsha. The three men spent most of the day digging into the ice-cold earth. A quiet and tearful funeral took place.

After the funeral was over, Zack approached Shireen to apologize to her but she wasn't interested in listening to anything that he had to say. She was still hurt by his words the previous day and just how deep they cut her. Their friendship had come to a standstill.

The stay ended up taking much longer than Drake had originally anticipated. One week turned into ten days and then, the ten days turned into two weeks. Then, two weeks turned into three.

Eventually they decided it was time to pack it up and go. The sleds were loaded with supplies, the dogs were harnessed and racing down the interstate once again. But this leg of the journey was quieter than the other legs. It would have to take place without Porsha.

9

Drake looked in his journal and wrote the date August 2nd, 2030. He sat in one of the three sleds, composing his thoughts for the day. Katie sat next to him, attempting to get a peek at what he was always writing about. Each time she leaned in and tried to get a glimpse, he'd quickly move the book away or slam it shut. "Come on, Drake, can't I have just a little gander?"

Drake knew this was driving her crazy. He smiled and moved the book away from her again and joking stated, "I'm sorry, Katie, you're going to have to wait for the movie."

Katie shook her head and laughed with him. Then, she shouted ahead to Shireen and Tony in the first sled. "Where are we?"

Tony pointed and hollered back, "I believe we're on the outskirts of Baton Rouge," as they passed the big green signs stating "Baton Rouge, next three exits".

Drake yelled, "This looks good! Let's pull in and find a shelter!"

Shireen steered the sleds toward the center of the city. As they moved into the heart of Baton Rouge, the sleds went down into a deep icy valley. The valley continued for miles. Granger looked around and asked Naomi, "What's the name of this valley? I don't remember ever learning about it in school."

Naomi informed him, "You didn't learn about it in school because it didn't exist when you were in school, Granger. I do believe this used to be the Mississippi River."

Granger and Naomi glanced around and saw that the entire Mississippi River was now void of any water. But riding through the basin where the river once flowed so mightily put them in awe of its magnitude. Naomi commented sadly, "I guess the Mississippi River belongs in the history books from now on."

They wandered through the city in search of a home or a building that looked sturdy and warm. Most of the area, like Lake Charles, and so many other cities, was almost completely devastated by the earthquakes.

After driving up and down the desolate streets for over an hour, they came upon an old southern home. It was a large place, that appeared to be intact.

They stopped and gazed at the home with a

sudden sense of wonder when they saw puffs of smoke billowing from the chimney. They knew someone was living in that house.

Drake had Shireen pull the sleds out of sight while he and Tony approached the home on foot. As they moved up the sidewalk, Tony reminded Drake, "Remember those freaks I told you about, the rain people? The ones with the red skin?"

"Yes, I remember."

Tony continued, "Well, this could be them. We have to be careful."

Drake and Tony moved very cautiously towards the front door. They noticed the windows were blocked off with cardboard, so no one could see inside.

Drake asked, "So, what are we supposed to do? Should we just knock on the door like it's any other day?"

Tony was as perplexed as Drake on how to handle the situation. "I guess we have to. We don't have any other choice."

Drake lifted his fist to knock on the door but then paused for a moment. "Tony, what if they have a gun? It's possible that they might shoot first and ask questions later."

Tony thought it over and said, "We better take our chances. Otherwise, we'll never find out who's in there."

Drake raised his hand to knock on the door and paused again. Suddenly, Katie hopped out of her sled, walked up from behind the two men, stood at the door, and remarked, "For Christ's sake, get out of the way," as she pushed in between them and knocked as hard as she could.

They waited to hear footsteps. They heard nothing. Katie knocked forcefully again and again as she hollered, "Is anyone in there? Hey! Is anyone there?"

Tony attempted to turn the doorknob but it wouldn't budge. "The door must be locked. Why would they lock the door?"

All of a sudden, the lock on the door clicked and the door began to creak open slowly. Much to everyone's surprise, when the door was finally open all the way, they saw a young girl standing there, by herself. Drake, Tony and Katie found themselves speechless. The girl smiled and asked, "Are you good or are you bad people?"

Drake knelt down to look her in the eye and calmly stated, "We're good people, sweetie, and who are you?"

The little girl smiled and gave a half curtsy to welcome them. "I'm Emily. Would you like to come in and visit for a while?"

Drake, in unfamiliar waters, glanced at the others before he accepted the invitation. "Sure, we'd love to come in a see your beautiful home, Emily."

She guided them down the hallway and walked into the living room, where a fire was burning in the fireplace. They were startled to see a man and a woman sitting on the sofa next to the fireplace.

The man was reading a book and the woman was making homemade jewelry. The couple stood up and greeted their guests. "Hello, I see you met our little Emily. I'm William Maddock and this is my wife Carly Riggs."

Carly smiled and said, "Hello", to each of the three guests. Drake introduced himself and the others. He told them that they were traveling in a caravan to Florida. "We have four other people with us … and about thirty dogs."

William and Carly were surprised at this news. Minutes later, they welcomed the other four and invited them to stay at their house. The offer was happily accepted. Shireen unharnessed the dogs and boarded the larger ones in the warm garage. The smaller dogs, as always, followed her into the house.

Carly made a big dinner with the assistance of Katie and Naomi. They all sat around the dining room table and discussed their futures and their pasts. Carly began telling her story. "I'm from Little

Rock, Arkansas. I worked as a waitress when Little Rock was still Little Rock. After the meteors hit, I found myself alone. I couldn't find anyone else, not a single human being."

Drake nodded and said under his breath, "I know how that feels."

Katie commented, "We all know how that feels, Drake. You weren't the only one looking for other survivors."

Carly listened to them for a moment before she continued with her story. "The cold was simply unbearable there. It was well below zero most days and the nights were bone chilling. After five or six months, I decided it was time to travel south to see if the climate was more tolerable."

Granger asked, "How did you travel?"

"On foot. What other way is there? After all, I couldn't just get in a car and drive here. Anyway, it took me a little over a year before I made my way here. I walked three-hundred and fifty miles. A few months after I got here, I found Emily and luckily William found us."

Tony commended her on her strength and courage. She replied, "It wasn't strength or courage that got me here. I was scared to death and tired of sub-zero weather. I can say, nothing about it was easy or pleasant. I had to travel by day and hide at night. I had a few challenging moments with some extremely large animals."

Drake turned his attention to William. "So, William, how did you arrive here in this beautiful city?"

"I came here from Lafayette. It took a few months but I made it okay. I didn't have nearly as many challenges as Carly had to go through. I guess I was as shocked as you were when I saw this house with a cozy fire burning. They both welcomed me with open arms."

There was a brief pause, a deep silence, as everyone wanted to hear more of William's story. Katie asked, "And what did you used to do for a living, William?"

"Oh, I was in the medical field."

Katie looked around the table at everyone waiting to hear more. No one said a word so, Katie asked, "Well, what did you do in the medical field? I was an ER nurse back in the day, in Texas City. No, I was the best goddam ER nurse in Texas City." She laughed at herself.

Carly interrupted, "He doesn't like to talk about the fact that he was a doctor. For some reason he feels he needs to keep it hidden."

"Yes, now that Carly spilled the beans, I was a doctor. I'd say I was doing pretty well too. I had my own practice and everything was beginning to look up for me."

Naomi turned and said, "Tell us about yourself, Emily."

Emily ignored Naomi's request. Naomi stared at her but didn't get an answer. Naomi asked Carly, "Is she alright?"

Carly told them, "When it all happened, the meteors, Emily was only nine years old. She was a nine-year-old trying to survive on her own in this big city. I don't know how she did it, but she did manage to get by for two and a half years before she met me."

Naomi had a tear in her eye. "Only nine years old? Such a shame."

Carly leaned towards Naomi and whispered, "When I found Emily, she wouldn't speak to me at all. She only spoke to the invisible friends that she invented to keep her company. She was angry, confused, scared and hungry. But, over the last eighteen months I, with some help from William, have been able to bring her back to a comfortable and stable life. She can still quiet at times but she's nothing like she used to be."

Naomi had tears running down both cheeks. "So sad, this poor little girl left alone in the world for all that time. My heart breaks for her. I know how hard it was when I found Granger. He was only twelve back then."

Carly stated, "I'm sure you know it's tough

but also very rewarding."

Soon, Drake told them about their days on the interstate. Tony and Shireen warned them about the rain people. They described their red skin and blisters. Emily commented, "Yuck! That sounds so gross!"

Tony and Granger cleared the table after dinner and everyone else moved to the living room to talk more. Zack still wasn't over Porsha's death and remained quiet most of the time.

Naomi excused herself to retire early. She grabbed Pierre and took him to bed as always. Carly and William tucked Emily in before they came back and joined the others.

William reopened the conversation, "It's funny. The other day, Carly and I were discussing moving out of Baton Rouge. The supplies are getting low and most of the businesses and grocery stores were flattened by the earthquakes. We just didn't know how we could travel to another city on foot with Emily. That's when you just happened to show up."

Katie volunteered, "Moving by dogsled is definitely faster and easier than travelling on foot. Most of our dogs aren't snow dogs though, but we can move about ten to fifteen miles an hour, and we always have room for a few more people. If you need us to get you somewhere, the door's always open. As you know, we're going all the way to Florida."

Granger was tired from the long day. He excused himself to go to bed and Zack followed soon after. Tony looked around the living room. "This is a nice setup you have here."

William smiled and said, "Thank you, but it was mostly Carly that did all this. I came along later."

Drake sat forward on the sofa, Chynna sleeping on his lap, and asked, "So do you think you might want to leave here with us?"

Carly confessed, "All I know is that the weather difference between Little Rock and here was drastic, almost fifteen degrees warmer. So, your friend in Florida is correct when she tells you it's even several degrees warmer there."

Unexpectedly, the ground began to shake fiercely. Pictures fell off the walls, glassware rattled in the kitchen, and the dogs began barking and howling. They sat tight and waited for it to subside before Shireen and Tony went to the garage to calm the dogs down.

William put his arm around Carly and revealed, "I have to admit that leaving here is going to be tough for a lot of reasons. After all, this is where I met Carly and Emily and we've been living as a family here for quite some time. It's going to be sad leaving here and knowing we'll never be coming back."

Carly asked, "How soon did you plan on hitting the road again."

Drake expressed, "We were planning on staying in Baton Rouge for about a week. One of the sleds needs to be worked on and Shireen likes the dogs to have some down time before they begin another long trek."

Carly gazed into William's eyes and said, "Only a week."

Drake added, "But if you need a little more time than that, we can always make it work. I want you to know, there's no actual schedule that we're bound to."

William looked at Carly and smiled. Then, he said, "It would take a little more than a week to get things wrapped up around here, maybe ten days to two weeks?"

Drake voiced, "That works. Ten days to two weeks. It'll give us time to get a little rest. It'll be nice to relax for a while."

William and Carly stood up. "Carly and I are going to hit the sack. It's been a long day and we're bushed."

After William and Carly left, Drake and Katie sat with Snickers and Chynna sleeping on their laps and Max was curled up on the end of the sofa. They spent the evening like they always did, talking about the day or what they had to do the next day.

Drake pointed out, "I'm a little worried. We have to do something about Zack. He's thrown himself into a deep and dark depression since he lost Porsha. I've tried to talk to him but he won't open up."

Katie cozied up next to Drake and said, "I know. I've tried too. He and Shireen haven't said one word to each other since the whole incident happened. I'm worried about her as much as I'm worried about him."

He returned, "I guess we'll just have to let nature run its course. I can't control what Zack or Shireen do or say."

"That's for sure. The two of them are strong spirited and stubborn."

A week passed as William and Carly packed up the things they'd need for their Journey. They decided it would be wise to stay with the others and travel all the way to Florida. Carly broke the news to Emily and let her get used to the idea. Excitedly, Emily said, "Alright mama, but, when we get there, I want to go to Disney World."

Carly laughed and put her hands on Emily's shoulders. "Of course, honey, we'll go to Disney

World." Both parents were both surprised at how she seemed to take the thought of relocating so well. She packed up her things too.

Drake repaired the third sled where some of the boards were loose. He asked Zack to help but Zack made excuse after excuse of why he couldn't. Shireen decided to take the dogs out for a walk. She opened the garage door and the pack marched out behind her They obeyed every command without hesitation. As she passed Drake and the sled, she shouted, "I'll be back in a little while. My kids need some playtime!"

"Okay, be careful, Shireen!"

She turned around and replied jokingly, "I don't have to be careful, Drake! I have thirty dogs here to protect me! You're the one who needs to be careful!"

Granger and Naomi stepped outside and walked over to see the progress Drake had made. Drake saw Naomi outside and said, "Well, this is a surprise. I'm glad to see you out, getting some fresh air, Naomi."

Naomi stated, "It's time I start taking better care of myself and stop hiding away in my bedroom all the time. Granger told me he wanted to go for a walk."

Drake grinned and winked at Granger, "Good job, buddy."

Granger smiled as he and Naomi took a leisurely stroll down the block. Drake went back to working on the sleds.

Inside the house, Tony and Katie were doing their best to persuade Zack to go out and hunt some game. Zack was still being distant and quiet. Tony said, "Come on, Zack, we haven't had a hot dinner from you in a long time."

Zack replied, "Then, go set some traps. I don't feel much like hunting today."

Katie said, "Please, Zack. You have to get out of this funk you're in."

He refused. Katie was at the end of her rope with Zack and Shireen being at odds with each other. She shouted, "This bullshit has to stop, Zack! You and Shireen are acting like teenagers! I need to know something and I want the truth."

"What do you want to know?"

"Are you more destroyed over Porsha dying or is it the death of your friendship with Shireen? Up until that day the two of you were as thick as thieves."

Zack sounded angry and aggressive when he warned, "Leave me alone, Katie. I don't want to talk about either of them right now. I lost them both in one day."

"I know you did, Zack. The funny thing is that one of them is still around and she's a great woman. You should remember how much joy Shireen brought you before Porsha's death managed to destroy your friendship. I don't like to speak ill of the dead, but Porsha was a messed-up girl. You knew that. Why would you still allow her to control your life from the grave?"

Zack bowed his head and stormed out of the room. Katie and Tony noticed William listening near the doorway. Tony said, "It's alright, William. You're part of this dysfunctional group now. We have no secrets."

William entered and said, "He has a huge chip on his shoulder. I feel bad for the guy. But I wasn't there so, my advice wouldn't really matter too much."

Emily came running into the room shouting, "Daddy, daddy did you see them? They're here. Did you see them?"

William lifted Emily up and held her in his arms. "Did I see who Emily?"

"Outside my bedroom window, in the yard, did you see them?"

"No, baby, I don't know who you're talking about. Who is them?"

"The rain people. The red skin people Tony and Shireen told us about."

Tony suddenly had a look of terror on his face. "Oh my God, where are they now, Emily? Are they still outside your window?"

The little girl shrugged her shoulders and replied, "I don't know."

Tony shouted, "Get everyone in the house!" before he bolted out the door. Katie and William moved into the kitchen. William called out, "Carly! Carly! Come downstairs!"

Katie opened the front door and screamed as loud as she could, "Everyone get back in the house now! Emergency! Get back in the house!"

Zack hurried downstairs and asked, "What the hell's going on?"

Emily blurted, "The rain people are here. I saw them outside my window."

Zack cried out, "Shireen's out there," as he raced by Katie and out the front door. He dashed through the yard and down the street screaming, "Shireen! Shireen!"

Drake watched as this transpired. Katie told him that Ganger, Naomi and Shireen were still outside the house. Drake ran down the sidewalk that Granger and Naomi had taken.

William noticed Carly didn't come down when he called to her. He tried again. "Carly! Come on downstairs!"

Katie recollected, "Didn't Carly say she was going to hang laundry this morning? That's in the backyard."

William, Tony and Katie ran to the back of the house. William flung the door open. They saw Carly in the backyard hanging the laundry. She was alone. She saw them standing in the doorway and asked, "Hey, why is everyone watching me hang the laundry?"

William asked, "Are you alright?"

She replied, "Of course I'm alright. Why? What happened?"

"How long have you been out here?"

"About ten minutes. Why are you asking me all these questions?"

Carly stopped hanging laundry and walked to the back door. William told her, "Emily said she saw the rain people in our backyard. She just told us a few minutes ago."

Carly said, "I was out there and I didn't see anyone else in the yard. Maybe Emily just let her imagination run away. You know how young girls can be."

William checked with Tony and Katie. Tony shook his head and said, "Why would she make that up? I have a bad feeling about this."

Katie added, "Actually, I do too."

They went back into the house. Carly left the rest of the laundry in the basket sitting in the yard. They went to the front door but didn't see anyone else. Tony wanted the truth. He knelt down next to Emily and asked, "Are you absolutely sure you saw those rain people outside your bedroom window?"

"I sure did. Swear to God."

"How long ago did you see them?

She giggled, "I told you, Tony, just before I came downstairs."

Tony stated, "Your mommy said she was in the backyard the same time you said the rain people were there. She said she didn't see anyone else in the yard."

Emily stated, "That's because her back was turned from them."

Carly asked, "What did you say?"

"I said that your back was turned. You were hanging the light blue sheets and they were standing right behind you."

Carly looked at William and confirmed, "I was hanging the light blue sheets on the clothesline a few minutes ago."

Emily continued, "That's right, mama. They were standing a couple feet away from you. There was a man and two women and they had red skin, and wigs. The women had their hands in their coat pockets but the creepy man had a black gun pointed at your head. When I saw that, I screamed and ran downstairs."

Carly gasped with shock. Tony told the

others, "I believe her."

Nervously, Katie said, "Where the hell is everyone else? They should have been back by now. What do we do?"

Tony put his hands up and ordered, "For now, we just wait. We don't know what these rain people are capable of. Drake, Zack and Shireen can take care of themselves."

Katie asked, "And what about Naomi? Can she take care of herself? Or Granger, he's a fifteen-year-old boy? Do you think he can he go up against three adults with weapons?"

Tony reasserted, "I say we wait. There's no sense in putting anyone else's lives in danger. They can take care of themselves."

Thirty minutes passed as Katie tapped her foot anxiously. William and Carly stared at the front door but no one entered. Soon, it was an hour. Then, it was two hours. Finally, Katie stood up and stated, "This is crazy! I'm going to find them." She walked out the door.

Tony shouted, "That's a bad idea, Katie!"

The others stayed seated and waited. They noticed that Emily had fallen asleep on the sofa with a few of the smaller dogs.

Katie paced quickly down the street. She didn't call out to anyone so she wouldn't attract any unwanted attention from the rain people. She tried to stay focused and alert but still managed to slip on the icy sidewalk once or twice. She kept her hands in her coat pockets, one hand was gripping a small concealed handgun. She continued down Orchard Street and then up Sherwood Avenue. She found no one. There were no traces of Drake or Naomi or the rain people.

She was a determined woman. She walked up Peach Road, South Street and Bent Creek Lane, and still, there was no one. She decided to take a chance and call out to her friends, "Drake! Granger! Naomi! Can anyone hear me?"

The air was still and Katie could sense a horrifying empty silence all around her. At one point she realized she had walked several miles from the house. She didn't want to but decided she had to turn around and head back, back down South Street, then down Peach Road.

She was becoming frustrated. She called out again, "Drake, where are you? Granger! Naomi! Can anyone hear me?"

She stopped for a minute to rest. As she stood there, she heard a noise, a whistle. She turned to look around but saw nothing. She waited to see if she'd hear it again. She did. Someone was trying to whistle to her. She peered around Peach Road again and saw someone in a dilapidated building waving to her. It was Granger. She carefully walked toward him. When she arrived, she saw Drake and Naomi inside too.

Katie entered the building and asked quietly, "What happened to you? You've been gone from the house for hours."

Drake asked, "Did you see them?"

Katie whispered, "No, I was in the house most of the time. By any chance, did any of you see them?"

Granger replied, "No, we've been hiding in here since Drake found us."

Drake asked, "Is everyone else okay?"

Katie said, "Zack ran out to find Shireen and the dogs. We haven't seen them either. I hoped they might be with you."

Sitting in a corner of the room and exhausted, Naomi questioned, "What do we do? We can't stay here all night without a fire. We'll freeze to death."

Drake could see the weakened state that Naomi was in. He agreed with her. "You're right, Naomi. I think we should take our chances and attempt to get back to the house. If we stay here for the night we'll die."

Katie, Drake, Naomi and Granger left the old building and walked back towards the house, taking it slow and easy. They arrived at the house and saw that everyone was alright but there was still no sign of Zack or Shireen. Tony asked, "Didn't you see them?"

Drake stated, "No, we didn't."

William questioned, "Doesn't that seem a little odd? Shireen had dozens of dogs with her and we haven't seen or heard a thing."

Drake answered, "Yeah, I thought about that too. Not even a howl."

Hours prior, about a mile away in an icy dog park Shireen and Zack stood completely still as requested by the rain people, who had loaded guns pointed at each of their backs.

All of Shireen's dogs had scattered away from the park. When she spotted the strangers, she commanded them to run, and they did exactly as they were told. Zack asked the rain people, "What do you want from us? We don't have anything. We never did anything to you."

One of the two women lowered her gun and stepped in front of Zack and Shireen. She ordered, "You'll do as I say or we'll kill you too."

Zack felt a chill run down his spine when she said this. He questioned, "Kill us too? Who else did you kill, lady?"

The woman responded, "Anyone who gets in our way dies."

Shireen said, "But we didn't get in your

way. You came to us."

"Shut up!" The woman shouted and raised her hand to slap Shireen. Shireen didn't flinch and the woman stopped herself.

Zack asked, "Who are you? What happened to your skin?"

She introduced herself and then pointed at the others as she said each name. "I'm Debra Elder, that's Eddie and Eleanor. What the hell do you think happened to our skin? It was that damned acid rain! We got caught in the rain!"

Compassionately, Shireen squinted her eyes and said, "It looks painful."

Debra responded, "It was painful for a long time but we've gotten used to it. It's like when you have a bad tooth and learn to live with it."

Zack loudly interrupted, "Look, Debra, what do you want from us? Tell us! We still don't know why you're here!"

"We want all the supplies you have and your sleds. well, just one of your sleds."

Shireen asked, "Why do you want one of the sleds? They're useless if you don't have a team of dogs to pull them."

Debra replied, "We'll find a way. Don't tell me what to do. Remember I have the gun, and we have all your weapons."

As if Shireen was keeping some deep dark

secret, she mentioned, "Well, not quite all of our weapons."

Eddie looked at Eleanor, then at Debra, and inquired, "What's she talking about? We checked them both."

Debra turned to Shireen and asked, "What did you mean by that? We searched you both quite thoroughly."

Shireen called out, "Mojo! Zeus! Einstein! Jackson! Holmes! Tonto! Trixie! Harry! Dante! Chi-Chi!"

Suddenly, Debra saw ten large dogs standing directly behind them. Ten other dogs followed a few seconds later. The intruders saw the Rottweilers, the German Shepherds, the Huskies, a Malamute, the Pit Bulls and other large breeds surrounding them with their teeth bared, giving off deep growling sounds.

Shireen mentioned, "I spent years with my babies, caring for them and making sure they were healthy and happy. They love me beyond anything else in this world and the loyalty that they show is simply indescribable. I trained them to sit. I taught them to rollover and even play fetch. I knew the day would come that they'd have to become my shields. So, I made sure to teach them one more command. It might be the most important one."

The dogs began growling even louder and

meaner as they shifted even closer to the strangers. Shireen asked, "Would you like to hear me give them that last command or would you rather drop your weapons and end this bullshit?"

Trembling, Eleanor dropped her weapon immediately. Debra looked at her and questioned, "What are you doing, you little fool?"

Eleanor stated, "I've been through enough misery to last a lifetime. I don't want this to be how my lifetime ends. Sorry, Debra, I can't do this anymore. I'm out."

Eddie glanced toward Debra and inquired, "What should I do?"

Debra scowled at Eddie. "Don't even think about it, Eddie."

"I agree with Eleanor. This isn't worth it, Debra." He dropped his gun and stood next to Eleanor.

Shireen addressed Debra, "The balls in your court, sister. What's it going to be?"

Reluctantly, Debra bowed her head, let out a long sigh and handed her gun to Shireen, mumbling. "This isn't over."

Shireen and Zack moved around freely as they searched the strangers for more weapons. Once they made sure they were clean, Shireen had the dogs back down. She told Debra, "Something really strange happened today. I learned a great lesson about love and loyalty. I never trained any of my dogs to do what they did today. I just made most of it up. They trained themselves to protect me. Isn't that an amazing thing?"

Angrily, Debra shouted, "What do you plan to do with us now?"

Zack put his pointer finger in the air and intervened, "Could you just hold on one minute, Debra?"

Shireen was questioning what Zack was doing. He faced her and gently put his hands on her shoulders. "You're an amazing woman! That was amazing! I want to thank you for saving my life, Shireen. And I'm so sorry about the way I treated you. Can you ever forgive me for the ugly things I said to you?"

Shireen felt uncomfortable. She whispered, "Zack, please. Not now."

Zack wouldn't stop until he finished what he had to say. "If I don't say it now, I never will. The reason Porsha followed me to that field the day she died was because she was jealous of our friendship. She believed it was more than we led her to believe. I denied it over and over. But the truth is that I did love Porsha, but she wasn't the woman I was in love with. That's the guilt I've been dealing with since she died."

"Oh, Zack, I don't know. After everything

that's happened between us. I just don't know if I have anything left."

He blurted, "I'll wait for as long as it takes you to decide. I'll wait for you."

Shireen smiled and kissed him on the cheek. "Why don't we start over and take it slow this time, Mr. Gunslinger."

Appreciatively, Zack nodded his head in agreement. Debra rolled her eyes and said, "Could you two just kill us or beat us or something? This is too much like torture."

Shireen giggled and said, "What I want to do is talk with you. We're going to sit down right here in this dog park and talk."

Eddie was puzzled. "That's all you want is to talk?"

Shireen and Zack sat down on the frosty ground. The three strangers sat down too. The team of dogs laid down next to the group and encircled them.

At the house, Drake was pacing back and forth. "This is stupid. We have to find Zack and Shireen. It's been hours and I know they're in trouble. I just know it."

Granger stood there, looking out the front door, and said, "I don't think they're in too much trouble, Drake. They look fine to me."

Everyone got up and looked out the front door. They saw Zack and Shireen walking up the sidewalk with the rain people, followed by the legion of canines.

As they entered the house, the others backed up and sat in the living room. Emily shouted, "Mama! Daddy! That's the rain people! That's the rain people!"

Carly quieted her down and sat her on the sofa. They waited for someone to say something as to why the rain people were standing in their living room. Shireen stood in the middle of the room with the strangers. "I want you to meet Debra Elder and Eleanor Parrish and Eddie St. James. Yes, the rain people have names."

Tony asked, "What are they doing here? What are you thinking? I told you these people are dangerous."

Shireen explained, "We had a little clash with them down at the dog park. Luckily my army is bigger than their army. Once we had a chance to talk, and we've been talking for hours, I found that they aren't what we think they are."

Katie asked, "And what exactly do we think they are?"

Zack said, "You think they're criminals and some kind of a threat to us. They're not. You think they're killers and they're not that either. They only killed once and that's because they were threatened by some madman who tried to kill Eleanor. They had to protect her. They're just trying to survive day to day like we are."

Twenty-eight years old Debra said, "We're just trying to find a place where we could live apart from the rest of the world. As you can see, the rain has made us quite different in appearance from you. This is one of the reasons why we became so hostile and guarded."

Eleanor added, "We never meant to hurt anyone. We really were good people before all of this happened. Then, the acid rain changed things. I'm only eighteen years old, Eddie's only twenty-three, and we're forced to wear a wig for the rest of our lives."

Eddie sat down on a chair and listened to Debra and Eleanor control the conversation as usual. He barely had a chance to say anything but eventually opened his mouth and said, "It was painful at first. The blisters were agonizing but we've grown accustomed to it."

William got up and walked towards Debra, he looked closely at her skin and he touched a few of the blisters, examining her. She asked, "What are you doing?"

"I'm William and I'm a doctor. I can't fix what's happened but I do believe I can minimize the appearance and lessen the pain, if you'd like me to take a shot at it."

Katie stepped up and agreed, "I've seen patients successfully treated for burns like these when I was an ER nurse."

Eleanor, desperately wanting her youthful beauty back, stepped forward and said, "Yes. I'd like that."

Debra questioned, "And just how are you going to do this? You don't have an internet to look things up anymore."

"I don't need the internet. We just need to find a pharmacy, some kind of pharmacy. There must have been dozens of pharmacies in this city. Perhaps one is still standing. Katie can assist me with your treatment."

Debra asked, "And then what?"

He expressed, "And then I can relieve some of your pain, get rid of those blisters and bring your skin closer to a normal color again."

Debra seemed hopeful. She looked to Eddie and Eleanor for an approving nod and they gave it. "Alright, Dr. William, we'll do it."

"Great, Katie and I will start looking for a pharmacy tomorrow."

Drake held up his hand. "Hold on, William. I need to know how long this is going to take. You know we're already behind schedule."

William replied, "It won't take anytime. I just have to find the correct combination of salves and medications. We can take them with us. So, don't worry Drake, it won't stop you from getting to Florida."

Eleanor asked, "Does that mean we're going with you?"

Zack added, "It doesn't make much sense for you to stay here. Besides, you have to go with us if you want William to help you."

Katie interjected, "They can go along but they have to understand we live by certain rules. If you can't agree to follow those rules, you can't go to Florida."

Eleanor begged, "I'll do anything you want me to. I'll go anywhere you want me to go. Just get rid of my pain."

Katie clapped her hands together and stated, "We operate as a family unit here. We talk to each other and we confer with each other in a calm and rational manner. We don't need any hotheads, no pun intended, or loose cannons to put us in harm's way. We saw that happen with someone else and she ended up dead."

Everyone in the house agreed to let the rain people join their excursion east. The following day, William gave everyone a list of the products he'd require to treat the rain people. Three sleds set out across the city to find pharmacies. Each group collected more than enough oral and topical medications to last for weeks.

The next day, hours before the sleds pulled away from Baton Rouge, William began the first treatment on Debra, Eddie and Eleanor. It seemed that the rain people would have to soon change their collective name.

The interstate was icy and tricky with many newly formed gorges. It forced the caravan to travel at only eight to ten miles an hour.

They continued onto Interstate 12 instead of going further south on Interstate 10. They knew that keeping above Lake Pontchartrain, instead of below it, would be safer.

The thirteen survivors knew that Interstate 10 would take them into the heart of New Orleans and most of them were positive the city would be underwater. New Orleans always seemed to be such a fragile city when disaster struck.

10

In mid-August 2030, once the sleds had made it around Lake Pontchartrain, they linked back with Interstate10 again. The winds were blowing so intensely, they were forced to stop in Hammond for one night.

The town was not hospitable. Most of the streets and avenues were sliced open with cracks caused by the earthquakes. The whole area was nothing more than a barren wasteland. Most of the structures had either collapsed or were getting ready to collapse. These buildings were just heaping piles of cement now.

They rode through the area for over an hour before they found an old red barn. It appeared sound enough to stay in. They were able to build a small fire inside safely.

Even with the fire, it was a cold night. The barn walls were lined with warped planks, leaving tiny cracks in between them. This allowed the frigid cold air to enter through. Everyone stayed close to one another and every blanket was used. No one got much sleep that night.

Katie was exhausted but she slept with one eye open most of the night. The howling wind created some persistent disturbing squeaking noises outside the barn.

At one point, she got up and sat closer to the fire with a small blanket wrapped around her entire body, shivering. She tried to keep as quiet as she could.

A few minutes later, Eleanor opened her eyes and noticed Katie sitting by herself and staring into the flames. She crawled over and sat next to her. Katie saw this, smiled and made some room for her. They whispered back and forth.

Eleanor asked, "Why are you up? You need your sleep too, just like the rest of us."

Katie looked at the creaky roof of the barn as she replied, "I couldn't sleep. Those sounds are freaking me out. I keep thinking the barn's going to collapse on top of us. Tell me, why are you awake, Eleanor?"

Eleanor explained, "I have a lot on my mind. I always have trouble sleeping whenever I have any kind of problem."

Katie whispered, "You do? Is it something you need to talk about? Something you need to get off your chest?"

Eleanor showed the top of her hands to Katie. "What do you think, Katie? Look at my hands. Look at my face."

Katie looked and responded, "Yeah, what about them?"

"Haven't you noticed that the blisters are beginning to fade away? The color of my skin isn't as red as it used to be. William's a miracle worker. He was right. We're getting better and it's only been a few days."

Katie smiled from ear to ear. "I know. I'm so happy for you, all three of you."

"It feels good to know I'm going to look like

an eighteen-year-old again. The past few years have been pure hell for me, for all three of us, just pure hell. I know I shouldn't care about my appearance as much as I do, but I can't help it, Katie. When I look good, I feel good."

Katie pulled her closer to help keep her warm. She asked, "Where were you when those fucking meteors hit?"

Eleanor stared at the flame and said, "I was on a boat in Galveston Bay. It was my parents' boat. It was a magnificent boat. It had four bedrooms and a full kitchen and even a hot tub. I have a lot of memories of being on the bay with my parents, good memories."

"That's a good thing to have. It seems all we have are memories now. Tell me more."

"You see, my mom and dad were always so busy with their work that, when we could finally spend some time together, we'd hurry up and head for the boat."

"That sounds like a nice time."

"It was nice. We loved to take the boat out on the water. But they didn't make it. The boat capsized and they were pushed out to sea. I swam toward the shore and eventually washed up on the beach. By the time that I finally made it to the shore, I didn't see anyone there. Galveston was a ghost town. Then, the tsunami came and I watched it all get washed away. It was as if Galveston never even existed. I was only fourteen-years-old when all that happened."

Katie inquired, "Explain the rain. When did you get caught in the acid rain?"

"I met Debra and Eddie about seven months later. Debra came from Shreveport and Eddie came from Oklahoma City. One day, we tried to get to the next town but we didn't get there fast enough and we had no shelter. We were stuck in the rain for hours and then days as we watched each other's flesh slowly burning."

Katie began to weep. "That must have been awful. I'm so sorry honey. But I'm glad we met and William's able to help you."

Eleanor smiled and put her head on Katie's shoulder. She whispered, "I'm going to make you my big sister. You can be the older sister that I never had."

Katie chuckled as she said, "And I'll make you my little sister, Eleanor. Just remember, the big sister gets to make all the rules for the little sisters." She laughed at herself.

Eleanor smirked and then the two of them stared into the fire until they finally drifted into a light sleep, sitting up with their heads on each other's shoulders.

The buckling winds continued to whip

around the loose boards well into the early morning hours. As expected, no one seemed to be able to get a restful night of sleep.

11

The next day they travelled as far as Slidell. It would be their last stop before they found their way out of Louisiana and into Mississippi. As they pulled into the city, Drake reminded everyone, "We need to find cases of bottled water while we're here. We're running low. I think we're down to one or two cases."

The sleds pulled up to an old mall. Zack and Shireen unharnessed the dogs and took them inside to run around, play and rest.

Katie led the smaller dogs in to join them. William turned to the rain people and said, "Let's go inside so I can apply your topical ointments. We can look around in here to see if one of the stores has a pharmacy."

Eddie asked, "I thought you said, when we started this, that we had enough medication to last for quite a while."

"We do, but if we have an opportunity to get more, we should. Who knows how many other pharmacies will be available to us down the road? There may be none. We just don't know. I say better safe than sorry."

Drake walked into the mall with the others. He peered around and noticed the enormity of the inside. "Let's pull the sleds inside and out of the elements. We can stay here for the night. With these vaulted ceilings we can even build a fire without any danger."

Tony said, "I'm going to look for some of that bottled water you mentioned. Granger, do you want to help me?"

"Sure, Tony. I'm coming."

Carly and Naomi took Emily through the mall to find something they could use for bedding. William took Debra, Eddie and Eleanor into a private area to apply their topical treatments. Within minutes, Carly came racing through the mall. She was hollering, "Hurry up! You have to see what we found!"

Drake ran toward her and then followed her to where Naomi and Emily were. Carly announced, "It's a furniture store. Real fluffy, comfortable beds again and no rickety barn with a hard floor. We hit pay dirt."

Drake congratulated her, "You certainly did it, Carly. Now let's get some of this stuff moved to the center of the mall."

Zack and Tony pulled the display beds and fluffy sofas into the middle of the mall and put them in a large circle. Shireen and Carly laid out blankets and mattress pads all over the floors for the dogs to rest on. Drake and Granger built a fire pit in the middle of the big circle. They surrounded the area with movable store partitions to help keep the area warm and dry.

The stores were full of canned goods and bottled water. There were two pharmacies where William found an abundance of medicines. The women went into the clothing stores and picked out new garments. As Katie and Shireen were in the dressing rooms and Naomi was picking out clothes with Emily, they could hear all of the dogs barking uncontrollably. They were sure the barking meant trouble was just ahead.

Suddenly, the ground began to shake. The shaking continued and got even stronger. Naomi put Emily in the doorway of the clothing store. Katie and Shireen stood in the dressing room entrances. This earthquake was the most powerful one they'd experienced in years.

Eddie and Eleanor frantically tried to calm the dogs as stones from the ceiling were falling nearby. Drake rushed over to help. Together they moved the dogs to another area where there was less debris dropping. Granger and Tony assisted Zack in protecting the smaller dogs. William and Carly made sure the fire didn't get out of control.

Stones continued to plummet to the floor and bounce as if they were made of rubber. A large stone came down and smacked Debra in the head, knocking her wig off. She felt the impact of the rock as she fell to the ground. Carly saw that she wasn't moving, but there was a lot of blood on the floor around her.

Carly shouted to the others. "Oh my God, Debra's been hurt!"

William attempted to walk through a clear path to her. Smaller rubble fell all around him and knocked him over for a moment. The shaking got worse as he crawled on his hands and knees to get to Debra. Carly screamed, "Be careful, William! Please, be careful!"

He ultimately got to Debra. He tried to check her head but the earthquake made this impossible. Instead, he grabbed her ankles and slowly pulled her into a cleared area. The blood from her head made a long red streak on the floor behind her. The shaking abruptly stopped. Drake ran to William to help with Debra. Soon, the others filtered in around her too.

Drake and William lifted Debra and put her on a bed. William checked her thoroughly and let everyone know she was still alive. "Her breathing is shallow and her pulse is weak. She has a nasty gash on her head and she lost some blood. She's still unconscious. I'll have to watch her tonight and monitor her condition."

William and Katie cleaned, stitched and dressed the wound and made Debra comfortable. Shireen spent an hour getting the dogs to settle in for the night, then, clearing rubble and waste from the quake.

Naomi curled up on a bed with Emily and Pierre. Drake and Katie found a bed that was large enough to accommodate the two of them, Snickers and Chynna. The air was still and everyone fell asleep quickly, except William, who sat with Debra until the morning came.

Eddie was the first to open his eyes to greet the new morning. He sat up and saw William was still wide awake, sitting next to Debra, holding her hand. Eddie stood up, yawned and stretched his arms. Then, he threw a few logs on the dwindling fire. He walked over to William and whispered, "How's she doing?"

"Still unconscious. I'm a little worried. I'm afraid the rock may have hit her head harder than I thought. I hate to say this but there is a possibility of permanent damage to her brain."

Eddie said, "I wish there was something I could do to help, William. It's times like this that I feel useless. I wish I took the time to learn some skills, even first aid or CPR, but I was too busy in college partying with my boys and failing most of my classes."

"What was your major?"

Eddie replied, "My major should have been architecture but it turned out to be endless days of drugs and alcohol. My first two years were great. I was at the top of my class in every subject. They all said I had a promising career in architecture, but I blew it. All through high school I won awards and a scholarship for my designs."

William consoled him. "No use in worrying about that anymore, Eddie. I don't think a degree matters too much anymore. Maybe when we get to Florida, you can be the one to design the new town we're going to build."

"We're going to build a town?"

William grinned, "Well, it'll be more like a little village. After all, we'll have to do something to keep everyone close and safe."

Eddie elaborated, "I think I see what you mean. I can design and build a working community, with a well and a circle of homes."

"Exactly."

Eddie expressed, "Thanks, William. I actually feel like I may have been put on this earth for a reason now."

"You're welcome, Eddie. And by the way, your skin is looking a hundred percent better these days. I think I'll start calling you the pink people from now on."

Eddie chuckled. "Funny."

The day moved forward with only a minor tremor and nothing else. After Katie woke up and got moving, she relieved William for a few hours. Debra remained in a quiet sleep.

As the evening approached, Drake's radio went off. "Drake, Drake, are you there? It's Carolyn calling. Drake?"

Drake swiftly took the radio and answered her call. "Carolyn, this is Drake. I'm here, and how are you this evening?"

"I'm doing okay. I haven't been able to get through to you in a while. Something happened to my radio and I had to repair it."

Drake replied, "So much has happened since we last spoke."

"You found other survivors?"

Drake calmly said, "We did, but we also lost Porsha."

Carolyn questioned, "You lost Porsha? But how? Where?"

He informed her. "She was mauled by a black bear in Moss Bluff. It wasn't long after you and I spoke."

"Oh, poor Porsha. How is Zack? How is he handling it?"

Drake stated, "At first, he wasn't dealing with it at all, but he's come around and realized he had to move forward."

There was a moment of silence before Carolyn inquired, "You said you found another survivor?"

"No, we actually found six more survivors."

"Six? That's remarkable, Drake. It sounds like you're collecting an entire village to bring with you to Florida."

Drake told her, "We found a doctor named William and a younger woman named Carly. They were also taking care of Emily, a little thirteen-year-old girl. The three of them were living as one family unit. It's quite impressive."

"That is impressive, and to have a doctor with you. He's a good man to have around. You mentioned you found six survivors. That was only three. Who else did you find?"

He spoke to Carolyn in private so he could explain who was traveling with him. "Do you remember a while ago when we told you about the rain people?"

"Yes, I do."

He whispered, "They were in Baton Rouge, almost stalking us. We had a little conflict with them. Well, it was actually Zack and Shireen who had a little conflict with them."

"What happened? Are Zack and Shireen alright?"

Drake added, "Oh, they're fine. Shireen used the best weapon she could to turn the tables in her favor."

"The dogs?"

"Yes, her little canine army marched into battle for her. But after speaking to and getting to know the rain people, we found they're no different than us. They were just bitter and angry over their own physical pain and sad appearances. They felt almost cheated."

Carolyn hinted, "So they've overcome that hostility?"

"Dr. William began to treat them for the problem and it appears as if they're going to make, what William said would be, about an eighty to ninety percent recovery. Their pain seems to have subsided by leaps and bounds."

"That's pleasing news, Drake."

He giggled, "Our numbers keep growing. If we find anyone else on the way, I might have to build another sled. I'm getting pretty good at this sled building stuff, you know."

Katie walked in and joined Drake for the remainder of the conversation. "Hello, Carolyn. It's Katie here."

"Hi Katie, Drake has been getting me caught

up on what's been going on in your world. I can't wait to see all of you."

Katie announced, "Well, I just found out there's going to be even more of us coming. Shireen just discovered the Huskies are pregnant."

"That's so sweet. New puppies are so warm and wonderful."

Katie, before leaving, said, "We'll see you soon, Carolyn."

Drake could hear how tired Carolyn was becoming. "Just to let you know, we're in Slidell. It's only a few miles from the Mississippi border. We've come over three-hundred and fifty miles at this point."

"I know that. I can't believe it, Drake. I'm anxiously awaiting your arrival."

The transmission ended and Drake put the radio in his pocket. He went back to the center of the mall to see if there was any change with Debra. She was still unconscious. Drake pulled out his journal and sat by himself on the north side of the mall and wrote his thoughts down.

They waited patiently for several more days, holding onto hope. Until, finally, Debra opened her eyes and gazed around at her surroundings. She was awake. William asked her questions and the others gathered around to observe her condition.

"Debra, can you hear me?"

She looked him in the eyes but said nothing. He repeated, "Debra, can you hear me? It's doctor William."

She opened her mouth and asked softly, "What happened to me?"

"You were hit by a falling stone during the quake. You lost a lot of blood but you're going to be alright. How do you feel now?"

Her faced showed a look of anguish on her face as she replied, "The back of my head hurts. It really hurts. I have a headache and I feel weak and a little dizzy."

He assured her, "You're feeling weak now because you haven't eaten in a few days. I'm sure the headache will go away over time. You still have some healing left."

Debra attempted to sit up, slowly. She did for a moment but collapsed back onto the bed. She said again, "I feel so weak."

"We're going to get you some food and water and then I have to check your wound. Like I said before, I think you'll be okay."

She smiled and said, "Thank you for taking care of me, William, for taking care of all of us. You're a good man."

William and Katie made sure Debra was fed and well hydrated. They watched the days pass as Debra regained her strength. Soon, she was sitting up, then walking around and gradually making a full recovery.

Shireen was worried about the sleds. She told Drake the expectant Huskies would only be able to pull them for a few more weeks. Then, they'd have to ride in the sleds. "This is going to slow us down a bit."

Drake commented with a positive attitude, "We'll just have to adapt. Don't we always find ways to adapt?"

Shireen was comforted to know that Drake saw the dogs were as an important part of the family as she did.

A few days later, the sleds were all packed, the dogs were leashed and the survivors were on their way out of Louisiana. William and Katie made sure to ride in the same sled as Debra so they could continue to monitor her progress.

12

Once in Mississippi, they noticed the Gulf of Mexico had risen so high that the Interstate 10 was only a couple miles away. The sleds crossed into a dark and heavily wooded area that seemed to go on for miles.

The first sled contained Drake, Shireen, Zack and Granger. In the second sled was Eddie,

Katie, Emily and Eleanor. The third sled carried Tony, Carly, William, Naomi and Debra and many cases of canned food and bottled water. Until then, the canines kept their steady pace.

Their trek through the dense woodlands was slow and careful. Zack and Granger had their rifles ready to shoot anything that tried to attack them from the front. Tony and Carly had their rifles to protect the rear of the caravan. Granger said, at one point, "Doesn't it feel like the weather's getting a little warmer?"

Shireen nodded and agreed, "It does feel like the temperature's rising."

The sleds continued through the wooded area with caution as the temperatures seemed to climb up above freezing.

Drake noticed the icy roads weren't icy anymore. The interstate looked like an interstate again. The heat continued to rise as they gradually made their way out of the woods and across the Mississippi state line. The bottoms of the sleds were taking a beating on the pavement.

The survivors realized the sleds and the dogs couldn't handle their weight anymore. Drake and Zack got out and helped pushed the first sled along. William and Granger pushed the second sled. Eddie and Tony pushed the third one. Shireen, Katie, Eleanor, Emily, and Carly tried to help as they got out and walked alongside their wooden vehicles. Debra and Naomi were too fragile to walk or push. They remained in the third sled.

The temperature had risen so high that the survivors removed some of their layers of clothing. Drake looked at his thermometer. The reading had shot from twenty-five to fifty-five degrees in a matter of an hour. Drake, walking next to Zack, remarked, "This shouldn't be happening. This isn't right. Something feels different."

Zack replied, "What do you think is causing the heat wave?"

"I don't know what it is but it's not normal in this new world. The world that we live in now is always supposed to be cold, bitterly cold. Look all around us. There're healthy trees and lots of green vegetation here. None of the lakes or the roads are frozen over."

The survivors continued walking along and forcefully pushing the sleds, questioning what they were walking into. The temperature had spiked at sixty-seven degrees. They found they were actually sweating underneath their heavy jackets and thermal hats. Granger and Eleanor noticed puffs of smoke off to the side, in the distance. Granger questioned, "Drake, what is that smoke?"

Drake peered into the distance. "I don't know. It must be some kind of fire."

They continued to drag along, noticing more puffs of smoke. The survivors were alert to the bizarre climate change and mysterious smoke. No one was able to explain why their surroundings were changing.

They also noticed they'd been moving up a slight incline for several miles, an incline that didn't exist five years before. Drake commented, "I don't like this at all. This is supposed to all be flat land. We shouldn't be moving uphill."

It was a long and strenuous climb for all involved. The dogs were tired and the survivors were exhausted but they knew they had to keep trudging ahead.

Granger kept staring at the puffs of smoke, trying to figure out what they were. Tony made the remark, "It's funny how we hated the cold for all these years and now it warms up and we're asking why. Let's enjoy it. We'll only worry about it if it becomes a problem."

Granger agreed, "Okay Tony," but still, he tried to figure out where the smoke was coming from.

The day was dragging on and everyone had to stop to rest. The dogs needed water and a break. Drake saw the temperature had climbed to seventy-five degrees. As they sat there, Granger stared at the strange puffs. It was then he realized what was they were. He grabbed Drake and Zack and pulled them off to the side so they could speak in private. "I can't believe I didn't figure it out sooner. I'm such an idiot. I know why it's been getting warmer and what's causing the smoke."

Seeing the look on his face, Drake asked, "What Granger? What do you think it is?"

"It's a volcano. We're on a volcano. That's the only logical explanation."

Eddie overheard Granger and shouted, "A volcano?"

Soon, the survivors were alerted to the fact that Granger could be correct in his assessment of the situation. Katie said, "It does make sense. The weather, the smoke, the hill we've been climbing. It makes perfect sense."

Tony questioned, "Correct me if I'm wrong, but don't volcanos occasionally erupt and destroy everything in their path?"

Drake raised one eyebrow and responded, "That's what they do, Tony. The problem is we don't know where the volcano is."

Zack pointed down the interstate and asked, "So, should we keep going that way or do we turn around and high tale it out of here?"

Drake replied, "I don't know, Zack. We know what's behind us but we have no idea how much worse the heat and the gasses can get if we keep moving forward."

Carly stated, "Then I vote we turn around. Turn around right now and go back to where we came from."

Fatigued and concerned, Shireen intervened, "Guys, I don't know how much more the dogs can handle. They're tired. I think we should go ahead. Once we reach the top and start downhill, it'll be easier on the teams."

There was a rumble! The ground shook! Naomi and Debra popped their heads up from their sled to see what was going on. Another rumble! Granger pointed and alerted everyone to the puffs of smoke that were getting larger.

Shireen walked to the third sled and took Pierre. "Naomi, I'm going to let the little guy walk around for a while and let him stretch his legs. He'll be right back."

Shireen unleashed some of the large dogs and they ran ahead with the smaller dogs. The ground shook again! The survivors saw that the puffs of smoke shooting higher were actually steam and gasses coming up from the ground. Drake said, "We need to figure out which way we're going! I think we should take a vote!"

The ground began to shake violently. Katie and Eleanor had to hold onto the first sled to keep from falling over. There was a cracking noise. The cracks already in the interstate behind them were growing larger. Granger pointed, "Look! The ground is breaking open!"

Shireen began to unharness all the dogs she could as fast as she could. Zack asked, "Why are you doing that?"

"I'm freeing them in case something does happen, they need to be able to save themselves. They can't be chained to these sleds. That would be inhumane."

Zack heard her and ran to the second sled and began untying those dogs.

Suddenly, a crack appeared in the road just beneath the tail end of the third sled. Tony noticed the crack as it started to widen. The third sled began to shift itself into the crack.

Debra and Naomi braced themselves when they felt the quick jerking motion. Their fragile states and the shuddering of the sled made it impossible for them to do anything else. Tony ran to the sled and grabbed the front. Eddie ran over to help. He grabbed the other side. The four dogs that were still harnessed to the third sled were being pulled backwards as they barked and clawed at the ground for stability.

Again, the ground shook violently and most everyone tumbled over or grabbed ahold of a sled. The ground behind the third sled began to crumble rapidly. Steam poured up from the gap. Tony and Eddie clutched ahold of the wooden monster in an attempt to help Debra and Naomi.

There was another rumble and the ground shook more violently. The third sled began to slide backwards into the huge gorge that was forming under it. Debra and Naomi screamed but couldn't do anything to save themselves. Tony realized his sleeve was caught on a few nail heads that were protruding from the sled. Eddie saw this, let go of the sled and tried to free Tony's sleeve. It wouldn't come free in time.

Another rumble! The steam shot higher from the ground. The gorge opened wider. No one could get to the sled fast enough as it dipped and then quickly plummeted into the gorge.

Eddie was thrown backward to safety. Tony remained attached to the structure as it plunged into its downward spiral.

The last thing the survivors saw was the four harnessed dogs clawing and yelping defenselessly. Shireen screamed in terror as she watched this. The rumbling continued.

Within a few minutes, it was all over. The survivors had lost Tony, Naomi, Debra and four of their strongest dogs. They were in awe over what had transpired but knew they had to move forward, whatever the circumstance they would face ahead.

The gorge behind prevented them from progressing any other way but straight ahead.

Everyone remained silent for a time. The shock, the loss and the devastation had each person tongue-tied.

Shireen realized she not only lost the four large dogs but two of the smaller dogs were killed during the disaster. She held onto Pierre and noticed how sad and shaken up Emily was from what she had witnessed.

She knew that Pierre had just lost his new best friend. Shireen asked Emily if she could take care of Pierre for Naomi. Emily cried as she took the French Bulldog from Shireen's arms, but she saw the comfort that he gave her as she hugged him closely and sobbed. "It's alright, Pierre. You'll see your mommy again someday."

The remaining people wasted no time in harnessing up the dogs on the only two sleds they had left. There wasn't enough time to mourn the horrible deaths that just happened. Shireen was deeply saddened with the loss of her six dogs, her children, her best friends.

The road continued to shake sporadically as they moved forward. Soon, they found themselves moving downhill. They noticed that the shaking had subsided and, as they spent hours getting to the bottom of the hill, the temperatures began to fall again. Drake checked his thermometer. It read thirty degrees. Strangely, they found the bitter cold was more comforting since it meant they were probably moving away from the volcano.

Eventually, the interstate became a desolate and icy roadway once again. The dogs had resumed their movement at a normal pace.

Drake and the others chose to travel further into the night than they usually would, in order to put more space between them and the volcano. As they progressed along, each one thought of what was lost that day.

13

The temperatures were back to where they should have been. The two sleds pulled into the Mississippi town of Diamondhead. As they were traveling down Main Street, Drake spotted a man walking. He stopped the sleds and got out to speak to the man. He yelled, "I don't want any trouble!" and ran away from them.

Zack hopped out of the sled and ran after him. Zack was fast but the man was even faster. He kept a quick pace even though he was sprinting on solid ice. Zack kept the same pace for a while but slipped on a patch of ice and the pursuit ended quickly. The man disappeared from view. When

Zack got back to the others, he said. "I can't believe how fast he was moving. He was actually able to outrun the Gunslinger."

Drake said, "You tried, Zack. I guess the guy just didn't want to be caught."

Irritated, Katie said, "Enough about the guy. We need to find a place to camp out for the night. I'm tired and so is everyone else."

Drake and Zack stopped talking about the running man and resumed their search for a safe place to go. Eventually, they turned down Pine Street. Granger called out and pointed, "Hey, it's that guy again!"

Zack hopped out of the sled again and began another foot race with the man. They made it three blocks before the man stopped dead in his tracks and turned around. Zack stopped when he saw the man had a gun pointed at his chest. Zack raised his hands in the air. "Come on, man. I'm unarmed. I don't have a weapon."

The paranoid man responded, "How do I know that? You could have a gun hidden in one of your pockets."

"No, really … I don't."

The stranger walked up to him with the gun still aimed at Zack's chest. He waved the gun and stated, "Don't make me use it 'cos I don't have any problem pulling the trigger."

Zack, still out of breath, said, "We just wanted to stop you to see if you needed any help, man. You look like you're alone here."

"Whether I'm alone or not is none of your damned business."

Zack asked, "Then you don't need anything? We're on our way to Florida. We just didn't know if you were interested in joining us?"

"Where the hell did you people even come from?"

Zack answered, "We started in Texas and have been working our way across the states. It's been slow."

"You saw the volcano? You made it past the volcano?"

Zack replied, "We barely made it and lost three of our friends in the process."

Suddenly, the man seemed friendlier, almost too friendly. "I'm Hal, Hal Reynolds."

"Hello, Hal. I'm happy to meet you. I'm Zack Strickland from San Antonio."

Hal inquired, "Just how many of you are there?"

Zack counted in his head. "Now, we have ten humans and twenty-six dogs. But we still have room for you if you want to go with us. It would be no trouble."

"Go back to your dogsled and follow me.

It's a few more blocks to the east."

Zack agreed. "Where are we going?"

"You'll see! Just go back and get your people to follow me."

Zack nodded. "Okay, I will."

Zack went back and told the others to follow Hal. Shireen questioned it. "We're going to follow this man we don't know? Isn't he the same man that had a gun pointed at your chest a few minutes ago? Are you sure about this, Zack?"

Zack answered sternly, "Yes, I'm sure. Now let's get moving."

The sleds pulled away and followed the man to an enormous warehouse. Eight of them got out and walked inside. Shireen and Eddie stayed outside with the dogs.

Drake and Zack were the first to enter the structure. Inside, they couldn't believe their eyes. Somehow, the man turned the warehouse into a beautiful home. There were separate bedrooms and bathrooms. He had running water and a furnace he had ingeniously linked from the warm steam of the volcano miles away that heated the entire space. He even had a place behind the warehouse he had turned into a greenhouse where he was growing his own fruits, vegetables and herbs. The beds were large and comfortable.

Hal took his layers of jackets and flannel

shirts off, revealing he was a man in his early sixties with gray hair and a matching beard and mustache. Drake said, "This is unbelievable. How could one man possibly do all this?"

Hal mentioned, "That's not even the best part. I have the furnace piped into an area out back. I have a chicken coop and pigs. I even built a dome where I keep cows too."

Drake asked, "But how?"

Proudly, Hal replied, "Well, first you need a lot of determination. Then, you need a strong back and a big plan."

Zack announced, "You have all that and more, Hal."

"It took years to create my own little utopia but I did it. You can all stay here for a rest, if you want. There's a separate space over there for the dogs. But I do have some rules!"

Drake murmured, "Rules? What are the rules, Hal?"

"You all clean up after yourselves and the dogs, and no stealing. If it's mine, it better not be touched by any of you. I don't like people who take what's mine."

Drake responded, "No problem. We're just thankful we found you."

Soon, the rest of the survivors came into the building. Shireen untied the dogs and brought them in. It was an early night. No one spoke too much. They were exhausted and still shaken deeply by the loss of the others.

The next morning, the survivors were invited to partake in a beautiful breakfast with fresh ham and eggs. The massive warehouse was warm and comfortable. So comfortable, that many of them could see themselves staying there with Hal instead of continuing onto Florida.

Eddie and Granger spent a lot of time with Hal as they learned exactly how everything was planned and built. Granger asked, "But what about the volcano? Aren't you dangerously close to the volcano?"

Hal answered, "No, the volcano is a good distance from here. Sometimes, it does help to bring the temperatures up around here. I remember one spell that happened. The warm wind was blowing this way and temperatures climbed into the upper fifties for nearly a month. That was a good time to get out and work on the dome. I remember, all the animals lived here in the warehouse with us until I built that dome."

Eddie questioned, "Us? You said us. Does that mean there were other people here that helped you create this?"

Hal stated, "Well, I had lots of help at first.

There used to be five other people that lived here with me. Three men and two women. They helped me to construct this monstrosity, but none of them are here anymore."

Granger asked, "What happened to them? Why are you alone?"

"Well, two of the men and one of women died over time. The other man and woman left Diamondhead a long time ago. They've been gone about a year now."

Eddie probed, "If this is all so wonderful, why did they leave?"

Hal snapped, "Why, because of the volcano of course. It's always about that damned volcano. They were afraid the volcano would erupt and kill them. I tried to convince them that the volcano is too far away to hurt us."

Granger was curious. He asked, "How did the other three die?"

Hal reflected, "Good old Roger died of a massive heart attack. Happy and healthy one day, gone the next. Charlotte got sick with a fever. I don't know what strain it was but it was strong enough to kill her in just a few weeks. A few months later Vic got the same fever and, boom, he was gone too. That's when Peter and Maddie decided it was time to go. They were only in their late teens. I couldn't convince them to stay. Wish I knew if they made it to a safe place. I guess I'll never know."

Zack mentioned, "You did a great job of making this into a working community. You should be proud, Hal."

"It's great but lonely at times, most of the time, actually."

Several days passed by. The survivors were happy and content. One day, walking in the back near the dome, Eddie and Eleanor noticed graves, three graves. Eddie commented, "These must be the graves of those other people that lived here. He told us that there were three others that used to live here but died."

Eleanor walked to the other side of the dome and noticed something strange. She asked, "Eddie, did you say there were three others who used to live here but died?"

"Yes, that's what Hal told me."

Eleanor pointed down at the ground and questioned, "Then what are these four graves I'm standing in front of?"

Eddie and Eleanor walked around the entire circumference of the dome and saw multiple graves. Eleanor announced, "Suddenly, I don't feel so safe here anymore."

"There must some explanation. Maybe they're graves of people who died in the original blast five years ago."

Eleanor smiled. "I suppose you could be right. After all, he's too nice to be a serial killer. Besides, this looks like a place he wants to share with everybody and killing them wouldn't make much sense."

Eddie asked, "Do you think we could keep this to ourselves for now, Eleanor? Everyone is having such a good time. I don't want this news to spoil it for them."

Eleanor conceded, "Agreed."

Inside the warehouse, Drake and Granger spent time repairing the slight damage the sleds had endured. Shireen and Zack played with the dogs and let them rest. William and Katie continued treating Eddie and Eleanor for their skin conditions. Carly and Emily continued to build their bond as mother and daughter.

Hal appeared to be the nicest guy they could have ever crossed paths with. But sometimes, things aren't always what they seem. After ten days, Drake told Hal they were planning to leave the next day. Hal seemed sad at first but, nevertheless, he wished them well.

The following morning, the survivors packed up their sleds and harnessed the dogs. No one had seen Hal since the night before. They were prepared to leave the comfort of Hal's place and face the uncertain road that stretched out in front them. They didn't get to say goodbye.

As they cautiously pulled down the road, Granger turned and spotted Hal. He was running out his front door and down the street, screaming and waving a shotgun in the air.

They could hear his words all too clearly. "You goddam bastards! You can't leave here! You'll tell other people I'm here and they'll come here to take everything I own! That's why I had to get rid of the others!"

William dropped his head and shouted, "He's got a gun!"

Hal pointed the gun at the sleds as Shireen commanded the dogs to run at top speed. A shot rang out. Then another, piercing the back of the second sled. As he took a third shot, he screamed, "I'll find you. I'll get you filthy bastards! I'll find you! You can't hide from Hal Reynolds! Nobody gets away from Hal Reynolds!"

The third shot just missed Emily and hit Carly in the shoulder instead. She gasped and slumped over onto William's lap. William shouted, "Keep going! Don't stop! I can still check her while we're in motion!"

Zack shouted, "What's going on? What's wrong with that guy?"

Katie said, "I do believe that's a textbook mental health disorder without medication. I'd say it's paranoid schizophrenia."

More shots rang out but were too far way to make any impact. They could still see Hal while he screamed and shook his fists high in the air. Drake looked in the second sled to see what William would say. William told them, Keep going for a few miles before we pulled over".

14

The sleds swiftly made it back onto Interstate 10. Shireen had the dogs moving at top speed but she knew they couldn't keep that pace for very much longer.

They traveled a little over two hours before they made it to Gulfport. To their surprise, Gulfport, a coastal city, wasn't covered with water. They pulled in and found the old Magic Lantern Casino still standing. They stopped the sleds and went inside to explore.

The interior was dilapidated but still livable. Zack and William lifted Carly and carried her in, where they took her to a guest room and laid her on a bed.

Katie and Eleanor walked to the main lobby where they saw a giant fireplace. Katie yelled to the others, "I think I found our spot!"

Drake and Eddie began dragging beds and sofas from the guest rooms into the main lobby. Granger took an axe and set out to find firewood. Shireen tended to making the dogs and made them comfortable. Katie grabbed Snickers in her arms and told everyone she was going to help bring in supplies.

In the guest room, William took a closer look at Carly's wound. Trying to hide her pain, she whispered, "Is it bad?"

He asked, "How do you feel?"

She confessed, "I feel terrible."

Zack looked at William and asked, "Well, is it bad?"

William said, "No, it's only a flesh wound. The bullet didn't go in. She's going to be just fine. I have to clean it and dress it."

Zack stated, "I'll let the others know," as he left to inform everyone.

The ground shook slightly. Carly said, in her weakened state, "Not now. I don't need this shit right now."

William comforted her. "It was just a little shake, Carly. We should be fine in this building. It appears to be sturdy enough."

Carly smiled and took William by the hand when he tried to dress her wound. "I was afraid for a moment, when I heard that gunshot and felt it hit me. I was afraid I wouldn't have the rest of my life with you and Emily."

Through his facial expression, William revealed the fear he felt too. "Carly, the good news is that we have many, many years left. We'll both see Emily grow up into a beautiful young woman. I promise. You're not going anywhere without me, my love."

The ground shook again. Carly declared, "I hate these damned tremors. Have I ever told you how much I despise them?"

William snickered and said, "I think you might have mentioned it once or twice. Now, let me dress the wound."

Carly grinned, but then flinched a bit when William applied the dressing to her shoulder. She said, "Easy, tiger, you're working with a fragile flower right now."

They laughed before another slight tremor happened. Carly sat up and said, "I think it might be better if I go to the lobby with the others and rest where it's warmer."

"That's a good idea."

A few hours later, a new transmission came through from Crystal River. Drake held the radio and said, "Hello, Carolyn? It's Drake. It's good to hear your voice."

Her voice had been getting clearer with each new conversation they had. "Hello, Drake. I'm here. How are you?"

Drake stared down at the radio, smirked and replied, "Hopeful."

She stated, "That's good. I'm still feeling hopeful too."

"Is there anything new happening in your little corner of the world?"

Carolyn laughed, "It's a beautiful day today. I went out the front door took a little walk. It feels like the temperatures are around fifty."

Drake was surprised and happy to hear they were on their way to a bearable climate. He told her about crazy Hal Reynolds, his strange warehouse and the many graves that he had. "We barely made it away from the lunatic. Sadly, Carly was hit in the shoulder but she's doing alright now. William made sure she was taken care of."

Carolyn said, "Thank God."

Drake went on to discuss the volcano and its impact. Carolyn listened and asked where they were now. "We stopped in Gulfport for the evening. By tomorrow night we should, God willing, be almost out of Mississippi."

"That's such great news, Drake. I don't know how much longer I can last here with no one to talk to. It's lonely here."

Drake mentioned, "We would have been much further along if we didn't keep running into these damned interferences."

Carolyn expressed, "You've had quite the time of it, but I do say a prayer for each of you every night before I go to bed. Is everyone else in your group doing well?"

Katie, standing nearby, walked over and shouted, "Hello, Carolyn! Everyone's doing fine. Little Max can't wait to meet you!"

Carolyn laughed, "And I can't wait to meet little Max."

There was a silence as if Carolyn was trying to think of something else to say. Katie murmured, "Carolyn, are you still there?"

"Yes ... I was just thinking about Max. Isn't it amazing how dogs can give such an unconditional love? No matter who you are or what you've done or how they're treated, they offer that breathtaking unconditional love that humans aren't capable of. Such extremely different animals we are ... dogs and humans."

Katie responded, "It's true, but I hope our journey to Florida, even though we never met you, is enough proof to show that we care about you, unconditionally."

Carolyn said, "Oh, I do. I've never felt this feeling before. You're all risking your lives for me.

I want you to know how much I appreciate you. I look at you as my brothers and my sisters now. You are my family."

Katie conveyed, "Exactly. Now, we have to change it from being a long-distance relationship." Katie laughed at herself.

Carolyn laughed too but then her tone became dark and serious. "Katie, I have to tell you, the animals have been coming closer and closer to the building every night. It's a well-built firehouse and I don't believe I'm in much danger while I'm in here, but I have to go out for supplies and firewood at times and that scares me."

"Carolyn, you just have to hang on. We've made it more than half-way there. It shouldn't be too much longer."

Drake added, "I promise you. We'll be there by Christmas."

Carolyn whispered, "I live with that promise every day. Each time I have to sit here alone or go outside and face the elements, I think of you and how much different my life will be in just a few short months."

He added, "All of our lives will be different in a few short months."

The transmission ended abruptly, but this one lasted longer than usual. What used to be a five-minute conversation had become almost twenty minutes.

The ground continued to quake slightly as the day became evening and the survivors settled into the lobby of the hotel.

As the night moved forward, Shireen was awakened by whimpering. Soon, Zack and Eddie woke up too. Shireen checked out which of the dogs was crying. She saw that it was Nadia, the expectant Husky. She told Zack, "You and Eddie should go back to bed. Nadia's not feeling well and if I don't stay with her tonight, she'll keep everyone up with her crying."

Zack and Eddie did as she requested. The rest of the night was quiet except for a few little whimpers and cries.

By morning, Zack and Drake opened their eyes and saw Shireen sitting with Nadia and six newborn puppies. She said, "I guess Nadia was farther along in her pregnancy than I originally thought."

Emily hopped out of her bed and shouted, "Puppies! We have puppies!" She was elated to see them squirming around next to their mother. Their mother exhausted.

Drake asked, "How could she have given birth and none of us heard it?"

Shireen replied, "It was a very quick and easy birth. She went into labor after everyone had turned in for the night."

He inquired, "When will it be safe to travel with the puppies? Is this going to hold us up a long time? Remember, I promised Carolyn we'd be there by Christmas."

Shireen seemed a little upset with Drake's question, on top of the fact she had been awake all night. "What are you asking me, Drake? I didn't promise Carolyn anything. I never said anything about Christmas. You did."

Drake responded, "I'm sorry, Shireen. I just asked how long …"

"I know what you asked and I don't know the answer. It could be a few weeks, Drake. For God's sake, they're only two hours old! Now, get off my back!"

For some reason, every time Drake opened his mouth to say anything, Shireen interrupted and became angrier. Zack eventually stepped in and told Shireen that she had been overreacting to his simple questions. She said, "I see what you're doing, Zack. You're taking Drake's side?"

"I'm not taking either side. He just asked you when it would be safe to travel with the pups. That's all, Shireen."

Shireen was clearly exhausted and upset. Zack took her off to the side and told her, "You need to get some rest. You aren't thinking clearly."

Shireen listened to him and took a long, sound nap for several hours while Emily kept watch over the puppies.

Zack turned to Katie and asked, "Do you know what that was about? Why did she lash out at Drake like that?"

Katie put her arm around Zack and replied, "You have to understand, Shireen spent years alone with these dogs. They were all she had twenty-four seven. They're her children. You can't treat them like pets where she's concerned. And remember, without her children, we'd still be on foot walking through Texas somewhere."

Zack said, "I knew she was close to her dogs but I never realized just how close until right now. We're going to have to figure something out. We can't stay here for weeks."

Shireen woke up three hours later and said she felt much better but still had no intention of confronting Drake and his questions again. Instead, she spent most of the day with Emily, the Huskies and their puppies.

A few days passed and Drake, along with several others were still wondering how long it would be before the Husky puppies were strong enough to travel. Shireen came up with the only sensible solution to the problem. "What if I stay here in Gulfport with the Huskies and some of the other dogs."

Zack was stunned by her suggestion. He gasped and asked, "What are you talking about Shireen? That's just crazy. We can't just leave you here in Gulfport."

"It's alright. I could keep ten of the dogs here with me. That would leave you enough dogs to pull the sleds. Maybe when the pups are strong enough to travel, I could build another sled and catch up with you."

Katie was angry at the fact that Shireen even concocted such a foolish plan. She stated, "There's no way we're going on without you. So, what if you keep ten dogs here with you. How is that going to keep you alive?"

Shireen replied, "I've done it before and I can do it again."

Drake pleaded, "Please, Shireen, think about what you're saying. You'd been left alone in this strange city. We'll change our plans and wait for the Huskies until they're ready to travel."

Zack stepped up and said, "If she plans on staying here, then so am I. There's no way in hell I'm going to leave my little lady behind."

Katie was getting angrier She put her hands on her hips and shouted, "Okay, now this is just getting stupid now! You're both staying in Gulfport.

Do you even know what you're saying?"

Zack asked Shireen, "If we waited for the pups to get old enough to travel, and Drake helped me build another sled, how far behind them would that put us?"

Shireen calculated the days in her head. "About ten days to two weeks. The pups should be fine by then."

Zack turned to Drake and asked, "Can you help me build a new sled?"

"I-I guess I could."

"Once the pups can be moved, we'll get on the interstate and travel longer days than we usually do. We'll catch up to you eventually or we'll find you in Crystal River someday."

Drake conceded, "This is crazy, but if that's what you want, I don't have much of a choice. Let's get to work on the new sled."

Granger jumped in. Me and Edward can go out and find some lumber."

The four men walked out of the hotel to find the materials they'd need to build a sled. Once they were gone, Katie approached Shireen and said, "I think this is a bad idea. So far, our greatest strength has been our numbers."

A week later, the sled was completed. Drake didn't realize how long it would take to find the products he needed to build it. The process was much longer than the previous sleds. It was then that Shireen figured out they would only be a few days behind the rest of the group.

October 2030 began with two sleds pulling out of the Gulfport area carrying only seven people and sixteen dogs. Granger chose, at the last minute, to stay behind with Zack and Shireen. The group collectively mapped out each place they'd stop on the coastal highway and Interstate 10 until they'd finally be reunited.

The sleds pulled out and Shireen told Zack and Granger they'd be able to exit four days later. Drake and Katie were happy to know they were going to only be less than two hundred miles behind them.

Shireen, Zack and Granger watched as the others pulled down Beach Boulevard toward Biloxi. Granger pondered, at that moment, if he'd ever see any of those seven people again in his lifetime. He hoped he made the right choice.

15

It was the day that the sleds only made it about fifteen miles into the city of Biloxi. The seven survivors found Route 90 was a gravelly and torn-up beach road. This made travel a little slower than the interstate.

After arriving at the edge of the Back Bay, they saw the water was not completely frozen over and the access bridge that used to be there had been completely washed away. This was the bridge that would have connected them to Ocean Springs and eventually the interstate again.

After traveling for a mere three hours, Drake decided they should stop, figure out their next step and take it easy for the rest of the day. "Let's pull in a see what's here."

They saw Biloxi as it was, loaded with half-standing casinos and abandoned gift shops at every turn. Drake pulled the first sled over, the second soon did the same. "Drake hollered back, "The bridge is gone. There used to be a bridge there but it's gone. We're going to have to head back north to the interstate."

William yelled back, "But it's already one o'clock. How long do you think it'll take us to get back to the interstate?"

Drake looked at Katie. She shouted, "About three or four hours!"

William jumped out of the sled and said, "It's a good idea to stay here tonight. We can head for the interstate first thing tomorrow morning. I think it would be safer."

Katie nodded her head and blurted, "Sounds

like a good idea."

Eleanor said, "Let's find a place for the night. We can probably stay in one of the casinos like we did in Gulfport."

Drake nodded, "Then that's what we'll do. We stay in another casino."

The survivors turned the sleds around and headed to the Treasure Chest Casino and Hotel. They proceeded to stroll through the enormous golden front doors and check the inside for safety and functionality. It looked good.

Once the sleds were unpacked, Katie and Eddie untied the dogs. They noticed the dogs were acting strangely. Drake said, "They probably miss Shireen. They know us but we're not their mother. They're going to be a little difficult for a while until they get used to us."

A fire was built and beds were pulled into the lobby, as with the previous casino. Everyone settled in, but being on the road for only a few hours meant they had a lot of spare time to waste before they went to sleep.

Drake and Katie took a walk up the stairs to the top floor of the building. This took a while since thirty-two floors was not an easy climb. Once there, they made their way to the roof where a pool and cabana bar used to exist.

It was cold on the roof, much colder than it

was on the first floor. Drake put his arm around Katie to keep her warm. They looked out at the horizon, what little horizon still existed, that is. They looked off each side of the property to see the landscape.

To the east, they could see the beginning of the mountain range that split the Gulf of Mexico in two. It was the same mountain range that Carolyn had spoken about. Katie said, "Well, isn't that a slap on the back, mountains in the middle of the gulf." She laughed at herself.

Drake reminded her, "Katie, like I've said before, this is a whole new world we live in today. It's nothing like we used to know. Nothing and no one are the same since that day the meteors hit the earth. We have to accept it eventually."

She looked Drake in the eyes. "I know how different things are, Drake. I mean, we're driving across the bottom of the United States. It should be flat and warm, but instead, we're riding through active volcanos and ice-covered mountain ranges on goddam dogsleds. I have accepted it, but once we get to Florida, will life be normal? What's going to be our new normal?"

He responded, "I don't know, Katie. I wish I could tell you, but none of us know for sure. We'll have to make the best of it and pray we can keep the human race alive."

The ground quaked. The building trembled. Drake held onto Katie. They waited until it stopped. He suggested, "Maybe we should get off the roof for now."

On the first floor, William gave Eddie and Eleanor their skin treatments, commenting, "I didn't even think this medicine would work so well or so quickly."

Eddie looked at his arms and then looked at his face in one of the lobby mirrors. "It's so slight, you can hardly tell anymore."

Eleanor took her wig and put it back on her head. "Except for our hair."

William stated, "I'm sorry, Eleanor. There's nothing I can do about that. You'll just have to learn to look in the mirror without your wig and realize what a beautiful woman you truly are, both inside and out."

Carly agreed. "He's right Eleanor. You and Eddie look perfectly fine without hair. Besides, it's our world now. It's all ours. We can make whatever rules we want."

Eleanor gazed at her reflection in the mirror, smiled and said with a new confidence as she took her wig off. "You're right. I don't need this stupid wig anymore. I'm beautiful with or without it. And I prefer without."

Eddie was glad to see Eleanor's confidence

was getting better. Emily ran into the lobby, wrapped her arms around Eleanor and said, "I want to be just like you someday."

Proudly, Carly leaned down to Emily and said, "You already are like Eleanor, baby. You already are."

Eddie said, "I'll feed the dogs tonight. I know they miss their mama but they'll have to put up with me until we're all reunited."

As the night came, Drake walked into a separate room in the hotel, lit a candle and took out his journal. He flipped through a few of the pages, rereading what he'd already written. Then he pulled out a pen and began to write in it. His words were mostly the feelings that he didn't like to speak aloud in front of the others, his trepidation over Shireen's decision to stay in Gulfport and even his concern over the thought of crossing over a mountain range in a few days.

He didn't like the survivors being separated into two separate units. He didn't like the fact that Shireen wasn't there to care for and control the entire dog pack. He worried about the future of his friends and the entire the human race, questioning how they would carry on.

Strangely, in his gut, he knew everything would turn out satisfactory. He saw a future with the ten survivors, Carolyn and anyone else who just happened to be out there, looking for a home and looking for a way to survive.

He thought about the loss of Porsha, Naomi, Debra and Tony. He still couldn't believe how a life could just be exterminated in a few short seconds. He knew people who died during his earlier life but not from bear attacks or earthquakes or volcanos. He shook his head.

He knew, once Zack, Granger and Shireen reconnected with them, that they had to make better time in getting to Florida. Drake was worn-out from traveling and drained from the unfriendly elements. He just wanted the journey to be over.

When he finished writing his daily thoughts in his journal, he put it back in the pocket inside his jacket and joined Katie and the others for a quiet night of sleep.

Drake curled up on the bed with Katie and softly put his arm around her, trying not to disturb her. He closed his eyes and wanted to sleep, but couldn't. Instead, he lay awake for hours staring at the back of Katie's head and the dogs.

In Gulfport, Shireen was standing at the front of the building staring out at the water. Granger had already gone to bed. Zack approached Shireen calmly and asked, "What are you thinking about, baby girl?"

She was more than willing to open up and share her thoughts. "I think about different things sometimes. I think about our future. I wonder where we'll be five years from now or if we'll even still be alive. We never know. I mean, five years ago, who on earth thought they were all going to die the way they did."

Zack whispered, "That's something we'll have to wait to find out. The future's never certain, Shireen. It never has been."

"And when we do finally get to where we're going, are we going to have to live like we do now, having to search for canned goods in the abandoned supermarkets, eating, sleeping and existing in one big space, worrying if the next person we meet is normal or a serial killer? I don't know if I want any of that."

Zack looked out to the water and mentioned, "We'll never know if we don't try. I, for one, am happy I met you and the others. I couldn't stand living out the rest of my life with no one to talk to or hold while I'm sleeping. Even though I don't know what tomorrow holds for us, I'm satisfied with today."

Shireen grinned and turned to Zack. She moved closer until he was holding her in his arms. "That's what I love about you, Zack Strickland, I mean, Mr. Gunslinger. You always see the positive in everything, in every situation."

He beamed as he responded, "And there's so many reasons I love you, Shireen Parker, I mean Dog Lady. I love your spirit and your drive. I don't want to see that ever disappear. Keep believing it's going to get better. It has to get better. I think we've already paid way too much for any of this to turn out badly."

She lowered her head and acknowledged, "You're right. I can't allow myself to become a negative person. That's not who I am. I never was that person. I guess I'm just a little rattled that we're separated from the others. It feels a little bit odd not having them here with us."

"Once the puppies can travel, we'll all be back together soon enough. Why don't we check on them now?"

Shireen nodded her head and they went to see the pups and the mother who were all sleeping peacefully. Zack took Shireen by the hand and said, "It's getting very late. We should probably get some sleep too."

16

The next day brought about another cold morning with gloomy skies and thrashing winds. Shireen woke up first. She made breakfast for the three of them before she fed the dogs and checked on the puppies. Granger had a full day with nothing to do. He told Zack he was going out to explore Gulfport. Zack ordered, "Don't stray too far away from here, and I want you back in an hour. I know best."

Granger agreed to Zack's terms before he bundled up and left. He decided to head to the east side of town. As he walked down the abandoned streets, he saw another casino that must have once been a bustling haven for the gamblers and all-night party animals.

The sign that was once sitting on top of the building was now hanging down by its old metal wires. The sign creaked and swayed a bit whenever a wind would blow through. The sign said the name of the casino was The Jackpot. Granger pushed the doors open and walked inside.

He entered the main casino area and saw the rusted-out slot machines and table games that used to be surrounded by excited risk-takers.

Granger continued to wander through the casino when he suddenly heard music. It was the beautiful sound of guitars playing along with each other. He walked out of the casino and into the auditorium where the music got a little louder with each step he took.

On the auditorium stage, he saw a young

man and woman sitting on the stage, strumming on acoustic guitars. As he came into view, they spotted him and abruptly stopped playing. They set their guitars down on the floor. The young woman stood up and asked, "Who are you? Where did you come from?"

The young man hopped up from his chair, pulled a handgun from his pocket and pointed it at Granger. Granger put his hands up to show he had no weapons as he walked a few steps closer. He said, "I'm Granger Thomas. I came from Austin, Texas. I'm on my way to Florida with my friends." He inched even closer.

The young man commanded, "Don't come any closer or I'll shoot!"

Granger stopped walking. He said, "I'm not here to cause any trouble. I was just exploring and I heard your music."

The gentle young woman asked, "Did you like it … our music?"

Granger replied, "It was nice. I haven't heard music in a long time. I forgot how much I missed it."

"Thank you for that."

Granger questioned, "Who are you?"

The young woman said, "I'm Madison Green. Everyone calls me Maddie. This is Peter Wilcox. We've been living here in Gulfport for several months."

Granger stated, "My friends and I aren't here to cause you any trouble. We just needed to rest, and then one of the Huskies had pups. We have to wait until the pups were strong enough to travel. Then, we'll hit the road again."

Peter was suspicious of Granger and his sudden appearance. He inquired, "You said you have friends. How many friends do you have and where are they now?"

"We're staying right down the road at the Magic Lantern."

Maddie questioned, "You said Huskies. You have dogs?"

Granger was volunteering too much info to complete strangers. "We have a lot of dogs, and we have a sled. That's how we've been able to make it from Texas to here, and then on to Florida, faster than walking. Our dogs pull the sleds."

Peter put his hand up and stopped Granger from talking. "Wait! A minute ago, you said you had a sled. Then you said sleds. How many of you are there? Really."

Granger clarified, "We had two other sleds with seven other people and even more dogs. But, because of the puppy situation, they went on ahead of us. We figured we'd reconnect with them in a few days, maybe a week."

The nineteen-year-old man asked, "Florida used to be nice. I lived there when I was a kid. Why are you going there now? I'm sure Disney World is closed for the season."

"We've been in contact with a woman there. She's all alone and we're trying to get to her. She told us that the climate is a little warmer there than it has been here."

Maddie suggested, "Maybe we should go over to the Magic Lantern and say hello to your other friends."

Peter appeared alarmed. He demanded, "No, Maddie. What if this is a trick? What if Hal sent them to kill us?"

Dumbfounded by the mention of his name, Granger exclaimed, "Hal?"

Peter turned to Granger and asked, "Hal. Do you know him?"

Granger explained, "We met some crazy man over in Diamondhead named Hal Reynolds. Is that who you're talking about."

Maddie, who had just turned twenty a few days before, said, "That's him. That's the ridiculous bastard we're running from."

Granger mentioned, "He seemed so normal and friendly at first. Then, he ended up taking shots at us. He shot my friend Carly in the shoulder and just missed hitting our little Emily."

Peter's heart was beating in double-time. He guardedly inquired, "Hal didn't send you to find us? You're not here to kill us?"

"Nope."

Maddie looked at Peter and said, "I have a feeling. I think he's okay. Why don't we give him the benefit if the doubt?"

Peter responded with a quick nod but was still undecided. He put the gun back in his pocket as he warned Granger, "This better not be some kind of setup."

Peter and Maddie picked up their guitars and followed Granger down the street to the Magic Lantern. He introduced them to Shireen and Zack and the dogs. Shireen and Granger made a hearty lunch for everyone. They talked. Zack and Shireen confirmed their story about Hal. Peter and Maddie then shared their story.

Peter initiated, "It was so beautiful in the beginning, true perfection. There must have been thirteen or fourteen of us living there. Hal had the idea of turning the warehouse into a compound, a work in progress. We worked, every one of us, day and night, building up the inside, building the dome for the animals, the greenhouse and laying the pipes to connect to the underground steam baths from the volcano."

Maddie added, "No one took a day off until

we finished putting that damned pipe in, miles of pipe we found and soldered together. We dug the trenches. The work was pure hell, but it paid off in the end. We had a picture-perfect little community until …"

Zack insisted, "Until? Until what, Maddie? What happened?"

Peter spoke up. "Until our people started dying off. They were suddenly dying one after the other. I know the first man was strangled. Hal said he had a heart attack. Then, suddenly, others were getting sick with high fevers. We believe they were being poisoned by Hal."

Maddie continued, "This kept happening. We noticed Hal was getting more paranoid and suspicious all the time. Finally, there was only the three of us left. We knew we'd be next if we didn't get out of there fast. We made a plan to sneak away one morning before Hal woke up. The plan didn't go as we thought it would. He woke up and came running down the street, shooting at us, screaming that he'd find us."

Shireen commented, "We've been in that same place with him. It must have been horrible for you."

Zack asked, "And you made it all the way to Gulfport on foot with no supplies or protection? How lucky is that?"

Peter stated, "We did. It took us weeks to get here. I remember, at the halfway point between Diamondhead and here, I wished I could just die already. The pain of walking all those miles and seeing the struggle Maddie was having just made me want to die. But we forged ahead and made it. And now, here we are."

Shireen asked, "So, what are your plans for the future?"

Peter appeared jumbled, "Our plans?"

"Yes, what are your plans for tomorrow and the day after that? Do you plan to stay in this area? Are you thinking about moving on from here or is this it?"

Maddie glanced over at Peter before she said, "We don't really have any plans. We're sort of living our lives day by day and trying not to think of the future."

Zack leaned in and whispered in Shireen's ear. Then, Shireen leaned in and whispered in Granger's ear. Granger smiled and said, "I like that idea. I think so."

Peter and Maddie sat in silence waiting to hear what they were whispering about. Granger said, "We're going to be here for a few more days. When we do leave Gulfport, would you like to come with us to Florida? It's no trouble. We have plenty of room in the sled."

Peter and Maddie didn't smile or respond at first. They just contemplated their choice to leave Gulfport or stay. They knew they had to tell the rest of their story.

Shireen could see, in Maddie's eyes, that she was holding something back. "You're not telling us everything, Maddie. I can see it in your eyes, there's more."

Maddie turned to Peter and said, "I have to tell them the truth."

Peter was apprehensive but then agreed with her. Maddie muttered slowly, "Peter and I found out a few months ago that I'm pregnant. He's the father. We're pregnant."

Shireen slapped her knee and said, "That's wonderful news! I'm so happy for the two of you. Imagine that, a brand-new baby."

Peter swiftly stopped Shireen and explained, "That's the problem. We don't know if Maddie can travel on a sled across all of the rough roads in her delicate condition."

Shireen said, "She's pregnant. It's not like she's on life support or something. Of course, she can travel."

Zack asked Maddie, "Do you know how far along you are?"

Maddie didn't answer. Instead, Peter replied for her. "We're not exactly sure. We found this test, a pregnancy test, a few months ago when she wasn't feeling so good. The test showed a positive result but that's all we know. She could be six months or it could be seven months."

Shireen turned to Zack and said, "I really wish William was here right now. He'd be able to help these kids out."

Peter asked, "Who's William?"

Zack said, "He's one of the men that we've been traveling with. He's a doctor. We picked him up in Baton Rouge."

Maddie timidly posed the question, "So you think it would be alright for me to travel with you in my condition?"

Zack said, "Absolutely! It's not as bad as you might think. We can take it slow to make sure you and the baby are okay."

Peter was elated to know they'd be leaving Gulfport, even further away from Hal Reynolds and they'd eventually be joined by Dr. William. He had only one more concern. "Do you think we can bring our guitars along with us?"

Zack said again, "Absolutely! Bring the guitars along. It'd be nice to hear some music once in a while."

Peter sat forward, let out a long breath and shouted, "Then I guess we're moving to Florida with you."

Everyone at the table smiled and laughed and celebrated their new union. After lunch was finished, Maddie helped Shireen tend to the dogs. With their departure only days away, Peter assisted Ganger and Zack with locating more provisions and packing the sled.

Drake and his companions found that the easiest way out of Biloxi was to travel north back onto Interstate 10. Once on the interstate, they continued east until they crossed over the state line out of Mississippi and into Alabama.

After being on the road for nearly seven and a half hours, they came upon a small town named Tillman's Corner. Drake was happy to know it was an easy day of travel. The sleds pulled in front of an old farmhouse for the night.

Eddie grabbed some firewood and Carly took some bottled water into the kitchen. Drake decided it was his turn to learn how to shoot a deer or catch a rabbit for dinner. He grabbed a rifle and left. Katie said to Eddie, "Would you go with him? He's a terrible shot. If you don't help him, we may never eat again."

Eddie laughed and agreed. William decided to tag along too. Katie told the women, "It must be a testosterone thing."

Carly, Eleanor and Emily laughed at Katie's

joke. The women noticed that Katie was unusually quiet for most of the day. Carly asked, "Is there anything I can do for you, Katie? Is there something you need to talk about?"

Katie shrugged her shoulders. And shook her head. "It's nothing."

Carly could sense her overwhelming sadness and concern. She knew the problem without having to be told. "They're going to be fine, Katie. They're only a few days behind us. Stop worrying. We'll see them soon."

A single tear ran from Katie's eye and down her cheek. "You're right Carly. I just miss my talks with Shireen sometimes."

Eleanor said, "You know, you still have us to talk to … anytime you need to."

"Thank you, girls, for trying to make me feel better." She lifted Snickers and went to the bedroom to nap.

Emily asked Carly, "Can I please go out and play in the snow?"

Carly gave Eleanor a troubled stare. Eleanor responded, "Sure. I'll go out with her. What are you going to do?"

"Oh, I found a bag with needles and thread. I thought I'd spend a little time patching up some of the holes is my old jacket."

Eleanor remarked, "I don't understand why

you keep fixing that old thing up. There're empty stores full of brand-new jackets. If I were you, I'd just toss that old rag in the garbage and find a better, warmer jacket."

Carly confided, "This is something I haven't told anyone else. I was wearing this jacket when the blast happened. I wear it to remind me of that day. I was waitressing at the Parkway Diner when I heard the announcement on the news."

"What did you do?"

"I told my boss that I was out of there. I took off my hat, grabbed my jacket and left to go home, or go somewhere, anywhere. Something told me not to stay at the diner. I remember, I was on my way home when the ground started to rumble violently under my feet. The shaking almost felt like the earth was rocking back and forth."

"Were you outside in the open when all this happened?"

Carly detailed, "Not for long. I could see buildings and houses starting to collapse. People were running past me, practically knocking me over. They were hysterical."

"It sounds all too familiar. I think we all went through a day like that."

"I was standing outside the high school when I spotted a drainpipe that ran underneath the road. It was wet and dark and tight but I didn't care about that. I just wanted to live. I jumped down and got inside the pipe. I must have laid in there for hours, listening to the screams of everyone around me dying, the sound of the crumbling high school being turned into a pile of rubble, the sound of the gas station down the street catching fire and then exploding like a bomb."

Eleanor nodded and consoled her. "Like I said, I know how you feel, Carly. We've all been through it, the misery of that endless day. We all have our own stories to tell."

Carly continued, "When the people stopped screaming, I finally pulled myself out of that filthy drainage pipe to get my first look at the new world. I noticed, when the gas station exploded, it also destroyed the business that was located just next door to it. That business was the Parkway Diner. I realized, if I'd stayed, that would have been the end for me too. This old jacket is the same jacket I was wearing that day in that disgusting drainpipe when our world ended."

Eleanor felt bad that she'd told Carly to get rid of the old jacket. She apologized, "I'm sorry, Carly. I had no indication what that old coat meant to you."

"It's alright. You couldn't have known, just like I don't know everything you've been through, Eleanor. That's why we have plenty of time to get to know each other. My jacket reminds me to never take anything for granted again. That's one of the many reasons why I take my bond with William and Emily so seriously."

Eleanor gave Carly a long comforting hug. After overhearing everything that had been said, Emily stood at the front door and asked. "Eleanor, are you coming or are you just going to stand there and talk all day?"

Eleanor giggled, "Hold your horses. I'm coming Emily."

Several miles from the farmhouse, Drake walked along with Eddie and William, each one carrying a loaded rifle. They passed smaller game on the way but were determined to find larger game like a deer.

Drake didn't like the hunting experience even though he knew it was necessary. He wanted to kill an animal large enough that they could smoke and then eat for a week and not have to hunt again for a while.

Eddie and William spread out in separate directions, so they were covering a larger area than just one small field. Unexpectedly, thunder began to burst in the sky. Eddie was petrified. "The rain! The rain is coming again!"

The men stopped what they were doing and began to race back to the farmhouse. The sky began to rumble more aggressively and a light drizzle started to fall from the sky.

Eleanor looked up and saw lightning bolts coming down all around the area and knew that the acid rain was on its way. She shouted out to Emily, "Let's get back in the house!"

Katie woke up and jumped out of bed when she heard the thunder and the hard rain hitting the windows. Carly opened the front door to let them in. They saw the light drizzle was turning into rain, heavy acid rain.

Drake and William swiftly sprinted onto the covered front porch. They looked behind them and didn't see Eddie. William questioned, "Where did he go?"

"I don't know. He was right behind us a minute ago."

The rains became a torrential downpour. William pointed to the far side of the property. "There he is!"

Eddie was standing inside one of the old outbuildings. The shed was damaged but provided Eddie enough coverage from the rain. He waved his arms back and forth at William and Drake. They saw he was safe but they knew there was no way to get to him without risking their own safety. They went inside to see how the others were holding up. William asked, "Is everyone alright?"

Carly answered, "We're fine."

Frantically, Eleanor looked around the room and asked, "Where's Eddie?"

Drake pointed out the window at the old outbuilding. "He's in there. He wasn't able to make it here before the downpour started. So, he parked it in the shed."

Eleanor, on her way to becoming hysterical, began to weep and tremble. Katie put her arms around her and tried to comfort her. "It's going to be okay, Eleanor. He's safe."

Eleanor confessed, "It's not Eddie. I know he'll be fine. He's a fighter. The sound of the rain brings back such clear memories of our past, what happened to us before, and the last time the rains came and trapped us."

Katie suggested, "Maybe you want to talk about it. I know talking about something makes me feel better."

Eleanor began, "It was horrible, probably the worst days of my life. We were still in Texas. We had just left Baytown, on our way to Beach City. We were about five miles outside Baytown and had five more miles to go. That's when we heard the thunder and saw the lightning. The rains had begun."

Carly inquired, "Wasn't there any shelter available?"

"No. It was a desolate area, no houses, no cars, no businesses. We began to run toward the woods. The forest there was thick with trees. Debra led us to the middle of the woods and had us hide underneath the dense trees. That helped us a little but the rain continued. It rained for days and days and we were only equipped with a small supply of drinking water. We had no food. So, we waited for the rains to let up a little."

Katie mentioned, "I think I remember that miserable storm. The rain didn't let up for eight or nine days."

Eleanor responded, "That was the one I'm talking about, Katie."

Emily, very interested in the story, urged, "So what happened next, Eleanor?"

"I remember everyone during that time. I watched Debra as she tried to devise a plan to get us out of there. Eddie was terrified. I believe he got the worst of the rains. He sat under that tree screaming each time a drop of rain would hit one of his open blisters. We were starving to death. We were dying of thirst. And the rain kept coming."

Eleanor walked over to the window and stared out at the outbuilding, knowing Eddie was probably scared and shivering as he waited. She turned back to the others and continued with her terrifying story. "Eventually, the rain slowed to a trickle. Debra took advantage of it and told me to help her lift Eddie. He was so weak. His skin was completely blistered and painful. We carried him out of the woods and onto the road. He tried to walk but he was slow and stumbling a lot. We must have walked for seven or eight hours before we came upon a little country store on the side of the road. If that store wasn't there, I'm sure we would have all perished that day."

Carly questioned, "Did you stay in the store for a while?"

Eleanor stated, "We did. We found bottled water and some canned goods, not much, but it was enough to sustain us. We remained in the store for a week until everyone felt strong enough to travel again. But the rain had burned our skin so badly, it even hurt to walk, to build a fire, to sleep. We were constantly tortured."

Katie rang in with a positive note. "But you made it through. You survived the rains and that's what's important."

Eleanor smiled and said, "We did survive but not without our struggles. When we finally made it to Beach City, we found out we weren't alone. There was a man there, an evil man who tried to kill the three of us."

Eleanor closed her eyes and thought back to their time in Beach City. "Debra and I walked onto the main street of the small town where we were hauling supplies on our shoulders. Eddie walked slower than us and followed behind. He couldn't really carry anything due to his fragile state. We found a small house and moved into it. We chopped firewood and found more supplies from the corner store. One day, I was standing in the front yard and I couldn't believe my eyes. A man was walking down the street as if he was taking a restful Sunday stroll. He waved and said hello to me as he passed by, like nothing was wrong, like the world hadn't been hit with meteors."

Drake mentioned, "With the world as it is, he just walked by ... unaware?"

"Yes. Eddie and Debra came to the porch to see it for themselves. The man was just as friendly as could be. He came to the front gate, introduced himself as Clayton Valentine and carried on quite a lengthy conversation with Debra. He was asking questions about what happened to our skin. Debra went on to explain the circumstances and Clayton seemed okay with that. He told us he was staying in a house on the next block and, if we needed help with anything, just to let him know. It was nice to know he wanted to help us."

Katie stated, "Something must have gone wrong or that helpful man would be here with us now. Right?"

Eleanor pointed at Katie and said, "Exactly. This is where the story took on a bizarre twist. He befriended us and came to visit us and acted as if he cared about our survival, gave us food, drinking water and firewood ... until one night."

"One night?"

"That night, Debra was awakened when she heard creaking noises coming from the front porch. She thought it might have been some wild animal. So, she grabbed a gun and walked toward the front window. Suddenly, out of nowhere, shots rang out and the glass in the front window shattered. Eddie and I jumped up and grabbed our guns and joined Debra. It turned into a shootout."

"A shootout with Clayton?"

"Clayton was crazy. He was shooting up the front of the house. I felt the bullets as they flew past my head several times. Finally, Eddie took a shot at Clayton and we watched him collapse in the front yard. We ran out to see if he was dead."

"Was he ... dead?"

"He was lying face down in the front yard. When we turned him over to check on him, he was barely breathing. His last words were something about all the freaks being wiped off the face of the earth, and then, he died. And that's what we had to live through before we met all of you."

William looked up at the ceiling and asked

everyone to be quiet. "Listen."

Carly paused and waited. She said, "I don't hear anything."

William excitedly said, "The rain. The rain stopped! We can get Eddie."

Drake and Katie bolted out the front door and to the outbuilding. They found Eddie curled up in a fetal position, shuddering.

Drake noticed that Eddie had wet himself during the storm. Katie overlooked his accident as not to embarrass him. She helped him stand up as she whispered, "It's alright, Eddie. The rain's over. It's gone. Everybody's okay and you're going to be just fine."

Eddie stood up and bowed his head. He was embarrassed that everyone witnessed him acting like a frightened little child, a weak little child. He whispered, "I'm so sorry about this. I can't help myself when the rains come. The rains are the one thing that seem to rattle me."

They gave Eddie a little while to collect himself and get his bearings. Katie ran to the house and grabbed another pair of pants for him to change into.

Again, Eddie felt the need to apologize for how he acted, "I'm sorry, guys. I don't know what came over me."

Drake patted him on the back as they walked

toward the house. "There's nothing for you to be sorry about, Eddie. You're only human, just like the rest of us. You've been hurt in the past and we're well aware what you've gone through."

17

Shireen and Zack had the strongest dogs harnessed to the front of the new sled. The pups were covered and carefully placed inside. Peter and Maddie's guitars were loaded along with essential supplies. Zack alerted everyone, as he stared at a map of the southern United States, "I think we need to skip the beach road and head back north to the interstate. It's not much further and it hasn't let us down yet. We could make some good time if we do it this way."

Shireen peeked over his shoulder at the map and agreed. "We could catch up with the others a little sooner if we listen to Zack's idea and get back on the interstate."

The sled pulled out of Gulfport early in the morning and traveled quickly for nearly nine hours until they eventually reached Mobile. Granger said, "Another state is checked off the list and only one more to go."

The stayed in Mobile for the night. Finding an old brick library was helpful. It was large enough to build a fire using many of the old books instead of having to search for firewood. Zack announced, as they settled into their new space, "This is just for tonight. We can't waste any more time. We need to get back on the road tomorrow if we're going to catch up with the others."

Peter asked, "How will we know where they are if we don't have a way to communicate with them?"

Zack responded, "We have a system. When they're about to enter a town, they leave a big red colored ribbon tied around the mile marker for that place. When they leave, they take the red ribbon away, put a blue ribbon in its place to say they've been there but left. Then, they save the red ribbon for their next stop. We'll follow the blue ribbons until we finally get to a red one."

Peter was impressed. "That's a smart way to do it, nice system."

Zack grinned as he said, "Now let's burn some books."

Granger stated, "Let's start with the history and math books. I always hated history and math back when I was in school."

Everyone laughed at Granger's joke. Shireen curled up on the floor next to the puppies, watching them play with each other but then run back to their mother for a quick snack and a nap. She informed

Maddie, "You know we're going to have to name these pups soon. They have to have names if we're going to train them right."

Maddie asked, "How many boys and how many girls?"

"Four females and two males. Do you want to name them, Maddie?"

Maddie was delighted to have this honor. At first, she was apprehensive and cautious. She didn't want to give one of them a name that might sound silly. "Well, I don't know, Shireen. I never named a puppy before."

Shireen said, "It's easy. Think of something you like and pick out some names. Trust me, there's no wrong answers here."

She expressed, "I like music. Maybe I could name them after musicians I like."

Shireen stated, "That's a great idea. Let's hear some names."

Maddie thought it over and said, "I could name the boys Simon and Garfunkel. I always loved their music."

Shireen clapped her hands, "That's very good. Then, Simon and Garfunkel it is. Now what about the females?"

Maddie mulled over names and names of musical groups. She declared, "I got it. I'll name them Go-Go and Bangles and Spice and Runaway after some girl groups."

Shireen was a little surprised by the names but she said, "Okay, we may have to get used to a few of those names, but I like them. In a few weeks we'll start to train them. You can help me out with that too."

Maddie shook her head and began laughing as Simon and Garfunkel decided it was time to play with her. Shireen reminded her, "Play nice with the boys. Let's not forget your delicate condition these days, Maddie."

Zack and Peter arranged the library sofas and chairs in a circle around the fire pit. Granger dropped dozens of books in the middle and lit the fire. Shireen and Zack snuggled up close to the fire and sat silently. Maddie quickly fell asleep on one of the sofas.

Peter didn't want to disturb Maddie's rest. He invited Granger to go out and explore the area with him. Granger was bored and more than eager to accompany Peter, but not without a shotgun. Before they left, Zack advised, "You two better be careful out there."

Peter and Granger left the old library and strolled around Mobile for nearly thirty minutes before they came upon a ghastly stench in the air. Peter pointed at a Catholic Church that was at the end of the block. "I think that smell's coming from in the church."

Granger pointed his shotgun as they walked up the long gray marble steps that led them into the sanctuary. When Peter opened the door, the smell got even worse, almost unbearable.

They had to cover their noses with their hands as they entered. The enormous room was dim and visibility was low as they crept in quietly. Their eyes opened widely when they spotted the dead bodies slumped throughout the pews. Peter looked down on them and said, "These people haven't been dead that long. They just started rotting."

Granger looked around but was so confused he couldn't count. "I-I can't think right now. How many bodies are there?"

Peter used his finger to point and count in his head as he walked up and down the aisles. He told Granger, "I counted thirteen people. It may be fourteen."

"What do you think happened to them?"

"I don't know, but whatever happened to them, only happened recently, last week or maybe the week before that."

Granger speculated, "I wonder what killed them. Do you think someone did this to them, like that crazy Hal Reynolds guy?"

Peter got brave enough to check some of the bodies. He noticed every person in the church had a small plastic cup tossed next to them on their pew. It was as if the cups were dropped. Dumbfounded, Peter said, "I believe that these people might have poisoned themselves."

Granger asked, "Do you think we should get Zack and Shireen?"

Peter said, "Yes. Now!"

Granger ran, by himself, back to the library to alert Zack and Shireen of what they had found. They let Maddie sleep while they followed Granger back to the church.

Zack walked around the sanctuary to check each body. The putrid smell was so overwhelming, Shireen threw up on the alter.

Zack picked up the plastic cups and smelled them. He agreed with Peter's theory that everyone ingested poison. He questioned, "But why? Why would fourteen people just decide to off themselves like that?"

Shireen looked green. She told the others she was going to take a slow walk back to the library to get some air. "You three sleuths can figure out what happened here. I need to go out and breathe before I heave again."

Zack and Peter searched around the church for traces as to why something like this could have happened. Peter commented, "It just doesn't add up. These fourteen people survived the meteors and lived almost five years since then. Why in the hell would they do this now?"

Zack placed his hand on Peter's shoulder and reminded him, "That's what we're trying to find out."

Granger walked to the back offices of the church to snoop around, hoping he might find something there that would shine some light on the situation. Nothing jumped out at him. He saw desks covered with files and dusty computers that had long since been touched. The offices had the usual paintings of angels and saints hung on the walls and religious books scattered about.

Peter checked the deceased's pockets for any type of clue. As with Granger, nothing was helping to give answers.

Zack noticed, on the alter, a hand-written sermon lying there. He picked it up and began to read it to himself. Before he got too far along, Peter hollered out, "Read it out loud so we all can hear what it says!"

Granger walked back into the sanctuary to hear the note that Zack was reading. "My brothers and sisters, we're here today with one sole purpose in mind. The purpose to selflessly give ourselves over to our maker. He left us in this world after the great rapture took place. We were left here to walk this earth as a punishment for all our unforgivable sins. We were chosen."

As Zack read on, the sermon took an unbelievable turn. He continued, "Our sins have been great and we were locked away in our prison cells when the world came to an end. But now, we're free and we've been left to suffer for five long years. It's time to leave this world and claim our place in heaven. We paid deeply for our sins. We didn't complain and we didn't back down. But now is the time to end this travesty and move onto our new life at the right hand of our father as his chosen ones."

Peter interrupted Zack by chuckling and then commenting, "Are you kidding me? Is this for real?"

Zack looked up from the paper and said, "And there's more."

Granger said, "Keep reading, Zack."

"We, the fallen angels, have done our due diligence and found we're worthy of transcending into the new world. We won't be jailed in heaven as we were on earth. We won't take other lives or steal or scorch that which doesn't belong to us. We'll drink from the cup and feel your abounding spirit rush into us like a brand-new life."

Zack stopped talking. Peter looked up and asked, "Is that it?"

"Yes, that's it. I suppose that would have

been the point when everyone picked up their cups and drank the Kool-Aid."

Peter needed more clarification. "You mean to tell me they were all convicts? They were in jail when the meteors hit the earth?"

Zack said, "That what it looks like. All ten men and four women were convicts, and I think they believed living in this new world took away their sins."

Granger questioned, "I wonder what they did to get locked up. I'm sure it had to be some real bad stuff."

Zack shrugged it off and said, "Whatever the case, let's go back to the library. Shireen didn't look too good when she left here."

Granger asked, "Do you think we can come back tomorrow to check it out more?"

Zack found the whole ordeal to be a waste of time. "No, Granger, we're finished here. The five of us are leaving first thing tomorrow morning!" Zack shouted this as he grabbed Granger by the ear and led him out of the church. Peter trailed behind, still chuckling.

Shireen entered the library, still a little sick from the stench of the church. As she walked into the center room to check on Maddie, she saw a man, an older man, maybe sixty or sixty-five, with salt and pepper hair, standing there, hovering over her.

Maddie was still in a comfortable asleep.

Shireen froze. She didn't know what to do. She was afraid, if she woke Maddie up, she might overreact to the man and get hurt somehow. Shireen slowly inched towards the man. Abruptly, he held his hand up and whispered, "Don't take another step lady, not another step."

Shireen stopped and waited to see what the man would do. She knew that she had a gun in her pocket and was prepared to use it if she had to. She also observed how strange it was that all the dogs were quiet and lying down. She saw they were breathing but didn't know if this man had somehow found a way to quiet them by giving them some kind of sedative.

Maddie rolled over, stretched her arms and looked up. She saw the man standing over her. Her eyes became wide as she gasped with horror. She saw Shireen standing across the room, wondering why she wasn't speaking or doing anything. Maddie remained on the sofa. Shireen asked, "Who are you and what do you want?"

He replied, "I'm Irwin Howard. Why are you in my city?"

Shireen answered, "I hardly think Mobile is your city. We just stopped over here, for the night, on our way to Florida."

Irwin insisted, "This isn't Mobile anymore. I

run this place now so, I renamed the city. It's now called Irwin's Landing."

Maddie didn't care about the name of the city. She sat up and questioned, "What do you want from us?"

Shireen saw the dogs pick up their heads and watch what was happening but still remained calm and content. Irwin said, "I don't want anything from you. You're the ones who came into my library and lit my books on fire."

Maddie exclaimed, "Your books? And what makes them your books?"

"They're my books! This is my city and you weren't invited to come here! I'm the only one who can do that now!"

The dogs began to stand up when the tension started to rise. Zack, Peter and Granger came in the library and spotted Irwin. Zack pointed and asked, "Who the hell is this?"

Shireen attempted to explain. "This man said that his name is Irwin Howard and that this is his city. He thinks we're trespassing because we're in his library."

Peter shrugged and said, "What? You have to be joking."

Irwin shouted, "This is my goddam library! None of you have any business coming into Irwin's Landing without my permission! You have to leave, all of you, including the dogs! I want you out of here by morning!"

When Irwin finished giving orders, he stomped past everyone and left the library. No one stopped him. After he was gone, Zack looked at Shireen with a curious gaze and said, "What the hell was that?"

Shireen shook her head in disbelief. Zack decided to scoot out of the library to follow the man. He observed him walking quickly down the street toward the church. Zack called out, "Hey, Irwin, I need to talk with you."

Irwin turned his head and saw Zack racing towards him. Irwin sped up his pace and ran into the church. Zack ran into the church behind him, the heavy stench hitting him again.

He looked in the sanctuary but didn't see Irwin. He crept slowly up the aisle, looking at each dead body, making sure Irwin wasn't trying to pull a fast one. Sure enough, there sat Irwin pretending to be one of the rotting corpses. Zack stood in front of him. "Get up."

Irwin suddenly wasn't quite as loud as he'd been before. He appeared timid and scared. "Please don't kill me, mister. They wanted me to die but I was smarter than they were."

Zack sat next to him as Granger rushed into the sanctuary. Granger stood in the back of the room and listened to the conversation between Zack and Irwin.

Irwin stated, "It was just crazy. They were crazy. I only went along with it because they were all such dangerous people."

Zack interjected, "You mean that they were all criminals?"

"More than just criminals. They were the worst of the worst. They were the child molesters and the baby killers. One of these women killed an entire schoolroom of children. Lit a match and let them burn."

"What about you, Irwin, what did you do that put you in prison?"

He seemed appalled by Zack's question. "I didn't do anything. I actually worked in the office on the men's side of the prison. None of them knew that. They never saw me before the meteors hit the earth. They thought I was one of them when the world came crashing down all around us and I let them believe it."

Zack questioned, "You mean that you were a secretary?"

Irwin was appalled that Zack categorized him as a secretary. "I was a file clerk, a file clerk and a damned good one!"

Zack grinned and giggled, "Alright, Irwin, you were a file clerk. What happened after you got out of the prison?"

Irwin said, "I got out. They got out. You don't understand. They were safe from the blast because they were all locked away in solitary. Two guards survived the destruction too, but the convicts killed them. That's why I led them to believe I was one of them too, a criminal. I wasn't ready to die. Soon, we began living in the same place. We started in a grocery store, then we moved to a big Victorian mansion. We moved around a lot. The last place we ended up was here in this church. That's about the time they started to believe the bullshit that they were forgiven for their sins because the served their penance on earth."

"What would make all of these hardened criminals believe they were some kind of chosen people?"

"It was some crazy cult shit they were talking. I don't even know how they came to that conclusion. Then, one day, they all drank the poison, everyone but me that is. I acted like I was drinking the punch but I poured it on the floor instead. By the time any of them saw what I had done, it was too late. It must have been a mighty powerful dose they took. It only took five or ten seconds and they were gone. That left me here, all alone in my city, Irwin's Landing."

Zack lightly slapped Irwin in the face and

stated, "Stop saying this is your city. This is Mobile, Alabama, not Irwin's Landing, Alabama. There's no such place."

"These idiots killed themselves about three weeks ago. Since then, I've been free. I don't have to pretend anymore and I don't have to be afraid of being caught. They can't do anything to me. Now, I just want peace and quiet. I just want you and your people to leave here. That's all I'm asking for. I just want to be left alone."

From behind, Granger asked, "Are you sure about that Mr. Howard? You know, we always have room for one more person on our sled. I don't think I'd want to live the rest of my life in a big city like this alone."

Irwin stood up and faced Granger. "Thanks for the offer, kid. That was a nice thing to offer, but that's not what I want. I don't care about Florida or building some new world or living with a dozen or so people that I don't even know. I just want peace, and the only way to get that is to keep everyone else away from me."

Zack got up and walked towards the front doors. Granger followed and said, "Have it your way, Mr. Howard, but if you do happen to have second thoughts and change your mind, we'll be here until tomorrow morning. I hope you do change your mind."

Once Zack and Granger left the sanctuary, Irwin sat back down in his pew and looked up at the big wooden cross suspended behind the pulpit. He looked up as if he was speaking to God and said, "This is what I wanted. I wanted them all to be gone but now there's more of them pouring in. What do you think I should I do?"

Drake's sled pulled off the interstate. He got out and tied a large red ribbon to the mile marker alongside the road. Katie shouted, "We're going to have to get more ribbon in the next town! We're getting kind of low!"

Drake came back to the sled and said, "We need to pull in and stop. I think we overdid it today. We've been on the interstate for ten hours and it's getting dark. This place is named Avalon. I say we go for it."

William yelled from the second sled, "Lead on, Drake! Lead on!"

The sleds moved toward the small unincorporated town of Avalon as the skies rapidly became black. They saw the main street was once a tiny historic district lined with antique shops and eateries. At the end of the street was, what used to be, a quaint little bed and breakfast. It seemed like the most sensible place to stop.

Once inside, a fire was started in each of the

five hearths, the dogs were fed and the survivors ate dinner. As they sat around the table, Eddie noted, "We went seventy-five miles today. I think that distance was way too much. We shouldn't be out on the roads so late. That's the time when the wildlife comes out to hunt for food."

Eleanor agreed, "I know. I was getting a bit paranoid the last few miles."

Eddie mentioned, "Isn't it funny, seventy-five miles. That would have taken an hour by car in the old days, but now it takes us a full day to get that far."

Drake, after taking a bite of food, said, "It's just one more thing we're going to have to adjust to, Eddie, one more of the many things we have to get used to."

A call suddenly came through on the radio. Drake and the others could hear the high-pitched squealing noises the radio often made just before Carolyn's voice would come through. Drake said, "Carolyn, it's Drake."

The squeal of the radio continued for several minutes. Drake couldn't understand what was going on. It didn't usually take that long for Carolyn to begin her conversation. He repeated, "Carolyn, it's Drake. Are you there?"

Finally, her voice came through. "Yes, yes, Drake, I'm here."

He asked, "Are you alright?"

She responded, "I'm the same. Nothing has changed on my end of the world. After all, nothing ever changes here. What about you?"

"I have some great news for you."

Her mood seemed melancholy and remained that way even after Drake tried to lift up her spirits with the announcement that they were in Florida. "We're just east of Pensacola. We're getting closer and closer."

Still, even with the amazing news she had just heard, her tone was soft and her temperament seemed sullen. "That's nice, Drake. I hope to see you soon."

He inquired, "How's the weather been in Crystal River?"

Carolyn replied, "It was about forty-five today with a hint of sunshine."

Carly mentioned, "Wow, I wish it was forty-five here. I think our high for today was about in the mid-twenties."

Carolyn responded, "See, if you'd hurry up and get here, you could experience all of this mild weather like I do."

Drake took control of the conversation once again. "Have you had any problems there since the last time we spoke?"

"Just the usual, cold nights and noises of the

animals hanging around outside my door. I think I'm going to have to leave the firehouse soon. My resources are getting sparse and the two grocery stores I go to are almost empty."

He asked, "You don't think your supplies will last until we get there?"

"Definitely not. If I'm lucky, my food and firewood will maybe last another week. I've used it all up."

Drake looked at the others with a great concern painted on his face. "You must be very cautious, Carolyn. Do you have any idea where you're going?"

"I've been mapping out the area in my head. There are a few places I have to check out before I actually move, make sure it's safe. I should know a little more in a few days."

Drake implored her, "Don't risk your well-being. Take your time, find something that's close by. Try not to travel more than a mile from your current location if at all possible and make sure you carry a weapon."

She laughed, "I know how this is done, Drake. Remember, I've moved many times in the last few years. I've taken time teaching myself how to shoot a gun and I think I've gotten pretty good at it. I just wish I had the skills to hunt for my own food like you do."

Drake, picking Chynna up and holding her in his arms, grinned, "Don't worry, as soon as we reconnect with the others and get to you, Zack will have a great meal on the table every night of the week."

"So, you're still separated from Zack and Shireen?"

Katie answered, "Not for long. They should have gotten back on the road by now. At least, that was their plan."

"That's good. I hate thinking you've all been separated like that. I liked it when I knew there was a cohesiveness. I'm going to begin searching for a new residence in the morning but I won't have the radio with me. I don't want to risk dropping it and breaking it. If something like that happened, you'd never be able to find me."

Drake agreed, "That's right, Carolyn. We want to keep our radios in good working condition. They're our lifeline."

"It's not like I'm going to …" There was the buzzing noise, alerting Drake that the broadcast was over again.

Katie confided, "I have to admit. She scares me a little bit."

Drake asked, "What do you mean?"

"I mean she scares me. Her mood seems to be getting more and more depressed with each call.

Even though we're getting closer to her, she seems like a woman who's given up all hope. I don't know if she believes we'll actually get there."

He expressed, "You read a lot more into her voice than I do."

Katie added, "And moving into a new place is dangerous, especially if it's only one person doing it. It's possible she feels so hopeless that she doesn't really care if she lives or dies. She seems to have sunken that low."

Carly interrupted, "I agree. I've noticed the same thing. Let's not forget, she's been alone for nearly five years and her only communication has been with a couple voices over a radio. That has to be like a prison sentence and exhausting to the mind. She's probably wondering what she ever did to deserve the fate she's been dealt."

Drake said, "We're doing all we can. We're moving as fast as we can. I think I need to remind her how many people have put their lives at risk to get to her, not to mention the lives that have been lost along the way."

Katie ordered, "That wouldn't be such a good idea. If you tell her that, she'll begin to feel responsible for their deaths. She'll think that she somehow killed them for her own personal gain and we all know that's not how it happened. That's not why we're doing this."

He responded, "Okay, I'll hold my tongue for her sake," as Snickers jumped up and down trying to get his attention.

Katie smirked and said, "Good, now pick up your little boy. He's been trying to get a hug out of you for a while now."

Drake picked up Snickers and held him on his lap. He scratched his ears and around his head as they continued their conversation.

Eddie questioned, "Are we hitting the road tomorrow morning or are we taking a break from the road for a day?"

William looked at Drake and Katie as he answered, "I think we should get right back on the road in the morning. There's nothing to keep us in this place. Hell, I didn't even see any stores where we could find supplies."

Eleanor said, "Then, I'm going to bed now. These long days on the interstate are just taking it all out of me."

Eddie inquired, "So, where's our next stop going to be?"

Drake pulled out the map and plotted their passage to the next city. After a few minutes of calculating numbers in his head, he stated, "Well, if we can get on the road tomorrow and go about as long as we did today, I think we'll end right around a little town called De Funiak Springs by tomorrow evening."

Eleanor, with very little enthusiasm, said, "Great, we get to spend another long and miserable day in the sled."

Katie reminded Drake, "We don't want to run the dogs too much. Remember, we promised Shireen we'd look after them. I say, once we get to this Springs place, we need to take a few days to let the dogs rest up."

Drake replied, "Okay, when we get to De Funiak Springs, we'll do what you think is best. Besides, that'll give Zack and Shireen a chance to play catch up with us."

Katie pondered, "I wonder where they are or if they've even gotten back on the road yet. I hope they're okay."

"Sweetie, those two going to be just fine. I don't have any worries. Don't forget, they have our secret riding along weapon with them … Zack, the Gunslinger."

Katie chuckled, "I guess you have a point. Who, in their right mind, would be crazy enough to tangle with Zack or Shireen for that matter?"

"I don't feel like going out and searching for supplies right now. Why don't we just sit back and close our eyes and relax?"

Katie smirked. "I like that idea a lot. I can certainly use some me time."

Katie sat back on the sofa. Drake put his arm around her as she slowly let her head drift onto his shoulder. He whispered, "This is very nice. It's just the kind of relaxation I need."

18

In the morning, William and Eddie were the first to step outside get the sleds loaded up when they noticed how low the temperature had dropped. Drake took the thermometer outside and noticed it was ten degrees below zero. Eddie commented, "That's odd. It shouldn't be that low. Usually, by this time of the morning, it should be a few degrees over the zero line."

They waited a few hours for the conditions to warm up but it didn't. The temperature remained below zero. Katie stated, "We can't travel when it's like this. It's too cold for us and way too cold for the dogs."

Drake said, "Then, I guess we're stuck in Avalon until it warms up. We might as well make the best of it."

He grabbed his many layers of clothing and coats and his shotgun. "Anybody want to join me for a little hunting?"

Eddie jumped up and volunteered. "I'll go," as he began to bundle up.

William took the axe and said, "I'll go out and get some firewood."

Emily asked if she could go along. Carly said, "No, honey, it's too cold out there today. I don't want you catching a cold."

Katie began putting on several heavy flannel shirts. "I'll go with you, William. Nobody should be out there alone."

Carly and Eleanor remained in the bed and breakfast with Emily and the dogs. She decided to clean things up since they could possibly be there for a while.

Eleanor sat and stared out the big picture window in the living room. She watched as Drake and Eddie trudged away with guns in their hands. She saw Katie and William in the yard next door, cutting down a good sized tree."

Suddenly, there was the sound of explosions in the distance. The ground began to shake. Eleanor watched William and Katie as they stopped cutting when they heard the noise. She saw them both fall over when the ground shook. Carly asked, "What the hell was that noise?"

"I don't know. I never heard anything like that before."

Another explosion rumbled far off in the distance. The ground began to shake again. They saw Drake and Eddie racing back towards the house. Drake pushed the front door open and shouted, "Did you hear that noise? Did you feel the shaking?"

Suddenly, the entire house began to shudder. Eddie ran into the house after Drake but fell as he entered the living room. They watched Katie and William trying to remain upright as they looked around the yard and then up at the skies.

There was another thunderous explosion, followed by a thick smoke beginning to roll in like ground fog. Scared and unsure, Eleanor ran to the center of the room and asked, "What is it? What's going on?"

Drake shook his head and answered, "I don't know what it is. This is the first time I've ever heard these sounds too."

It stopped just as quickly as it began. The house was immediately calm, the ground was still, and the black smoke began to rise.

Watching out the window again, Eleanor noticed, that when Katie fell over during the final quake, she didn't get back up. She saw William down on his knees next to her, as if he was trying to wake her up. She shouted, "Drake! Drake! I think there's something wrong with Katie!"

Drake and Eddie rushed out to the yard to help William. Eleanor continued to watch through the window as the three men lifted Katie and carried her into the house. They laid her on the sofa and began removing her layers of clothing. Drake sat on the sofa next to her and whispered, "Katie? Can you hear me, sweetie?"

Katie didn't respond. William asked Drake to move out of his way so he could examine her. Drake moved a few inches down the sofa. With a sternness, William stated, "You have to give me some room to work if you want me to find out what's wrong with her." Drake moved to another seat nearby.

William felt the chill on her skin when he opened her eyelids. She stared straight ahead with a lifeless gaze. He checked her vital signs and then shook his head.

Drake stood up and walked to the picture window and stared outside. Eddie approached and said, "He's going to do everything he can, Drake. You know that. William is an amazing doctor and a good man."

Drake responded, "I know that, Eddie. I just wish I knew what the hell happened to her out there. She was perfectly fine one minute and then, on the ground, the next."

Once William finished his examination, he announced, with a tone of urgency, "We need to find a hospital or a medical center or even an urgent care. I don't have all of the materials I need to run a thorough examination."

Drake asked, "Can't you just give us a list of what you need and we'll go out and get the stuff for you?"

"No, that would take too long. Let's get her bundled up. Eddie, could you get one of the sleds ready for travel?"

Eddie did what William requested. The women dressed Katie warmly and she was loaded onto the sled. Drake got into the sled with William and Katie. He informed the others, "I want you all stay here and don't go outside. We'll be back as soon as we know something." They rode away into the abnormally bitter cold seeking help.

Eddie ignored what Drake asked him to do. He waited until they were out of sight before he started to bundle up again and said, "I'm going to finish cutting down the tree. No matter what, we still need firewood."

William and Drake drove the sled up and down the streets of Avalon, searching. They saw stores and restaurants and bakeries but no medical centers. They continued on, up and down, side to side, until they saw a run-down building and a sign for the Avalon Emergency Clinic. Drake stopped the sled at the front doors. They unloaded Katie and unleashed the dogs.

The clinic was cold, very cold. Most of the

instruments were frosted over. Drake said, "This is stupid. I have to find some wood that we can burn in here. If I don't, we'll freeze to death before you can help her."

William agreed. Drake set out to find something, anything that he could burn. William attempted to check Katie out more thoroughly but the cold was hindering the procedure. He waited for Drake to return.

Thirty minutes later, Drake entered the building holding a medium sized metal garbage can that he set it in the middle of the examination room. He left again and came back with large branches of wood, books and pieces of wooden furniture. He lit a fire and waited for the temperature of the room to climb. Drake mentioned, "Once you start the exam, I'll head out and get more wood. I found a furniture store down the street."

William began his examination, while Drake collected more wood, some bottled water and a few bags of canned food, including dog food.

During the examination, Katie began to roll around on the table and moan for a minute, but then, returned to a silent state. Drake waited to see what William would say. He noticed it was beginning to snow outside. This meant they couldn't travel until the snow stopped. Drake knew the acid snow was almost as dangerous as the acid rain.

Eventually, as the day moved forward, Katie opened her eyes. She was unsteady and a bit out of touch. Drake could she was weak. William told Drake, "At first, I thought that Katie could have had a heart attack but it appears more likely she only experienced an angina."

Drake said, "What exactly does that mean? I need it in simple words, William."

"An angina has the same symptoms of a heart attack but it's not. It was most likely caused by the combination of cold weather and chopping of the tree. It doesn't mean she's never going to have this happen again."

Drake questioned, "What about having any permanent damage?"

William told Drake, "There's no permanent damage. She'll be as good as new in a few days, but she does need to rest now."

Katie smiled up at William and Drake and coughed before she muttered, "Thank you. You're like my white knights in shining armor."

Drake chucked some more wood on the fire as Katie drifted back into a comfortable sleep. They knew it was going to be a long night.

At the bed and breakfast, they saw that the snow was beginning to come down even heavier. Eleanor said, "I hope they're safe."

As Carly was heating up a pot of stew. She

said, "Of course they're okay. If they didn't find a place to help Katie they would have turned around as soon as they saw the snow. I'm sure we won't see them tonight."

In Mobile, the same snowstorm was hitting hard. Zack put a hold on their plans to leave that day. Instead, they spent the afternoon getting to know the mysterious Irwin Howard. He came to visit them before the snow began to fall. He brought food and gifts.

As they sat around the living area, many questions were asked but not a lot of clear answers were returned.

Zack, sitting comfortably on a cushioned chair in the middle of the room, began, "So, Irwin, is that what you always go by?"

"Is what, what I go by?"

"Is that the name you go by or did you have a nickname people used to call you? Maybe your family or your wife?"

Irwin stated bitterly, "I didn't have a wife. That money hungry bitch left me twenty-one years before the blast. I hope one of those meteors landed right on her head."

"No children?"

"No. I never got the chance to have kids. We were only married for a couple years. No parents, no brothers, no sisters."

Maddie said, "That's sad. Everyone should have someone."

Irwin seemed angry. "Well, I didn't, so why don't we change the subject?"

Shireen asked, "Did you like your job at the prison?"

This question seemed to calm him down again. "Oh yes, it was a wonderful job. I had my own office and no one ever bothered me there. It was nice and quiet."

Shireen, suspicious he was making the story up as he went along, asked, "So, you like everything to be quiet?"

"I do, very much. See, the world before was noisy and full of people. Our new world is calm and there aren't too many of those loud individuals left. That's the way I always wished the world could be and my wish finally came true."

Zack and Shireen glared back at each other as if they knew they were speaking to a delusional man. Shireen inquired, "Are you sure you don't want to come with us, Irwin? It feels wrong leaving you here all by yourself."

He blurted, "Dandy."

Shireen looked at Zack again. She had no idea what Irwin meant when he said, "Dandy". Zack asked, "What's Dandy?"

"My nickname. You asked me if I ever had a nickname. I did and it was Dandy. But they stopped calling me that a few years back."

Granger questioned, "Why did they stop calling you Dandy. It's a little strange but I could get used to it."

He became angry again. "Stop asking me so many goddam questions. They just stopped calling me Dandy one day. I don't know why. They just did. There doesn't always have to be a reason why people do the things they do. That's what's wrong with the whole goddam world. Everyone needs a reason for thing to be the way they are. They all someone to blame!"

Granger mumbled, "I'm really sorry, Irwin. I didn't mean to upset you."

And just like that, Irwin was calm again. "Don't worry about it, Granger. I know you meant no harm."

The snow continued falling. Shireen insisted that Irwin stay in the library with them until the snow stopped but he declined. "I'd rather be at home in my own bed. If the snow stops and you leave, I'll say goodbye now. Be safe and I hope you get to where you're going to."

Peter and Maddie sat and watched the storm as it eventually turned into a blizzard. Peter stated, "Look at it out there. I don't know if we're going to get out of here anytime soon."

Zack leaned in the front door of the library and watched Irwin walk swiftly down the street towards his home. He wondered why the man was being so difficult about leaving Mobile. "I'm going to that prison tomorrow to see if he's really who he says he is. It's probably the same place we passed on our way into town, about a mile or two up the road. I can walk it, no problem."

Shireen asked, "Is it really that important to find out his past? After all, no one ever bothered to learn more about me, or you, or anyone else that's traveling with us."

19

Another blustery morning rolled around in Mobile and Zack saw that the blizzard was slowing down considerably, but not enough for them to get back on the interstate yet.

He was damned and determined to find out the truth about Irwin Howard, or Dandy, or whoever he really was. He bundled up, put a handgun in his coat pocket and headed to the door. Peter stopped him and asked if he could tag along. Zack agreed and they left for the prison.

Shireen fed the dogs and then exercised the puppies in her usual morning routine. Maddie posed a question to her. "Why do you think all the dogs stayed so calm and cool when Irwin was here. It was if they hardly even noticed him. Don't you find that strange? They're usually alert to everyone and everything around them."

"I don't know. I was wondering about that myself. It's like he was here but the dogs weren't aware of his presence."

Maddie commented, "Maybe he did drug them without us knowing. I wish I could figure the guy out."

Shireen decided to have a little fun with Maddie. "There is one other explanation that would make sense."

"What's that?"

She joked. "Maybe he wasn't actually here. Maybe he's a ghost or a spirit that's haunting this old library. Perhaps Irwin died in the church along with those other fourteen people."

Maddie appeared alarmed and worried. She didn't say a word but she did gasp for a moment. Soon, Shireen giggled and confessed, "Oh, Maddie, I was only kidding, just having a little fun with you. We all know ghosts don't exist."

Maddie laughed along with the joke. Shireen went into a separate room to fix breakfast for them. Maddie sat in her chair thinking about Shireen's joke. Maddie rubbed the goosebumps on her arms and whispered, "She was only trying to scare me. Ghosts don't exist."

They heard a hard and abrupt knock on the front door of the library. This startled Maddie. Then she saw Irwin enter the building. He asserted, "I see you haven't gone yet. When do you think you'll be out of my town?"

Maddie didn't know the answer to that particular question. "You'll have to ask Zack about that. I have no idea."

Crossly, Irwin waved his hand in the air and insisted, "I need one of you to give me some kind of idea when your departure is going to take place! It's of the upmost importance. If you can't answer that, then what good are you?"

Maddie noticed the dogs were all standing but calm again. She whispered, "If I knew, I'd tell you, but I don't."

Shireen, hearing the conversation, walked into the room and Granger came in behind her. She scolded him. "Firstly, don't ever walk in here and speak to Maddie like that again. As far as I'm concerned, you're a silly little man. And secondly, we'll leave when we want to leave, not when you tell us to leave … Dandy."

Irwin glared at Shireen with an intimidating gleam of hate in his eyes. She wasn't frightened or scared by this. Instead, she walked over to him and glared back. She pointed her finger at his face and ordered, "Either you're going to treat everyone here with some semblance of respect or you're not going to walk in this library at all!"

Irwin was fuming. He put his hand in his pocket where he kept a small pistol, just in case he needed it.

Zack and Peter made their way to what used to be the maximum-security prison. Most of the old buildings had been ripped apart by the earthquakes and the meteor strikes. They found what used to be the main admissions and records building. There wasn't much was left standing.

Peter found his way to rows and rows of file cabinets that were lying on their sides. He had a gut feeling and decided to follow his instinct. He started opening the cabinets. None of them were marked on the outside anymore. Whatever used to be labeled had faded from the storms and snow. Zack asked him, "What are you doing?"

Peter explained, "I'm looking through these cabinets to find a file. There could be a file on Irwin Howard. If he worked here, he'd have an employee file. Right?"

"Great idea, Peter. I never thought of that," Zack said as he began to open file cabinets and check through files to find the "I's" for Irwin or the

"H's" for Howard.

Peter searched through several cabinets with no luck. "Almost everything in here is the prisoner files. There should be a cabinet where they kept the employee records."

Peter and Zack combed through more files, overturned cabinets and stumbled over office chairs and broken computers.

Finally, Zack opened a cabinet and saw the "H" flies. He found a file marked Howard, Irwin. Zack stated, "I think I got something here. I found it. I found his file, Irwin Howard."

Peter was relieved to know he could stop looking as he walked over and said, "Thank God, you found the employee files."

Zack looked up and explained, "I didn't find the employee files. I found him in the prisoner files, Peter."

"What?"

Zack opened the file and began to study it. He repeated, "It's definitely the inmate files. He wasn't an employee. He was a prisoner here, with a life sentence."

Peter took half the pages from the file and began to read through them. As he read the fourth page, he stopped. Zack asked him, "Why'd you stop reading?"

Peter's eyes grew wide as he announced,

"He was sentenced to life in prison for murder. He's a killer, Zack!"

Zack grabbed the papers from Peter's hand and said, "Come on, let's take this file back to the others. We'll finish reading it on the way."

Shireen stood eye to eye with Irwin. Maddie and Granger stayed off to the side. The dogs stood near Shireen sensing that something wasn't right. Irwin shouted, "You'd better stop telling me what to do, little girl! I don't like being told what to do in my own city!"

She asked, "Then, why did you come here? We're not bothering you. You're the one who came here to us. The snow should stop soon and we'll be on our way."

He let out a breath. "Thank the lord! I can't wait to get rid of you rude and filthy people. Just your presence makes my skin crawl."

Granger walked over and inquired, "Why do you hate us so much? We've never done anything to you, Irwin. And Mobile is such a big city, you could just go away and we'd never have to see you again. There has to be something else. Why do you want us out of here so fast?"

"Little boy, can't you see? I never wanted any of you here to begin with."

Shireen deduced, "I get it now. You want us

gone because you're hiding something. There's something about all of those dead people in the church that you don't want us to find out about. Yes, that's what I think, Irwin or Dandy or whoever you really are."

He was beyond furious. He was red in the face. "I told you to get out of my town! Gather up your boyfriends and get the hell out of here before you end up like the others!"

Shireen, Maddie and Granger believed, at the exact same moment, they were dealing with a man who might have murdered fourteen people. Shireen reached down to put her hand in her sweater pocket. Irwin shouted, "Don't move your hand!"

Irwin pulled the gun from his pocket and pointed it at Shireen's chest. Granger and Maddie backed up. Shireen slowly took her hand away from her pocket. The moment became tense. The dogs began to make a whimpering sound as they stood around the room. Shireen could hear herself breathing heavily. Irwin could feel his heart beating faster. It was a showdown.

Shireen gulped and then whispered, "I told you, as soon as the snow stops, we're out of here. I don't know what else I can say to you."

The dogs began to growl, from the largest to the smallest. Irwin glanced around the room at them and quietly demanded, "You'd better make the dogs back off, or else."

Shireen stood there, with a gun aimed at her chest, but didn't say anything to the dogs. Granger and Maddie inched away even more.

Irwin watched the dogs carefully. Shireen said, "Tell me more about all those people in the church, Dandy. I want the truth. Were they really convicts from the prison?"

He hesitated but then answered her question. "Yes, they were!"

"Why did they die and you didn't?"

"I told you what happened. I swear that everything I told you was the God's honest truth. They killed themselves."

She questioned, "What about you, Dandy? Were you really a file clerk?"

His voice got a little deeper as he stared in Shireen's eyes and finally spoke the truth. "No, I wasn't a file clerk. I was an inmate."

Shireen remarked, "I'm not surprised at all. Somewhere, in the back of my mind, I knew that you weren't who you said you were."

He pleaded, "Can't you see that I'm finally free … finally. The other inmates killed themselves. The prison is gone. I'm free."

Granger stepped closer and asked, "Why did you go to prison?"

Irwin hung his head and shamefully said, "Murder. I was in for murder."

Granger didn't seem shocked by his answer. "Who did you murder?"

Irwin kept his head bowed as he spoke. "It was my cheating wife and her boyfriend."

"You're wife?"

"You see, I came home one day from work early, because I thought I was coming down with something like the flu, and there they were, in our bed. I was in shock, but they didn't notice I was in the house. All these emotions took over my body, anger, sorrow, hurt. It wasn't me who killed them. I don't even remember doing it. All I know is that I passed out and when I eventually woke up, I was lying on the bathroom floor with blood all over myself. The police kept me face down while they were putting the cuffs on me."

Maddie asked, "So, how did you kill them exactly?"

"They said I used the black iron poker from the fireplace. I don't remember doing it or even having the poker in my hand. That was an hour of my life that I can't recall. They tried everything to help me remember, even hypnosis."

Shireen asked, "So, you got a life sentence in prison?"

Irwin threw his gun on the sofa and gazed at

the three of them. He was sincere when he said, "Yes, I got life. And I'm sorry Shireen, Maddie, Granger. I was just so afraid of being found out. I didn't know what to do. I can't believe I could ever be capable of what I did but the courts said I did it so, I must have done it."

Zack and Peter hurriedly raced into the library just as Shireen commanded the dogs, "Lie down."

The dogs laid on the floor and remained calm. They saw that Irwin was hugging Shireen. Zack held the file up and shouted, "Shireen get away from that man right now! You don't know who he really is!"

Shireen looked over Irwin's shoulder, smiled and whispered, "Yes, I do. I know exactly what he is."

Maddie walked over and gave Irwin a hug too. Peter and Zack were confused as they watched Irwin begin to cry. He bellowed, "I was trapped in that place for twenty-four years, twenty-four long, miserable, lonely years, for some damn crime that I don't even remember committing."

In Avalon, William and Drake saw that the snow had ended. Katie was still weak but she able to walk to the sled with Drake's assistance. They loaded the needed medical equipment and headed back to the bed and breakfast.

Carly and Emily stood at the window and saw the sled pulling up in the front. Carly hurried outside to greet them. She embraced William and put her head on his shoulder. "I don't like being separated from you."

He replied, "I don't like it either, Carly."

She said, "Come on inside. Emily's waiting to see you. How's Katie?"

William said, "She's going to be alright. I told her she needs to take it easy for a while, no more chopping down trees, but you know Katie. You know how she is."

Carly laughed. "I sure do."

He continued, "So, whenever she tries to go above and beyond the call of duty, don't be afraid to tell her to sit down and relax.

Carly grinned and said confidently, "Oh, I won't."

Katie, walking behind them, commented, "I'm right behind the two of you. I can hear you talking about me."

They made their way into the house. Katie removed a few layers of clothing, laid down on the sofa and fell asleep quickly. William sat the others down and told them, "She has to take it easy. It's imperative. Her body has been dealt a horrible blow. I don't want her overdoing things around here. She was lucky this time. She may not be as lucky the next time."

An hour had passed. Eddie continued to watch through the front window to make sure the snow had actually ended. Carly and Eleanor fed the dogs. Each person would check on Katie as they passed the sofa. Eddie appeared impatient. Drake noticed this and asked, "Are you alright, Eddie? You seem annoyed."

With a concerned expression on his face, Eddie pulled Drake to a corner of the room, away from the others, and tried to explain, "I know that Katie's fragile right now, and you know how much we all care about her well-being, but when do you suppose she'll be strong enough that we can get back on the road again?"

Drake nodded for William to join in their conversation. William said, "We can leave here today if you want, but I suggest we make our travel time shorter than usual, much shorter. We shouldn't be on the interstate for more than, say five to six-hour intervals."

Drake asked, "Is everyone ready to go?"

"I believe so," Eddie said as he glanced around the room at the other faces wanting to leave Avalon.

Drake approached Katie and sat down next to her on the sofa. He lightly rubbed her shoulder and watched her open her eyes. She stretched her arms out and laid her hands down on Drake's legs. He asked, "How are you feeling?"

She smiled at him and replied, "It's funny but I feel surprisingly well, considering everything that's happened to my body in the last twenty-four hours."

"We were all talking amongst ourselves and William says that you're well enough to travel. He told us we have to be careful and, for now, it would be wiser to only go about five or six hours a day. I don't want to make that decision until I hear you tell me it's okay."

Katie sat up and said, "Come on, Drake, I'm fine. Sitting in a sled for five hours isn't going to hurt me. And, if I happen get tired, I'll go to sleep on the road."

Drake, being extremely overprotective, asked again, "You're absolutely sure?"

She smiled and kissed him before saying, "Absolutely."

Drake announced to the room, "Did you hear that everybody? It's time to pack up and get the hell out of this place."

Within an hour, the sleds were packed, the dogs were harnessed and this group of survivors were on their way. As the exited Avalon, Drake pulled over to the mile marker, took the red ribbon down and put a blue ribbon in its place.

The interstate was smooth and easy to travel on. At one point, Katie did lie down to take a rest. Ultimately, they pulled off the road, tied another red ribbon to a different mile marker and pointed the sleds towards the heart of the town, passing a green sign that read "Elgin Airforce Base". And then, they saw another sign one read "Crestview City Limits - Population 24, 922".

They found a row of good-sized houses in the middle of what appeared to be an old shopping area. They saw several grocery stores, clothing stores, a few hardware and farm supply stores and various other businesses.

Drake steered the dogs into a subdivision and stopped. He got out and entered the first house. When he came out, he looked at Eddie and said, "No good." He went to the next house, and then the next, finally settling on the fifth home.

They unpacked the sleds and entered the residence. Eddie knew Drake was checking for a sound structure with fireplaces and lots of sturdy furniture. Katie woke up and tried to help them unpack but Eleanor stopped her. "Go in the house and take it easy. We can handle it without your help for a day or two."

Katie nodded her head. She walked into the living room and went to sleep again. Drake decided, since they still had a lot of day hours left, he'd take a look at the sleds and make sure they were still safe. Eddie went outside with him just in case he needed help. Drake knelt down and pushed his hand over the bottoms of the sleds to feel for smoothness and making sure there weren't any loose boards. "It all seems to be alright."

Out of the blue, Eddie said, "I have a great idea, Drake."

Drake stood up, wiping the dirt from his hands. "Let's hear it."

"Didn't we pass some hardware and farm supplies stores before we pulled in?"

"I think so. What's your idea?"

Eddie didn't announce his plan at first. Instead, he told the others he and Drake would be back in an hour or so. As they trudged through the snow, Eddie proclaimed, "I can't believe I didn't think of this months ago. This is going to change everything for us."

They left on foot and collected materials to help execute Eddie's plan. The others could hear banging and sawing and hammering in the yard. Eleanor came out the front door, at one point, and tried to peek at their secret project but Eddie yelled for her to get back in the house.

Hours later Eddie and Drake entered the house and announced, "We're done! Everyone can go outside and take a look at it."

The others went to the front yard to see Drake and Eddie had turned their sleds into wagons. They found a way to attach wheels to the bottoms of each. Eleanor stated, "You put three wheels on each side. That's amazing."

Eddie explained the benefits of the wheels. "It's going to be much easier on the dogs. We'll be higher up off the ground and able to move even faster now."

Katie hugged Eddie and whispered, "You see, I knew you could build anything if you applied yourself. I guess your days studying to be a designer are finally paying off."

Drake commented, "Once the others join us, we can convert their sled. We brought extra wheels and everything they'll need."

William said to Eddie and Eleanor, "I have an announcement of my own. I think it's time for your skin treatment ... and I believe this will be the last one. Your blistering has completely faded and your skin looks healthy again."

Emily stood between Eddie and Eleanor and smiled. "I knew you'd get better if you just trusted my daddy."

Carly interrupted, "I'm think I'm going to make some dinner. Everyone's got to be famished by now."

As they started to file into the house, Eddie stood there, staring at the sleds, proud to have given such a contribution to the group.

In Mobile, the other survivors sat with Irwin as he told the story of his adulterous wife and the years that he struggled to make their marriage work. Again, he reminded them he didn't recall killing her or her boyfriend.

Shireen sat down next to Irwin and held his hand. "I think you should go with us to Florida. No one's judging you here. No one will judge you there."

Peter glared from across the room and said, "I think maybe we should talk this over before we doing something we may regret, Shireen. After all, the man was serving a life sentence for murdering two people in cold blood. Then, we show up and find fourteen poisoned people in a church but he somehow survived. I don't want to put Maddie or our baby at risk. We shouldn't make any decisions right away."

Shireen said, "But, we have to decide soon. We're leaving in the morning and I'd like him to go with us. I can't leave him here alone. He's been by himself for way too long already."

Irwin interjected, "Please stop arguing over me. I don't want to cause any problems for any of you. I never did. I planned to stay here all along, so, I think you should go and stop worrying about me. I'm going to be just fine."

Shireen took the floor again. "No, I'm sorry, Irwin. I'm not going to let that happen. I trust you. I know I can trust you because the dogs trust you. If you weren't a good man, they would have been all over you, but instead they stayed quiet and peaceful. Dogs can sense danger and bad people a lot better than any human can."

Zack commented, "That was odd how the dogs seemed to accept him, even in the beginning, when he was standing over Maddie."

Peter was still not convinced. "I don't know. I still have a girlfriend who's carrying our unborn child."

Irwin whispered, "Peter, I would never hurt Maddie or your baby. But I understand what you're saying. You have my file there and it's all in black and white. There's nothing else I can say to defend myself. Besides, I have no desire to go with you to Florida. My time would be better served here in Irwin's Landing. I mean Mobile."

Zack stepped up and suggested, "Why don't you head on home now, Irwin. We need to get some rest tonight. We're going to have to leave early in the morning if we want to make some time on the road tomorrow."

"I understand, Zack. I was just getting ready to leave anyway. You folks have a good night and a safe trip. It was nice meeting you. I hope you find what you're looking for."

They watched as Irwin hung his head down and ambled out the front door of the library. Shireen turned and scowled at Zack and Peter. "Do either of you want to know what I think? I think you are way off the mark about this. You're dead wrong about that man."

20

Each of the survivors detected the unusually warm temperatures and brighter skies. The sled was loaded up and Shireen had harnessed the dogs. As she did this, she checked the street to see if Irwin had changed his mind, but she didn't see him. She went back into the library to see if everyone was ready to go. Peter leaned in to Zack and whispered. "I need to speak with you before we go."

Zack and Peter strolled off on their own. Zack asked, "Yeah, what's up?"

Peter pulled out Irwin's file and told Zack he had stayed up most of the night reading through it. He stated, "I read the history and the transcripts of the trial. I think Irwin was set up to take the fall when it wasn't him who really did it. I think he might be innocent."

Zack put his hands up and asked, "What are you talking about?"

"They found Irwin with his wife's blood on his clothes but, the murder weapon, the poker from the fireplace, had no fingerprints on it. They found no traces of her boyfriend's blood on Irwin. I find that a little bizarre. If you're hitting someone with a poker until you kill them, there would be some of the victim's blood on you."

Zack agreed, "That makes sense."

Peter continued, "And there was one other person who testified against Irwin at the trial, the wife of the boyfriend, who claimed she knew about the affair. Irwin wasn't a rich man. He could only afford the cheapest legal team in the area, maybe a public defender."

Zack paged through the file. "So, what do you think happened?"

"I think the wife of the boyfriend did it. She had no alibi for her whereabouts at the time of the murder. She knew the affair was happening. Irwin didn't. And she came from an extremely wealthy and powerful family who would have done anything to cover up the real truth. They must have spent hours convincing Irwin that he was the true killer, but he wasn't."

They noticed Shireen and Maddie standing

over their shoulder. Shireen muttered, "You see, I told you he didn't do it. My dogs are never wrong about someone's character."

Zack expressed, "The problem now is what are we going to do about it? He's already spent too many years paying for a crime he probably didn't commit."

Maddie shrugged her shoulders and said, "There's nothing we can do. He decided he's guilty and is prepared to remain here, in solitary, for the rest of his life."

Shireen mentioned, "Can't we go looking for him at his house? Then, we can convince him to leave with us."

Zack said, "The only problem with that is he never told us exactly where he lives. It could be any one of a hundred or more houses. I wouldn't even know where to start."

Peter crossed his arms and firmly stated, "Well, we have to do something to make this right. I feel so stupid. The things I said to him last night were thoughtless."

Granger intervened, "Guys, I have to make a confession."

Everyone turned their attention to Granger. He continued, "I didn't trust Irwin at first, so last night, when you four were standing here arguing over him, I slipped out and followed him. I only got a few blocks but I know which street he lives on. I don't know the exact house, but I do know he lives on Lincoln Circle."

Zack looked at the others and stated, "What are we waiting for. Let's go. Let's get out there and find him and explain what we discovered before it's too late."

Maddie questioned, "I don't understand. Too late? Too late for what?"

Zack clarified, "Irwin was very depressed when he left here last night. I think that he was depressed enough to want to harm himself ... to kill himself."

Hearing this, everyone moved faster than they had before. They got into the sled and followed Granger's directions to Lincoln Circle. They rode up and down the street, hopping out and banging on front doors, shouting out Irwin's name at the top of their lungs.

Eventually, the sled arrived at 121 Lincoln Circle. They shouted and ponded on the front door. The door began to open and a sleepy Irwin stepped out, appearing confused by their visit. Peter ran up to Irwin, which frightened him at first. He wrapped his arms around the sixty-four-year-old man and whispered, "I'm sorry, Irwin."

Irwin was startled by Peter's closeness. He backed away and questioned, "What are you sorry about, Peter?"

"I'm sorry because I know, we know, that you never murdered anyone. I know that you're an innocent man."

Irwin was perplexed. He asked, "How could you know that?"

Maddie moved closer and suggested, "Why don't we go inside and explain what we're trying to tell you. It might take a few minutes."

Everyone, including the dogs, ended up in Irwin's cozy little house. They saw it was clean and warm inside. He was told what they believed had actually taken place during the investigation and the trial. This saddened him. Maddie asked, "Why are you so sad, Irwin?"

"I can't believe it. I knew I couldn't have killed my Arlene. I cared for her, why would I kill her, even though she was cheating on me. I spent twenty-four years in the tiny grey cell, twenty-four years. But now I know someone else believes that I was innocent."

Shireen asked, "Does that mean you'll come with us?"

Irwin bowed his head and folded his hands. "I've spent so many years separated from society. I just don't know if I'd fit in anymore."

Maddie commented, "Come on, Irwin, don't make this bigger than it is. Society in this world is only going to be ten or twenty people. Besides, I may need someone to teach our baby the meaning of right and wrong and nobody knows that lesson better than you."

It took them another thirty minutes until they could finally convince him to pack the items he'd need for the trip.

Zack observed that Irwin made sure to pack a picture of his late wife. He put his hand on Irwin's shoulder and told him to get in the sled. As Irwin walked out, he passed each one of the harnessed dogs and scratched their heads. They, in turn, licked his hand.

Shireen glanced over at Irwin, as they were beginning to pull away from the city, and shouted, "Let's get the hell out of Mobile! I mean Irwin's Landing!" She and Irwin laughed.

Drake and the others realized how much smoother and faster the sleds, turned wagons, were sailing down the interstate. The weather conditions were comfortable and the winds were low. Eddie, proud of his accomplishment, asked, "What kind of time are we making now?"

Drake returned, "It looks like we increased our speed from seven to thirteen miles an hour. It's cut our time almost in half."

William shouted, "There's a sign for an exit!

I think we should take it!"

The newly built wagons pulled alongside the interstate. Eleanor hopped out and tied the bright red ribbon around the mile marker for De Funiak Springs. As they moved past the sign, Katie said, "Well, we found it. But what a weird name for a town."

As they entered the town, they saw large old plantation homes and blue sign that read "McCarthy Carriage Museum and Equestrian Center".

Most of the houses had suffered severe trauma from the natural elements. They forged on until they came upon one that appeared to still be inhabitable. They pulled up and did their usual unpacking, chopping wood, finding canned goods and settling in.

They noticed that the weather had become milder that day. Eddie and Eleanor were actually so excited to see the temperature rise above freezing, they went out for a walk.

As they sauntered along the streets, they talked about the newly altered sled wagons and the fact that their skin treatments were finally complete. They walked several blocks when they spotted, in the distance, two horses running through a half-frozen pasture. Eleanor pointed and shouted, "Look, Eddie! Horses!"

As they got closer, they saw several more

horses running on the same land. Their curiosity got the best of them. They continued on until they saw the sign again that read "Carriage Museum and Equestrian Center". Eleanor said, "This must be where all these horses are living."

Several other horses ran through the grassy fields, looking healthy and fit. They saw smoke puffing from the chimney of one of the property's many buildings. Eleanor got eager. "Come on, let's check it out."

Eddie agreed as they marched quickly to meet whoever was there. They arrived at the front door and knocked. There was no response. Eddie's eyes searched the vast property to see if there were any signs of life other than the horses.

Eleanor knocked on the door again. No one answered. Eddie spotted someone in a barn several hundred feet away. He nudged Eleanor. "Hey, over there, I can see someone."

They hurried towards the old barn. "Hello! Hello!" They shouted out over and over. As they advanced a little further, they saw an older woman step out from the structure. She shouted, "Stop right there or I'll shoot!"

Eddie and Eleanor stopped. The woman was shocked and amazed but stern and suspicious at the same time. They noticed she didn't have a gun. She said, "Other people, I can't believe it. I haven't seen another living soul in five years. What do you want from me?"

Eleanor explained, "We stopped here to rest for the night. There's a group of us, well two groups of us, traveling to Crystal River. I'm Eleanor and this is my friend Eddie."

The older woman introduced herself, "I'm Gwen McCarthy and this sad wasteland used to be my museum. There's not much of it left anymore. Two of the three buildings were destroyed years ago. But I still have one building left, and I have still some of my horses."

Eleanor, a bit baffled, said, "I don't know how the horses have been able to survive in these frigid temperatures."

Gwen explained, "Not all of my horses were able to handle this new climate. I lost most of them when the thermometer dropped, but I still have my Arabians and my Drafts. It seems they can make it through any climate. At night they stay in the barn, it's completely closed in and I keep it toasty warm for them."

Eddie asked, "Exactly, how many horses do you have here, Gwen?"

Gwen replied, "I still have six of my drafts and four of my Arabians. They're all the company I've had for all these years."

Eleanor looked at Eddie and grinned. "Yes,

we know someone else who's had the same experience with her dogs."

Gwen, the sixty-six-year-old woman with white curly hair, commented, "I'll bet you two are hungry. Would you like to come back to the main house with me to get something to eat? I've got plenty, believe me."

The pair accepted her invitation and they went to Gwen's for a hot meal and coffee. At one point, Eddie reminded Eleanor that they'd have to go back and let the others know where they were. Gwen bluntly inquired, "What happened to your hair? Why are you both bald?"

Feeling almost ashamed again, Eleanor brushed her hand over her scalp. "We got caught in the acid rain several years ago. It lasted for days and we had no protection. My appearance used to be a lot worse than it is today but William, he's a doctor, has been doing treatments on our skin for the past few months."

Gwen put her hand on the top of Eleanor's and commented, "Well, I think you look lovely just the way you are."

They talked for almost an hour when Eddie announced, "We've been gone too long. We really have to get back to the others. They do worry about us from time to time."

Gwen proposed, "How about I go with you

to meet them. I was thinking, this house is so big, five bedrooms, I have running water from the huge well on the property and plenty of firewood. Maybe you should all come and stay here. You'll be my guests for the night."

Eleanor was elated. She said, "That would be wonderful."

The threesome bundled up and went to see their traveling companions. After meeting Gwen, they all decided to pack up and move into her home. She was quite accommodating as she gave them a tour of what was left of her once thriving carriage museum.

Gwen still knew the history of every wagon in the place. They saw restored wagons from the old west, garishly painted carriages that had once been owned by royalty, even what used to be a horse drawn bus. Gwen reminded them, "There used to be so much more in this museum. My family poured millions of dollars into the place. But now, this is all I have left."

Carly and Eleanor took Emily out to see the horses. The gentle giants were approachable and quiet. Emily was excited when she got the chance to feed a few of them. Carly asked Gwen, "How do you keep them so healthy?"

"It's the grass. It never goes dormant and it can survive most climates. They have almost fifty fenced acres here."

She questioned, "And they've never been attacked by any wild animals?"

Gwen replied, "They have. Unfortunately, I lost several of them to animal attacks. I also had my last four Paints break out and run away. I had to kill quite a few bears and coyotes over the years. I don't like to brag but I'm a perfect shot."

Carly asked, "Are any of those carriages able to be driven?"

Gwen responded, "Of course, they all are. What are you getting at?"

Carly added, "Would these horses be able to pull them?"

"Yes, that's what horses do. Every one of my horses is capable of pulling any one of those carriages."

Carly turned to Eleanor and said, "Do you see what I'm getting at?"

Eleanor replied, "Not really."

"We don't need the dogs to pull the sled wagons anymore. We have horses that can pull much bigger wagons even faster."

Gwen abruptly threw her hand up to halt the conversation. "Hold it! You want to take my horses and my carriages to Crystal River?"

Carly added, "We want to take you with us too, Gwen."

Gwen paced around the pasture for a minute. "It does make sense and some of these carriages are three times larger than those tiny sleds you pulled up in."

Carly asked, "Exactly how many horses do you need to pull one wagon?"

"Not many. I have enough horses to pull three or four wagons."

Carly nodded her head as she continued to gather information. "And which of these wagons are large enough to hold several people, supplies and the dogs, and are the best for travelling in a horrible climate like this?"

Gwen responded, "That would probably be the old pioneer covered wagons. They called them the Prairie Schooners."

Carly questioned, "How many of them do you have?"

"Plenty. I believe I still have seven or eight of them."

Eleanor suggested, "Wait a minute! First, we have to be sure that Gwen's okay with this. Then, we have to find out if everyone else is okay with it. Don't forget, Carly, we decided a long time ago, we're a democracy."

Gwen glanced around at her vast property and said, "I was born here. I've lived all of my sixty-six years here. I don't know if I'm ready to change that now."

Eleanor begged, "Please, Gwen, think about it. I wouldn't want to remember you out here in this place all by yourself."

Gwen smiled and said, "Thank you, Eleanor. I'll give it some thought."

The house was warm and inviting. At one point, during the afternoon, Drake and Eddie went out into the fields and caught a few rabbits that were later prepared for dinner.

After Emily was put to bed, the other seven sat around the huge dining room table and talked and told stories well into the night.

As everyone became friendlier with Gwen, she pulled out a bottle of old Kentucky bourbon and poured seven shots. They toasted, "To life," and drank the alcohol. Soon, Gwen poured a second round of shots.

Zack steered the sled into a place named Harold. They had crossed into Florida several hours before and tried to make up some time, but found themselves in a town that wasn't even a town. As they pulled down the road that led to Harold, they saw what remained of a convenient store and an old post office.

The post office appeared as if it was still intact. Shireen said, "We shouldn't have kept going.

That was a stupid move. We should have stopped at one of those towns twenty miles back."

Zack raised the question, "Do you want me to turn around? If you want me to turn around and go back, I can do that."

Shireen stated, "No, it's much too late for that and too dangerous. Let's see how we do in this post office."

Granger took over and pulled the sled to the post office. They went inside to see what they had to deal with. It was small, very small. Zack said, "I guess we're going to have to make the best of it for the night."

The entire interior of the building was only twenty by thirty feet. They unloaded the supplies, unleased the dogs and built a small fire in the corner of the room. They ate cold food out of the cans and slept close to each other hoping the night would go by quickly.

21

Morning couldn't come fast enough after a lengthy and excruciating night. Everyone felt stiff and tired. Granger scratched the top of his head and yawned before he said, "I never want to sleep on a cold concrete floor again."

Irwin commented, "Wait till you get to be

my age, kid. It's no picnic."

Shireen was shivering. "It's so cold here. No matter how much I covered up last night, I was still freezing. I can tell it's October."

Maddie agreed. "I'm cold. I'm tired. I'm hungry. I never want to go through another night like that again."

Zack said, "I'm with you. I guess the good news is that we're in Florida and about forty miles through already."

Shireen looked out the post office windows at the frozen town and pondered. "I wonder how far the others have gotten."

Zack stood behind Shireen with his arms around her. "Who knows."

"Well, wherever they are, I hope they're safe and warm."

"They're fine. You need to stop worrying about them so much. I bet they slept in a nice warm house on comfortable beds last night. We're the idiots that ended up sleeping on cold floors a town with one standing building."

Shireen giggled. "Yeah, I guess you have a point."

"So, why don't we get up and get the hell out of this place. The sooner we hit the road, the better it'll be. I'm sure the next town will be a little more welcoming than this one."

Granger blurted, "I'm positive it'll be better. After all, it couldn't be any worse."

Even though they were all exhausted and hungry, they quickly packed up the sled and got back onto the interstate.

Zack examined the map and said, "If we can maintain a good speed today, we could make it to the next town before nightfall. Maybe in seven or eight hours."

Shireen asked, "And what's the name of this next town, Mr. Gunslinger?"

"It's a strange name. It's called De Funiak Springs."

Surprised when he heard the name of the town, Irwin blurted, "I know that place. I've been to De Funiak Springs many, many times. As a matter of fact, my first girlfriend lived there."

Granger asked, "Your first girlfriend? Was she pretty?"

Irwin gazed up at the sky and stated, "She was so very beautiful and rich too. Yes, she was the one that got away. Her parents owned a museum there."

Granger commented, "Too bad you didn't end up with her, Irwin. Your life might have turned out a lot different than it did."

"She was actually the one that nicknamed me Dandy. We had four wonderful years together until it ended."

Maddie joined in the conversation. "That's so sad. Why did it end?"

He replied, "There were a few reasons. You see, I lived in Mobile and she lived there. It was hard to see her a lot of the time. That was quite a distance in those days."

Maddie asked, "What else?"

"The other reason we didn't make it was because her parents didn't like me. They tried to break us up. They said I wasn't good enough for their daughter and their plan worked. We broke up and I never saw her face again."

"Oh, Irwin, I'm so sorry. It's sounds like she was your one true love."

"I still wonder what would've happened if we had stayed together. I still wonder if she really loved me the way that she said she did. There's so many unanswered questions."

Zack commented, "I guess that's something you're never going to know, Irwin. You'll just have to believe she did."

Peter noticed that the temperatures were slowly beginning to rise again. He looked up and actually saw the sun attempting to peek through the dusty clouds for a brief moment. "This is the second day in a row we've seen temperatures in the forties. What do you think that means?"

Zack commented, "It doesn't mean a thing. We just had a freak warmup for a day or two. That's all there is to it."

Peter expressed, "We can hope. Hey, Zack, how far is it to this next city?"

"About fifty, fifty-five miles."

The weather was so mild, Katie decided to take a stroll along the pastures with Gwen for a while. She admired the property and how well it had been kept up. "I just can't believe you took care of all this plus the horses. You must have one hell of a lot of energy."

Gwen said, "When it's all you have left, you tend to care for it even more. I've been working this property since the first day I could walk."

Katie asked cautiously, "I don't want to sound pushy but what did you decide on with the horses and the wagons, or haven't you made a decision yet?"

"You all seem like wonderful people, hard-working and loyal to each other. It's nice. But I've never known anything but this place."

Gwen looked at the pasture and noticed the frost from the night before had already melted away. "I've never seen the grass without a covering of frost this early in the day. This certainly is a beautiful morning."

"Yes, it is."

Gwen continued, "Even if I don't go with you, I'm going to give you some of the horses and covered wagons. I can't use them and it's the least I could do."

Katie smiled and said, "Thank you, Gwen, but I'd rather you went with us. The wagons aren't the important thing, you are."

Gwen brushed her hand down Katie's cheek and whispered, "You're such a sweet young girl. I guess Drake was lucky the day that you wandered into his life."

Katie blushed at the compliment. "He doesn't have a clue just how lucky he is." She laughed at herself.

Gwen hinted, "I'm getting a little hungry. Why don't we get back to the house and have some breakfast?"

"That sounds like a plan. I'm a little hungry myself."

They took a slow stroll back to the house. When they went inside, they saw that Drake and Peter weren't there? Katie asked, "William, where are the other guys?"

William replied, "I think they went up to the museum. Drake said he wanted to take a closer look at the covered wagons."

Gwen asked, "Did everyone eat breakfast

already?"

Carly mentioned, "We did but we left some in the kitchen for you."

Katie and Gwen grabbed some food and sat down at the table. Emily sat down next to Gwen and inquired, "Miss Gwen, can we go out and look at the horses today?"

"In a little while, sweet pea." Gwen leaned over and pinched her cheek.

Katie remained at the table as she looked at the map of the southern United States. She tried to calculate their route and figure out how many miles were still left in the trip. "It looks like we have less than three-hundred miles to go. I can't believe we're that close. It means we've already traveled over six-hundred miles."

Gwen leaned in and looked at the map. She commented, "Katie, that's a map of the world five years ago. I hope you know that the landscape is quite different these days."

Katie inquired, "How do you mean?"

She answered, "It should be smooth sailing for a while but you also have to factor in that there's a mountain range situated right between you and Crystal River."

"How do you know there's a mountain range there?"

Gwen stood up from the table, took Katie by

the wrist and guided her to the windows on the east side of the house. She pointed toward the horizon. "Do you see it. The peaks of a mountain range in the distance. I'd say they lie somewhere between here and Tallahassee, but I couldn't begin to guess how tall or wide they are."

Katie squinted and saw what Gwen was talking about. "Oh my God! If we can see them from here, they must be massive!"

Gwen added, "That's what I'm trying to tell you. Even if you're less than three-hundred miles from your friend Carolyn, you still have to cross those mountains. Even with the horses, it's going to be a very slow ride."

"I wonder if Drake has noticed them."

Drake had already entered the house when he asked, "If Drake noticed what?"

"Those mountains out there, they're coming up soon. They must be the same ones that Carolyn said rose up from the gulf."

Drake peered out the window and saw them too. He didn't act excited over this. Instead, he said, "It's just one more obstacle that we're going to have to overcome."

Gwen asked, "Did you have a chance to see the wagons?"

Drake announced, "I did. Eddie's still in there but it looks like two of the wagons wouldn't be roadworthy. They must have been damaged during one of the quakes. I think there's five of them that'll work for the trip."

Gwen questioned, "Do you think that you'll need all five of those wagons? Even if your friends do return, that would only be ten of you, and all those dogs."

Drake muttered, "But not you?"

"I don't think so, Drake. Like I told Katie, this is my life and it would take a strong, strong wind to blow me out of here. It would take some kind of miracle."

Drake expressed, "I really wish that you'd change your mind, Gwen. Remember, if you come with us, you'll be a part of a family again and you'll have all your horses." Gwen bowed her head but didn't give him any kind of response.

Soon, Eddie came back from the museum and announced, "I found a problem with another wagon. That means were down to four, but those four are solid and ready to roll."

Later that day, Eleanor was helping Gwen clean up around the house when she found several pictures sitting on the mantle. She picked them up and asked Gwen, "Who are all the people in these picture frames?"

Gwen walked over and took each on from Eleanor's hands as she explained who they were.

"This first one is my parents. They passed away so many years ago. They were both quite young when they died. My father was fifty-seven and my mother was fifty-one. It was a tragic automobile accident. It seems like yesterday."

Eleanor asked her about the second picture. Gwen responded, "That's a picture of my brother. He was younger than me. It's the only picture I have of him. He died of leukemia when he was only fifteen. I hated that I lost him so young. I miss him every day."

Eleanor held up the last picture and asked, "Who's he? He's quite the handsome and dashing young man."

"He's the boy I was in love with many years ago. He was twenty and I was twenty-two. We had been seeing each other for four years and I thought he was going to ask me to marry him."

"What happened? Why didn't he pop the question?"

"I don't know. He simply disappeared from my life one day and I never saw him or heard from him again. I guess I never got over him. I never met anyone else like him and I never married. At first, I believed he'd come back for me but that just turned out to be wishful thinking."

Eleanor reflected, "That is so sad. I had a boyfriend once, when I was fourteen, but he was killed during the blast like everyone else. He was so good to me."

"Isn't Eddie your boyfriend now?"

Eleanor was perplexed. "Eddie? No, he has no interest in me. We're just very close friends, I think."

Gwen treasured Eleanor's naive innocence. "You'd better take a better look at how he watches you when you talk. I know all the signs of true love and that boy is in love with you."

Eleanor blushed when she admitted, "I've always liked him a lot too."

Gwen pushed, "Then you shouldn't waste any more time. If we learned anything from what happened to this world, it's that time is more precious and important than anything else and it's never promised."

Eleanor commended Gwen. "You're an intelligent woman. I just hope I can be half as wise as you are someday."

Gwen laughed and put her hand on Eleanor's upper arm. "But you already are, sweet girl. You already are. Now, why don't we get Emily and take her out to visit with the horses as we promised."

Eleanor hollered up the stairs. "Emily! Emily! Come on! We're going out to see the horses! Emily!"

They waited a few minutes before they saw Emily come rushing down the stairs while buttoning her thick jacket.

Eleanor mentioned, "Oh, honey, I don't think you're going to need to wear a jacket that heavy. It's a beautiful day. I'll find you something a little thinner."

The survivors were relieved that the day had gone by so quickly as Zack pulled the sled down the interstate towards De Funiak Springs.

Shireen asked, "I'm so tired. How much further is it?"

"I'd guess that it's a mile or two. It should be coming up."

She stated, "I have to say, even given the fact that we're all exhausted, this has been the most pleasant ride we've had since we started the trip. The weather is beautiful and the sky is so clear, I feel like it's almost like a daytime we used to have in the old days."

Granger mentioned, "Let it stay like this forever. As long as I don't have to sleep on cold concrete floors again, I'm good."

Zack and Shireen laughed at Granger's grumpiness. Then, Zack commented, "You have to learn to let things go, Granger, or it'll just eat you up inside. We had one bad night."

Granger leaned back down in the sled and watched for any signs of De Funiak Springs. Peter pointed at the mile marker as they got closer. He shouted, "Look a red ribbon!"

Elated, Shireen clapped her hands together. "They're here! They're here! We finally caught up to them!"

Zack smiled as the sled pulled onto the ramp toward the town. He said, "That was the easy part. Now, we have to find out where they're staying in De Funiak Springs."

Shireen opened her atlas and read some information on the town. "It says that the town had a population of five thousand back in the day. It's not a great big place and they shouldn't be too hard to locate."

Granger said, "Just watch for the house with smoke coming out of the chimney."

Zack turned and said, "I already figured that out, smart ass."

They rode through the streets, up and down and across. They saw nothing, no dogs, no sleds, no smoking chimneys. They passed grocery stores, old schools, a police station and a winery. Still there was no sign of life.

At one point, Peter remarked "Maybe they already left and just forgot to take the ribbon of the mile marker."

Zack was hoping this wasn't what happened as they continued to ride down Orange Street and then onto Old McCarthy Road. As they pulled down Old McCarthy Road, they saw horses galloping in a pasture. Granger pointed towards them and shouted, "Look! Horses!"

Soon, they spotted the big brick house with the smoking chimney, the barns and the carriage museum. Irwin laughed and said, "Huh, this is the place where my old girlfriend used to live. Isn't that the strangest thing?"

They pulled the sled to the front of the house. Zack and Shireen were the first to get out and walk onto the front porch. They knocked as Granger crept quietly onto the steps and stood behind them. The others waited in the front yard. The door opened and a stunned Katie didn't know what to say. She gasped, put her hand up to her mouth and began to cry. The others gathered behind Katie at the door. Then, she put her arms tightly around Shireen and whispered, "You made it here. You're back."

Drake stepped forward and hugged and shook hands, as did the rest in turn. The survivors at De Funiak Springs were then introduced to Peter, Maddie and Irwin. As Irwin stepped into the house, he saw a woman step out of the crowd, staring at him in disbelief. His mouth hung open when he saw it was the one that got away. He advanced towards her cautiously. Everyone quieted down. "Gwen, is that really you?"

She gasped, "Dandy? I can't believe it. Am I dreaming?"

He got even closer and muttered again, "Is that really you?"

She smiled and replied, "It's me ... but how? How, after all these years, could you be standing here now?"

The room was so quiet, every breath could be heard from the ex-lovers. He said, "So many years have slipped away, forty years. I've waited for this moment."

She backed off a few inches. "But you left here and never came back. You disappeared without a trace."

Gwen peered at Katie and Drake as a signal to take the others out of the room to give them a little privacy. They left and Irwin tried to explain, "I didn't leave you. I'd never leave you. Your parents forced me to stay away. They threatened me and lied to me. A few years later, I tried like hell to see you but they said you had already been married to someone else."

A tear ran down Gwen's cheek. "I never married anyone, Dandy. I waited for you through all the years, wondering if you'd ever find your way back to me. Eventually, I just poured myself into life around here."

Irwin stared at Gwen. He could see the years were good to her. He wished he could say the same about himself. She commented, "I remember my father going to Mobile many times about thirty years ago. I asked him to check on you, to see if you were doing alright. He said that you had gotten married and you were very happy and had moved on. I think he said you went to the west coast. I believe he said California."

Irwin was puzzled, "I never moved to the west coast. Why on earth would he make up a story like that?"

Gwen commented, "Perhaps it was his way of making sure we stayed permanently separated, a final nail in the coffin."

He confessed, "Gwen, I spent twenty-four years in a prison for a murder I didn't commit. If your father came to Mobile that often thirty years ago, he would have known about everything He would have …"

Gwen had a look of disbelief on her face. "Oh no, not my father. He would never have been involved in something so diabolical."

Irwin mulled over what Gwen had said. He thought about it. Suddenly, he hollered to Peter and Zack to come back into the room. They entered and

Irwin asked, "Do you still have that file you found on me in Mobile?"

Peter announced, "I do. Do you need it?"

"Please. It's very important."

Peter, Zack, Irwin and Gwen sat at the dining room table reading through page after page of the transcripts of the trial. Most of the reading was boring and repetitive but they continued to mull through it anyway. Gwen mentioned, "This is a very thick file, Dandy." She smiled. "You must have been a very bad boy."

She got to read how there was no real evidence and it was all circumstantial. As they flipped through each paper, they'd pass it to the person who was seated next to them. Finally, Peter shouted, "Here it is! I found it!"

He handed the paper to Irwin. Gwen leaned in to read it at the same time. Zack asked, "What does it say?"

Gwen's eyes opened widely as she recited, "This says that Roland McCarthy III gave a private deposition to the court in order to maintain his confidentiality. He told the court he believed Irwin Howard was guilty of the murder of his wife, Arlene Howard, and her alleged lover, Dominick Moore. He's the one who hired the attorney to defend Dominick's wife."

Gwen let the paper fall from her hand and

onto the floor. She turned to Irwin and, in a deep sorrowful tone, whispered, "I'm so sorry, Dandy. My father did that to you."

Irwin was astounded at the discovery that the entire ruin of his life had been orchestrated by one spiteful man, Gwen's father. He bowed his head and announced, "I have to go for a walk. I need to think for a while."

Gwen didn't say another word. She didn't know what she could say to make it better. She was embarrassed and stunned at what had been revealed that night. She watched Irwin as he bundled up and walked out the front door. Zack turned to Gwen and said, "This wasn't your fault. None of this was your fault."

In the barn, Shireen and Katie walked by the horse stalls talking about their adventures since the last time they were together. Shireen looked out and saw Irwin walking through the pasture with his head hung down. Katie said, "I wonder what's wrong with him. I thought he'd be jumping for joy finding Gwen after all these years."

Shireen noted, "He's a funny little man, a little strange but he has a heart of gold. I guess being locked in a prison for over twenty years can bring on new behaviors. It must be hard to break that pattern of being a solitary man."

They glanced over at the front porch and

saw Maddie and Peter sitting and strumming on their guitars. This brought a smile to Katie's face. "It's nice to hear music again. I forgot how nice it sounds."

Shireen added, "And in a few short months they're going to have to put their guitars down to take care of their baby."

"She's pregnant?"

Shireen nodded. "She is. Can't you tell? I guess it's a sign that life will go on in this world, and evolve and hopefully it'll thrive."

They began walking again, glancing in each stall as they passed the regal horses. Katie inquired, "So tell me your plan with the covered wagons and the horses again."

"We have enough working covered wagons and horses that we don't need to use the dogsleds anymore. That's good news. Finally, the dogs get a chance to rest."

They looked toward the museum and saw Eddie and Eleanor exiting. Katie asked, "Don't they look great? Their skin is almost as normal as ours now."

Shireen probed, "Haven't those two gotten together yet?"

Katie let out a chuckle. "No, I don't think so, but I wish they'd figure it out already. The way they look at each other and talk to each other. I'd guess they're the only ones who can't see that they belong together."

As Eddie and Eleanor strolled across the grounds on their way back to the house, Eleanor asked awkwardly, "Eddie, can I say something? It's kind of important to me. It may sound dumb but I'm going to say it anyway."

"Sure, you can ask me anything."

Eleanor hesitated at first. She found it difficult in finding the right words but she tried. "Do you ... I mean, are we ... are we more than friends in your eyes?"

Eddie was pleased to hear Eleanor was finally picking up on the signals he'd been giving her for years, signals that usually went unnoticed. He questioned, "Would you like us to be more than just friends, Eleanor?"

She stopped marching. He stopped as soon as he saw this. She turned and commented, "I've always cared about you. I just never knew how to go about showing you this. Remember, I was only thirteen when the meteors hit. I never had a real boyfriend before. So, I never knew what to do or how to let you know."

Eddie said, "I've always loved you, Eleanor, from the first day I saw you but you were so young then. I recall you were about fifteen and I was twenty. I didn't want to cloud your judgement so, I stayed in the background when it came to love and romance. But the feeling was always there. It never went away."

"Well, I'm not a little kid anymore, Eddie. I'm eighteen. I'm a woman and I want to see if we can become a couple and still remain best friends. I want both, not one or the other. We've been through so much together. It would be a huge loss to throw either one away."

Eddie's faced beamed with hopefulness as he took Eleanor's hand and they began to walk towards the house again. He whispered, "I'd like to give it a try."

In the living room, Drake began to receive another transmission from Carolyn. He heard the static and the buzzing at first before her voice came through loud and crystal clear. "Drake, it's Carolyn. Are you there?"

William and Carly sat on the sofa while Emily sat on the floor playing with the Husky pups. They listened as Drake returned, "Yes, Carolyn, I'm here."

Her voice was sad, as it was during most of their conversations. "Where are you now? I've been trying to contact you."

"We stopped in De Funiak Springs. We're less than three hundred miles away from you. It shouldn't be much longer."

She questioned, "Tell me what's been happening in your life. Have the others joined with you again?"

He answered, "As a matter of fact, they have. They got here just a few hours ago."

She tried to sound happy but wasn't putting up a good front. "That's wonderful, Drake. And is everyone in good health?"

"Well, Shireen and Zack seemed to have picked up three more survivors during their time apart from us. One of them is a pretty young girl named Maddie and she's pregnant. She's extremely pregnant."

"That's so nice to hear. At last, good news. New life is a beautiful thing."

He added, "We also met an older woman here in De Funiak Springs who has given us the most amazing gift."

She mumbled, "An amazing gift? What could that be?"

Drake declared, "We have horses, ten of them, all healthy and happy, and we have covered wagons."

"No more sleds pulled by dogs?"

He laughed, "No, the dogs get to go along for the ride instead."

There was a moment of silence before William walked over to the radio and said, "Hello,

Carolyn. It's William."

She replied, "Hello, William, it's good to hear your voice."

"I just wanted to give you an update on everyone here. Eddie and Eleanor have completed their skin treatments and seem to be doing very well. Katie managed to give us a little scare with her heart. We thought she had a heart attack but it wasn't quite so serious. You'll be happy to know that I'm still keeping a close eye on her."

Carolyn praised William, "I know you will. It was good speaking with you."

Drake took over the broadcast again while William went back to the sofa. "What's been going on in Crystal River?"

"I'm not in Crystal River anymore. I had to leave there."

"Why?"

She explained, "For the past few weeks, the temperatures have risen. I actually have days where it climbs into the lower sixties. The ice is melting fast and there's been a lot of flooding in the area. So much flooding, that Crystal River is now a swamp. I moved east about twelve miles. I'm in a small town named Citrus Hills. It's all dry land and I feel much safer here."

Drake pondered, "So, the climate there has changed in that short amount of time? We've seen the same thing lately up here in the panhandle. What about the nighttime?"

Carolyn said, "At night it still drops to the twenties and teens but it warms back up again every day. It took me a few days to realize the melting ice was causing the water to rise but I got out in time. It took me a few weeks to get everything packed and moved but I made the transition."

"And where are you living?"

"I found a beautiful house on North Pave Avenue. It has a well and a septic system all in good working order. I have comfortable furniture, plenty of good books to read, two fireplaces and a whole lot of firewood. When I got here, I came upon some grocery stores, so I took a page out of your book and I built a little sled to transport supplies. I spent days dragging those cases of bottled water and canned goods back to the house."

Drake was thankful to know Carolyn had taken charge of the situation and did what needed to be done. "Any problem with animals?"

She chuckled, "Believe it or not I haven't seen or heard any since I got here. There's a tiny lake near the house and I decided to teach myself how to fish."

"And how's that working for you?"

Carolyn said, "I've actually caught fish. I caught them and cleaned them and cooked them all by myself."

Drake was proud of her. He inquired, "Is there any chance you might have bumped into any other survivors?"

"No, I'm still alone, but it's not nearly as bad as it was. The mild weather has helped a lot. Some days, I even see the sunlight for a couple hours. It helps me to ignore the grey skies that happen the rest of the time."

Suddenly, the static and then the buzzing came and Carolyn's voice was lost to the airwaves again. Drake was satisfied with their conversation. He told Katie, Zack and Shireen that he could hear a change in her mood. She sounded stronger. She was finally fighting to make things better for herself instead of simply existing or surviving.

Zack turned the conversation around when he asked, "When do you think we'll be able to hook the horses up to the wagons and go?"

Drake recalled what Carolyn had said about the warmer climate and the flooding, and pondered if that could become a problem for them down the road. He said, "Let's take another day here and see how things go."

Katie bent down and scooped Snickers up in her arms and agreed. "I think we have some people here that still might have some issues to work on ... or work out."

Zack stated, "Alright. We'll stay one more day and then we're out of here. Don't forget we still have a mountain range to cross."

Shireen gazed out the front window as she noticed the frost covering the grounds again. She questioned, "Has Irwin come back yet?"

Gwen muttered, "No. I haven't seen him in hours. I don't know what I can do or what I can say to make it better."

Zack stated, "This is just something he has to work out on his own. I don't think any of us can offer sound advice to him right now because none of us have been through what that poor guy's had to go through."

Maddie entered the room and asked, "Has anyone seen Granger?"

In a small, cold, dark outbuilding, Irwin sat on an old, rickety wooden chest, rocking back and forth, lost in thought. He heard footsteps and saw Granger as he slid open the door. He grimaced at Granger and shook his head. He asked, "How did you find me?"

"Just lucky, I guess."

Granger, wiser than his fifteen years, sat on the chest next to Irwin. "I wish I could tell you that I know how you feel, but I don't."

Irwin agreed, "No, you couldn't know how I'm feeling right now. You're just a little too young to help me with this one, kid."

They sat and stared at the dirt floor while Granger figured out what to say. "Remember when the meteors hit the earth?"

Irwin replied, "Of course, I do."

"I was only eleven years old when it all came crumbling down around me, eleven years old. You're whimpering over losing your girlfriend, but you don't know loss until you lived what I lived through. I was in school that day. During science class, the principal rushed into the classroom and told everyone to go home. The busses were waiting outside. Kids panicked and screamed as they ran out of the building, but I didn't get on the bus. I froze in my seat."

"You weren't able to move?"

"No. Everyone was so worried about getting out of there, they never noticed me still sitting in the science lab."

Irwin asked, "What did you do?"

"I didn't know what else I could do. When I heard the first loud crash, I leapt out of my seat and ran to the basement of the school. That's where the lavatories and the music rooms were. I heard every one of the explosions and felt the building and the ground rocking, and the gurgling screams. I stayed there for hours, until the ground stopped shaking. Then, I left the school to find my way home. I ran, no waded, through hundreds of dead bodies. It took me two hours to get home. When I got there, I saw the house was just a pile of rubble. My mother, my father, my two brothers, all dead."

Irwin was feeling embarrassed for being so selfish. He tried to intervene but was cut off by Granger. "Poor boy …"

"So, I knew I was by myself. I left there and wandered the streets. I must have walked those streets for days without any food or water. Then, the freezing cold came, and more earthquakes. I spent months trying to find someone, any other survivor. Eventually, I met Naomi and she took care of me and helped me. It took us nearly three years but we walked to Houston. That's when we met Drake and the others."

Irwin asserted, "I was wrong. You lost so much more than I could ever imagine. You lost everyone and everything, and you were just a child. I can't blame Gwen for what her father did to me thirty years ago. I should be thanking the lord above that this bizarre twist of fate has brought us back together again."

Granger stated, "That's what I'm talking about, Irwin. You have to let her know what you're feeling."

"We may not have many years left on this earth but, at least, we'll be able to spend that time together. That's all I need."

Granger stood up from the wooden box and asked, "What are you waiting for? The love of your life is only a few hundred yards away."

Irwin stood up and put his arm around Granger's back. He smiled at the boy as they left the outbuilding. They made their way back to the house but found most everyone had already turned in for the night. Granger questioned, "What are you going to do, Irwin?"

He whispered, "She's asleep and I don't want to wake her. I can wait until tomorrow to tell her how I feel."

Granger smiled. "Are you sure?"

Irwin responded, "I've waited almost thirty years for the moment. I think I may be able to wait nine or ten more hours."

22

The survivors were awakened at five by the slight rumblings of another earthquake. Then came another tremor. Carly was the first to roll out of bed. "I'll make the coffee."

Each person eventually woke up and came downstairs to the dining room. Zack asked, "Do you want me to cook?"

Carly was more than happy to turn that

chore over to Zack for a day. "That'd be nice. I'd appreciate if someone else took charge of the kitchen for once."

Katie stood at the kitchen door and heard what Carly had said. Caringly and with a hint of her usual humor, she said, "Hey, that's not fair, Carly. You know that I'm always here to help you in the kitchen, so you don't burn things."

Carly joked back, "In your case, Katie, it's not that you don't want to help, it's that I've tasted your cooking. You can stay in the dining room and leave the cooking to us."

Zack and Katie chuckled. Shireen came into the kitchen to gulp down a cup of coffee and then tend to the dogs. She told Zack she had planned to spend the entire day with them outside.

Irwin came into the kitchen and saw Gwen hadn't come downstairs yet.

Eddie, Drake and Peter skipped the coffee and headed right to the museum to finish getting the wagons prepared for the next day.

Eleanor, William and Granger lent a hand and loaded the transports with supplies and personal effects.

Drake announced that it could all be done with four wagons. He told then that he'd be leading the first wagon with Katie, Eleanor and Eddie. The second wagon would be Gwen, Irwin, Maddie and

Peter. The third wagon would carry William, Carly and Emily. He felt the last wagon should have Zack, Shireen and Granger to keep watch on the rear of the caravan. Of course, they had to make room for all the dogs too.

Gwen came to the dining room and drank her coffee. Irwin waited for her to finish before he came in and sat next to her. They didn't speak at first. There was an uncomfortable silence that lingered around the room. Gwen shifted in her seat a few times before she opened her mouth. "Dandy, I've had all night to think about this. I don't think I slept a wink."

He replied, "I couldn't sleep either. I just kept thinking about you. I have to get some things off my chest."

She asked, "And what have you come up with, Dandy?"

"I realized a few things last night. I realize that I was weak back then. I know that I should've fought harder to be with you, but I didn't. I allowed your father take control of the situation, a situation he had no business interfering in, and that's why I lost you. That's why my life was filled with chaos and regret."

She looked bewildered. "Are you actually blaming yourself for all of this?"

He nodded his head. "If I hadn't listened to

your father, if I hadn't been so afraid of him, we'd have been together all those years."

She whispered, "But we still have so many wonderful years ahead of us. Why don't we stop dwelling on the past? I'm so sorry for what that man put you through."

"It wasn't your fault, Gwen. You couldn't have control over something you never even knew was happening."

She bowed her head. "But I should have had more faith in the strength of our love. I was such a foolish young girl."

"And you never courted anyone else, never got married?"

"No, I waited and waited. I lived a fantasy that you might come back to me one day. I guess it's not a fantasy anymore."

Irwin put his arm around Gwen as they sat at the table and gazed at the world outside the large window. They saw a hint of sunshine that tried to break through the clouds. They watched Shireen in the pasture running with her dogs, even the Husky pups. Gwen commented, "They're good people, each one of them. We got lucky to be blessed with such an amazing family."

Irwin held her hand and said, "I think you may be right about that."

In the pasture, Shireen was joined by Emily

who wanted to run around with the Husky puppies. She said, "Hey girl, I've missed you."

Emily responded, "I missed you too, Aunt Shireen. I missed you a lot. Do you think I can I play with the puppies?"

"Of course, honey. I think they need to run around a little bit. But remember, they're still only babies and we need to keep a watchful eye on them. Don't let them get too rough with you."

Emily said, "I won't. I promise," as she began racing through the pasture with the puppies following closely behind.

Shireen knelt back on the ground and started brushing the big dogs. She looked at Abby, the Chocolate Lab, and said, "You don't have to pull anymore sleds, baby. It's all smooth sailing from here on out."

Abby put her paw up as Shireen ran the brush down her back. The other dogs almost formed a line behind Abby, anxiously waiting for their turn. She noticed Eddie and Eleanor taking a break from their morning routine and taking a stroll in the back pasture, seeing Emily and the puppies catch up to them and join in on the walk.

Katie came out of the house and approached Shireen, asking, "Do you want some help? I can get another brush."

Shireen said, "Thanks, Katie. I got this. Why

don't you go in the house and relax a little bit? We have a long trip tomorrow."

Katie seemed upset and anxious. She turned and started to stomp back to the house. Then, she stopped for a moment, turned around and marched her way back to Shireen. She asserted, "I'm tired of being treated like an invalid."

Shireen looked up and replied, "No one's treating you like an invalid, Katie. But you can't overdo it. Remember, you just had a huge scare with your heart."

Katie attempted to explain, "But I'm fine. William said not to overdo it, but I'm still capable of doing some things. No one wants my help in the museum or the stables. No one wants my help in the kitchen or with the firewood. Jesus Christ, I don't think brushing a few dogs is going to send me into cardiac arrest!"

Shireen observed how frustrated and angry Katie was becoming. She knew that Katie didn't come there to brush the dogs. She came there to let Shireen know exactly how infuriating her lack of involvement was getting.

Katie knew Shireen had a way about her. It was a persuasive manner, and perhaps she could tell the others to back off a little. Shireen looked up at the sky. "It sure is some great weather we're having again today."

Katie agreed, "Yes, it is."

Shireen gave Katie a look that she should grab a brush, kneel down and help groom the dogs. She smiled. "Well, what are you waiting for? You said you wanted to help me."

Katie smiled back and felt a little relief. She got down on her knees and began brushing one of the Otterhounds. "Thanks, Shireen."

Later that day, Zack and Granger decided it was time to follow Carolyn's lead and head out to catch something for dinner. Gwen told them about the springs several miles up the road. Peter and Drake tagged along with them.

The four sat along the banks of the water holding their fishing poles, enjoying the beautiful weather and captivating serenity. Zack commented, "It doesn't get much better than this, guys. I could live like this forever."

Drake cast his line and agreed, "And it's getting better all the time."

They found it to be a successful day once the tenth largemouth bass was caught. Even though their fishing jaunt was finished, they chose to stay there for another hour, enjoying the peacefulness, before they gathered their tackle and carried their buckets back to the house.

Shireen cleaned the fish. After talking to Carly, they allowed Katie in the kitchen to prepare dinner for everyone. Drake could see the world that had become so cold and isolated was beginning to develop into an inviting place.

23

The wagons began moving down the road, but at an exceptionally slow pace. Once they hit the interstate, they sped up quickly. All four covered wagons trotted down the highway at fifteen miles an hour.

Drake was sure they'd be in Citrus Hills by Christmas. He knew they were going to be faced with the obstacle of a mountain range that would be coming soon. But he felt confident they could cross it without danger.

The day was, once again, partially bright, and unseasonably warmer. The survivors didn't question it, they simply enjoyed it as they hurried down the interstate to the next destination.

They saw the mountains were getting closer with every mile they travelled. The formations were towering. Their magnitude was beginning to terrify most everyone.

Occasionally, they pulled over to take the chance to get out of the wagons and take in what would be an extensive climb upwards, and then a lengthy descent back down.

Three and a half hours had gone by before they were almost face to face with the new obstacle. Drake called out, "We're only a few miles from a town called Cottondale! We may need to stop there for a few minutes!"

Suddenly, Katie screamed out and the first wagon stopped abruptly and slid a little on the still icy roads. Wagon two did the exact same thing but bumped into wagon one slightly. The third covered wagon, riding off to the side, attempted to stop but couldn't. It continued to slide, horses and all, into the new gorge that had been carved out of the earth when the mountains formed.

William and Carly tried desperately to stop the horses but it wasn't the horses' call. Emily grabbed ahold of Carly, closed her eyes and screamed out.

The gorge was cavernous and deep. The horses finally found their footing as Zack, Granger and Shireen watched from the halted fourth wagon. William's horses came to a standstill but the wheels of the third wagon continued to slide them to the edge of the gorge.

The third wagon stopped but left the back of the cart teetering on the edge. Everyone could see that one unwise move could have sent Carly, Emily, William, five of the dogs and several of the horses plummeting into the deadly abyss.

Zack hollered, "Move yourselves and the dogs to the front of the wagon!"

Carly pushed Emily forward. The unstable wagon wobbled a bit.

Zack shouted, "Just go slow and take your time, Carly!"

He could see the look of terror on Carly's pale white face. She listened and just nudged Emily and herself forward, inch by inch.

Drake and the others moved their wagons to a safe place before everyone got out and loomed towards William and Carly's wagon. Zack and Granger got out of their wagon. They watched as Carly and Emily made it to the front.

Zack, Drake and Eddie moved closer to the one side. Peter, Irwin, Granger and Eleanor moved closer to the other side. Kate, Gwen and Shireen stayed near the front of the wagon.

Carly announced, "Okay, William, you have to move towards me. Bring one or two of the dogs with you."

The wagon stopped teetering for a moment as William climbed forward to Carly and Emily. He gently slapped his leg and commanded the dogs, "Come on. Let's go."

All five of the dogs listened and began walking towards the front. The other survivors grabbed the wagon and helped to keep it steady.

Suddenly, the wagon jerked back for a moment, creating a horrible creaking noise, as if it was ready to tumble backwards into the gorge.

William stopped and moving for a moment. He was trembling. Droplets of sweat fell from his forehead. He crept a few more inches, then a few more. The dogs gradually made it to the front with Carly and Emily.

In a brave moment, Irwin hopped onto the front of the prairie schooner. Gwen gasped when she witnessed this. His weight steadied the wagon and William made it to the front. Gwen called the horses to move forward. They walked step by step as the back of the wagon progressively made it onto steady ground again. Once the wagon was pulled to safety, William, Carly and Emily got out. They were relieved, elated and thankful they were back on solid ground.

Irwin stepped out of the wagon and watched as Gwen approached. She said, "That was a brave thing you did, Dandy, and stupid, very, very stupid. Don't you realize you could have killed yourself and left me alone again."

Irwin smiled and put his arm around her. He glanced at the other twelve people standing there and whispered, "Don't you see, Gwen? We'll never be alone again. We're part of a family now and I don't plan to screw that up."

Zack walked over and shook Irwin's hand. "I thought about doing that, but you actually had the balls to follow through with it. You're a good man, Irwin, brave too."

William and Carly acknowledged him for his courageousness. Emily ran to him and hugged him. "Thank you, grandpa Irwin."

Irwin grinned at Gwen when he heard the touching new title Emily had given him. He added, "Well, if I'm grandpa Irwin, I guess that makes you grandma Gwen."

Gwen smacked him playfully in the stomach and specified, "I didn't think I was that old but, for Emily, it's okay."

Drake approached Zack and Eddie. "I think we need to find a different way to Citrus Hills. This gorge is impassable."

Zack asked, "And just what direction do you think we should go?"

Katie pulled out the map and handed it to Drake. He scanned the area and decided, "It only makes sense to go north."

Zack questioned, "Why would we go north and not south?"

"Because Carolyn told us these mountains extended into the Gulf of Mexico. That could also mean this gorge is just as extensive. Plus, with all the warmer weather, we could possibly hit flooding if we go south."

Zack agreed, "Okay, we go north. How far north do you think we'll have to go, twenty miles, fifty miles, a hundred miles?"

Drake explained, "We have to go as far north as it takes, until we can safely cross over the mountains without a canyon to fall into. Just so you know, if we go north, we're going to be back in Alabama again. It looks like there's a small town about two hours from here. It's called Dothan. I say we just follow the gorge north until it ends, or at least until it gets smaller."

Eddie said, "Makes sense."

Zack expressed hesitantly, "If that's the way you think we should go, then so be it. I'm just along for the ride."

The fourteen survivors loaded back into their wagons and headed north toward the Alabama border and then into Dothan. As they traveled, they kept a close eye on the gorge to see if it was getting smaller as they continued.

After thirty-five miles and two and a half hours, they arrived in Dothan. Shireen mentioned at one point she noticed the gorge wasn't as wide as it was in Florida. She also took into account that the mountain range wasn't the same extent as before. She knew then that the mountain range would end eventually if they continued on their path.

In the city of Dothan, they found many structures on the east side that were damaged and flattened, which most likely happened when the mountains and the gorge were formed. They also noticed it was becoming noticeably cooler as they moved northward.

On the west side of the city were several large homes still left intact. On the outskirts of the area, they found an old plantation, large enough to house fourteen people, the dogs and the horses. They pulled onto the property and claimed it as home until they could figure out what their next move would be.

Gwen and Irwin put the horses in the pasture and Shireen found a safe place in the house for the dogs to eat and sleep and keep warm. She noticed the skies weren't as clear as they were in the south. They were gray again.

Drake, Zack and Katie sat at a kitchen table and figured out where they'd travel next. The worn map was laid out on the table as each one slumped over to get a better look at it. Katie said, "We know that the gorge can't last forever. We're just going to have to do what we have to do to get around it. No questions."

Eddie suggested, "When we're ready to move again, Columbus is only about a hundred miles north. By then, maybe things will look a little more promising."

William and Peter unloaded food and water from the wagons. As they put things away in the kitchen, they eavesdropped on the discussion that was still happening.

Zack stated, "The mountains are getting lower and the gorge is getting thinner the further we go north. If we get a hundred more miles, it could be crossable."

Katie zipped up her jacket and began shivering as she announced, "I'm cold. It's freezing in this place. I think we need to get more of these fireplaces lit."

William and Peter went to wagon four and unloaded the firewood. Granger jumped into help them out. Soon, four of the fireplaces on the first floor were burning.

Carly, Eleanor and Maddie went up to the second and third floors of the house to take a look around. Maddie counted bedrooms as she walked. They spotted, in one of the bedrooms, human bones on the floor.

Maddie turned and walked up to the third floor. Eleanor and Carly followed her. As they checked things out, Eleanor asked Carly, "Are you doing alright, Carly?"

"Yes, I'm feeling a little less shaken."

Eleanor commented, "It's understandable,

and you handled it well. You made sure that Emily was alright."

Carly answered, "Of course I did. She's my little girl."

Eleanor whispered, "It was almost the same scenario when we lost Debra, Tony and Naomi. I remember a gorge opened up behind them, but with the earth shaking like it was, none of them ever stood a chance."

Maddie intervened, "Well, I'm happy that this one had a different outcome. I couldn't imagine losing any of you. You're all such an important part of us."

Carly smiled and responded, "They are both very important. After all, William's a physician and Emily's just a sweet thirteen-year-old girl, soon to be fourteen."

Maddie seemed confused that Carly left herself out of the equation, "What about you? You're just as vital to us as anyone else. You're always the first one up in the morning making everyone coffee and breakfast. You always make sure we have plenty of food and beverages. You take care of Granger and Emily and you always make each place that we stay into a warm and inviting home. I don't think you give yourself any credit for all things you actually do."

Carly blushed. "I just do what I need to. I

want everyone one of us to be happy and healthy. That's all."

Eleanor stated, "Perhaps someday you'll realize the glue that holds us together begins with your actions. You've created this family and now, with each person we come upon, you add them to our family."

They continued investigating the house when they came upon a tiny wooden staircase at the end of the third-floor hallway. They saw a closed door at the top. Maddie looked at the others and suggested, "That must be the attic. Should we check it out?"

Eleanor and Carly approved and, together, the three of them crept up the narrow staircase, wondering what was on the other side of the door. When they pushed the door open, they saw another bedroom. The attic was actually made into a huge bedroom. They stepped inside and explored. They saw a bed so big it could fit five or six people. The room was decorated with ornate eighteenth-century furniture and carpets.

On the floor, next to the bed, they saw more bones. Carly began to weep because they were the bones of a young child who once wore the plain white dress that surrounded her skeleton. "So very sad. We've lost so much. We lost a world full of people, of children who never had the chance to become adults."

They stood silently for a moment before Maddie knelt over the bones and recited the Lord's Prayer. Eleanor and Carly felt compelled to bow their heads and join in. A few minutes later, the women left the upstairs and returned to the first floor. Peter noticed their saddened state and asked Maddie, "What happened up there? You look as if you just lost your best friend."

Maddie rubbed her baby bump and gave Peter a half smile when she answered, "It was just a little reminder of the past and a warning for us to remember that it can all be taken away from us in a split second."

She took a moment to think about what she said before she changed the subject. "I couldn't believe the size of the bedrooms. This house has twelve of them. It must have been astonishing back in its glory days."

Peter agreed, "Yes, it is a lot of house to take in."

Carly, still upset over the incident on the interstate and then finding the young girl's skeleton in the attic, knelt down and asked Emily, "Want to go for a walk?"

Emily said, "Are you sure? It's so cold out there today."

Carly convinced her with, "We can bundle

up like we used to do and I wasn't planning on
going very far anyway."

Emily nodded her head and put on her layers
on coats. They walked into the front yard and
waved when they spotted Shireen, Gwen and Irwin
admiring the majesty of the grand old plantation.
Carly took Emily's hand as they continued through
the pasture. Emily asked, "Where are we going to,
mommy?"

"Just for a walk, nowhere special, baby girl.
I just wanted to take a look around."

Emily squirmed, "But it's so cold out today.
I think I'd rather go back to the house now. Is that
okay with you?"

Carly let go of her hand and said, "Sure, I
just didn't want to be alone, honey. You go back to
the house."

Emily began to walk toward the house. As
she looked back, she could see Carly was still a
little torn up over her near-death experience. She
turned and walked back to Carly, took her hand and
said, "I can handle the cold for a little while longer,
mommy."

Carly was happy to see that she changed her
mind. They kept walking passed the grounds of the
plantation and saw a partially frozen lake only a few
hundred feet away. "Emily, let's go down and take
a look at the lake."

She nodded her head and walked with Carly to the shore of the lake. Carly put her foot on the ice but it was thin, very thin. The ice cracked into many pieces and sank into the water. Emily yelled, "This lake is huge!"

They stared at the water for a while, sitting down on the frozen embankment. Carly looked at Emily and asked, "Are you happy … with William and I? I mean, do you like it that we're your mom and dad now?"

Emily kicked her feet, "Of course I do. I love you and daddy."

After a short time, they noticed that Peter was walking toward them. Carly pointed and said, "Here comes Peter."

He stood behind them and asked, "What's up guys? What're you up to?"

Carly answered, "We're just enjoying the nature. How about you?"

Peter replied, "I just decided to take a walk. William's back at the house examining Maddie and I needed some air."

He thought he saw a figure move through the trees on the other side of the lake. He looked again but didn't see anything. Carly asked him, "What wrong?"

At first, he shrugged it off and told her, "It was nothing important."

There was another movement. He pointed and asked, "Did you see that?"

Carly and Emily were confused. They didn't know what he was talking about. Carly questioned, "Did I see what?"

He pointed again, "Over there, on the other side of the lake, I thought I saw something."

Carly muttered, "I didn't see anything."

Soon, no one was talking and the three of them had focused their eyes across the lake to watch for any sign of movement. Something moved again and this time they all saw it. Carly whispered, "I don't like this, Peter. What if it's a bear?"

Emily stood up and began shaking as she took Carly's hand. "Can we go back to the house now? I'm scared."

Carly turned to Peter and said, "I'm with Emily. Let's get out of here. We don't know what that is."

Peter stated, "Good idea. You two go back to the house. I want to watch what's going on over there."

Carly was shocked. "I'm not leaving you here alone!"

They spotted another movement in the trees. Peter asserted, "Get back to the house. Let Zack and Drake know where I am and tell them to bring a few of the shotguns."

Carly whimpered, "I don't like this, Peter."

He gave them a hand signal telling them to leave, before he whispered, "Go."

Carly took Emily by the hand. Peter watched them as they ran back to the house. As they opened the front door, Carly hollered, "Zack! Drake! Eddie! You have to go down to the lake!"

Zack could perceive the sound of panic in Carly's voice. He asked her, "Lake? What lake are you talking about, Carly?"

She replied frantically, "It's right behind the pasture, a few hundred yards away. Emily and I just discovered it. You have to hurry!"

The men stood up and questioned, "What happened? What's going on?"

Once Carly was able to catch her breath, she explained, "Peter's down there by himself. He saw something moving on the other side of the lake. It looked like it could be a wild animal! He said to bring your shotguns with you."

The men grabbed shotguns and coats that they threw on as they exited the house. Everyone else in the house looked at each other in horror. Carly sat down and pulled Emily close by. The house was quiet.

Zack arrived at the lake first. The others followed a minute later. Zack looked around at the perimeter of the water. "Where's Peter? I thought

Carly said he was here."

Eddie ran back to the house to get Carly for clarification. Soon, they were all standing at the edge of the lake, looking for Peter. Carly said, "He was right here where I'm standing, but I don't see him anywhere."

Drake had two working flashlights. They split up and began to walk around both sides of the lake. Zack walked with Carly, and Drake and Eddie went in the opposite direction. They could tell it would be dark soon. Each couple had a flashlight to shine around them. Carly said, "I don't understand how he just vanished into thin air."

They moved quietly but swiftly. Gradually, they made it to the other side of the lake, but there was no Peter. They shined the flashlights into the woods, looking for any type of movement. There was no movement. Drake shouted, "Peter! Where the hell are you?"

They continued to search for almost an hour until the skies were pitch black. Carly asked, "What are we going to do? He's not here."

Drake said, "We can't stay out here all night. These woods are full of nocturnal hunters at night. I guess we're going to have to go back to the house and pick up the search in the morning. I don't know what else we can do."

Eddie asked, "What do we tell the others?

What do we tell Maddie?"

Drake responded, "We tell them the truth. They'll see Peter's not with us."

They walked back to the house and broke the bad news to the others. Maddie was heartbroken and, at one point, hysterical.

As the night moved forward, most everyone retired for the evening. Drake remained in the living room with Katie, Shireen and Zack. Katie alerted them that she was joining the search in the morning. Drake said, "Absolutely not. You don't need that kind of stress right now."

Angrily, Katie looked Drake in the eye and stated, "Absolutely not? Don't tell me what I'm doing or not doing."

Drake backed up an inch. He could see Katie was fed up with the constant coddling. "I'm sorry, Katie ..."

"I love you, Drake, but don't ever attempt to order me around again."

Soon, Shireen volunteered too. Zack huffed and rolled his eyes and said, "Like I could ever keep you away."

Drake whispered, "All I know is that we have to find him. He has to be out there somewhere. He couldn't just disappear without a trace."

Zack added, "There has to be a reasonable explanation why he'd just leave and not say a word to any of us."

Drake nodded. "As soon as the sky lightens up in the morning, we have to move. The longer we wait, the worse the outcome will be. I can feel it in my bones."

24

The first signs of light filtered through the dust clouds and everyone was up and stirring about. Drake told Maddie they needed her to stay at the house incase Peter came home. Emily would remain there too.

They broke into four separate groups. Zack and Shireen were by themselves with several of the larger dogs. Drake and Katie took Carly with them. Eddie, Granger and Eleanor formed a team. Irwin, William and Gwen were the last group. They held shotguns, pistols, knives and clubs, not knowing what they could possibly face.

They started at the lake and planned to work their way deeper into the woods and then towards the main streets of Dothan.

Soon, Zack and Shireen found themselves deep within the threatening dense woods calling out to Peter with no response.

Irwin, Gwen and William walked down the main street, checking inside shops and diners with no luck.

After five hours, the survivors were getting tired and cold. Each party headed back to the lake where it all began.

Shireen ran with her dogs, calling them and petting them as they ran by. Shots rang out and Shireen saw three of the dogs drop to ground with blood on their fur. She ran to check them and heard more shots. The other two dogs fell over as Zack ran as fast as he could towards Shireen. She was leaning over one of the dogs where Zack caught up to her.

The other dogs began running towards Zack and Shireen. She gazed down at one of the German Shepherds and then a Rottweiler and began to weep. She knew they were all dead. Zack said, "Shireen! Your back is bleeding!"

Shireen fell over on top of the German Shephard. Zack shouted out to the others for help. "We're under attack!"

Everyone pulled their guns out. Drake pointed at Shireen on the ground and ordered, "Katie, Carly, Eleanor, Gwen get her back to the house and take William. He'll be more help at the house than out here."

Eddie, Drake, Granger, Irwin and Zack stayed at the lake and began shooting back in the direction that the shots had originated from. The four women lifted Shireen, who was squirming. More shots rang out. William took Shireen's legs. The men continued to shoot toward the woods. The same shots rang back their way.

When they got closer to the house, Katie glanced across Shireen's injured body at Carly and noticed there was blood all over the bottom half of her blouse. Katie shouted, "Carly, you're stomach! You're bleeding!"

Carly looked down at her stomach and fell to the ground. The others dropped Shireen when Carly let go. William grabbed Carly, lifted her in his arms and took her inside. Gwen, Katie and Eleanor were able to get Shireen on her feet, but she was still dead weight. They dragged her into the living room.

Inside the house, Emily saw that Carly was bleeding as William laid her on the sofa. Then, she saw them putting Shireen on the other one. Emily ran over to Carly and cried, "Mama! Mama, what happened?"

William worked fast with Katie assisting. He checked both women. He found Shireen had only been hit in the shoulder. After he examined Carly, he realized that she had taken a bullet in the stomach. William shouted, "Clear off the dining room table!"

Maddie stood in the background, rubbing

her stomach, sniveling and wondering where Peter had gone.

Hurriedly, Eleanor and Gwen pushed everything from the table onto the floor. Maddie stopped crying and threw a white sheet on the table. William lifted Carly and put her down on the sheet. She squinted her eyes listlessly as she stared up at William and mumbled, "What happened to me? Why am I so cold, William?"

He suggested, "Don't talk right now, honey. Just stay quiet and be still. I'm going to take care of you."

Katie leaned over his shoulder and inquired, "What about Shireen?"

William became annoyed. He asserted, "One patient at a time, Katie. Take Shireen and get her to the kitchen table. She'll be next, but I need you to assist me here first. I need water to be boiled! I need bandages and my bag!"

At the lake, the shots ended on both sides. During the storm of bullets, Zack and Eddie were able to sneak around to the other side of the lake without being noticed. Each one moved through the thick woods, carefully watching each step they made.

Soon, they noticed shadows near a cluster of pine trees. They saw a man and a woman standing in, almost hidden by, those dense trees.

Eddie made hand signals to Zack. They separated and crept deeper into the woods until they were only a few yards from the shooters.

Shots were still being fired across the lake at Drake, Granger and Irwin. Zack could hear the man and woman talking to each other. The woman said, "I think we better get out of here, Johnny, before they get any closer to us. There's way more of them then there are of us. Let's go."

Johnny replied, "Just one more. I just want to get one more of them, Betty. Tomorrow we'll take care of a couple more."

Impatiently, she muttered, "But, Johnny, they're shooting back at us. We should get back to the cave and hide out for now."

Johnny demanded, "Shut up, Betty, you big cow, or else!"

"Or else what, Johnny?"

Zack could see the couple in plain view from behind. They appeared to be a large couple in their mid to late fifties. Their attire was camouflage pants, t-shirts, jackets and hats. The woman wore her hair in pigtails and the man was completely bald with a beard so long that it covered his chest. They spoke with a deep Ozark twang.

Johnny and Betty Jones kept their focus across the river as they took shots at each of the men. Betty suggested, "Look at the kid. He don't even look like he's sixteen. I bet that he'd be an easy kill."

Johnny and Betty aimed their shotguns in Granger's direction. As they were about to fire, they each heard the click of a gun behind them. Zack and Eddie were standing a foot from each of them with their shotguns pointed at the back of their heads. Eddie said quietly, "I wouldn't do that. I'd drop the guns if I were you."

Johnny and Betty turned around to see their captors. Zack shouted across the lake, "It's alright! We got them!"

Granger, Irwin and Drake lowered their guns and began to make their way around the lake. As they approached, Granger stopped and gazed at the lake. He called out, "Drake! Drake! Get over here quick!"

They could see, floating partially under the ice, Peter's body face down. They knew he was dead.

Granger, in a panic, stepped onto the ice in an attempt to fish Peter out of the lake. The ice began to break and Granger had to hop back onto the shore.

They continued walking around the lake until they reached Zack. By then, Zack had Johnny and Betty on their knees with their hands folded on the top of their heads, asking, "Why? Why did you do this?"

Johnny, with no sign of emotion, responded, "Because we could, asshole. You're nothing more than target practice to us."

Distraught, Drake pointed and said, "Peter's body is floating over there under the ice. He must have been dead since yesterday."

Johnny laughed, "He was fun. That little pansy begged for his life over and over. I finally got tired of his whining."

Betty began to giggle hysterically. "What a wimp. He even started to cry."

Drake had to turn away. He was becoming infuriated by their answers and attitudes. Betty unfolded her hand and scratched her nose. Then, she put her hands back where they were supposed to be. She mentioned, "You can't hurt us. You ain't got the guts to kill us. You ain't the first. You won't be the last."

Eddie questioned, "You mean to tell me there have been other survivors that came through here?"

She giggled like a twelve-year-old. "They was coming through here and they never knowed it was gonna be their last stop."

Eddie faced her and requested, "How many? How many others have you killed?"

Betty Jones, with an obvious challenging

mentality, stated, "Well, I can only count as high as twenty, but I'd say that's a good number, twenty. Or maybe a couple more."

Johnny ordered, "Shut up, Betty. You got a big fucking mouth!"

He lowered his hands. Zack clicked his gun. Johnny said, "My legs is itchy." He acted like he was going to scratch his leg. But instead, he quickly pulled a handgun from his jacket pocket.

Zack didn't hesitate or ask him to stop. He shot him in the back of the head. Johnny dropped forward onto the ground. Betty screamed, "What did you do! You killed my husband, you bastards! You done killed my Johnny!"

She stood up and tried to run but Eddie grabbed her by the upper arm and pulled her back. She began kicking and swinging at Eddie, slapping him in the face several times.

Zack made a fist and punched her, as hard as he could, right between the eyes. She dropped over, almost unconscious. He said, "Let's get this bitch back to the house. I need to see what's going on with Shireen."

Zack speedily raced back towards the house, not waiting to see if anyone else was following him. Granger pointed at Johnny's carcass and asked Drake, "What about him, and what about Peter and the dogs?"

Drake pointed down at Johnny and said, "Leave this piece of shit for the wild animals. I'll help you get Peter out of the lake so we can give him a proper burial."

Irwin mentioned, "I'll round up the dogs. I don't know her that well, but I'm sure Shireen is going to want to bury them too."

Drake confirmed, "I was about to say the same thing."

Eddie and Drake lifted the overweight woman and walked her towards the house. When they arrived on the front porch Drake dropped her in a rocking chair, grabbed some rope and securely tied her up.

Drake went back to the lake to help Granger retrieve Peter from the water as they watched Irwin dragging each dog into the front yard.

Eddie came into the house and saw Carly lying on a table. Eddie asked, "What happened to Carly?"

Eleanor explained, "We're not sure. We think she got hit by a bullet when we were carrying Shireen to the house."

He probed, "How is she?"

Eleanor bowed her head and began to cry. "Not good. William said that she's lost a lot of blood. It's touch and go for now. I can't believe he's strong enough to take care of Shireen after everything that's happened."

"What about Shireen?"

Eleanor said, "It's a shoulder wound. Katie said it wasn't a fatal one. He just needs to extract the bullet and, with a lot of rest, she should be fine in a couple days."

Eddie pulled Eleanor to the side. "I have to tell you what's going on. We found Peter in the lake. He's dead. We're pretty sure he's been dead since last night. Zack killed one of the shooters and we have the female shooter tied up in a chair on the front porch."

Eddie looked over his shoulder and saw that Maddie was standing behind him. Maddie asked, "Did you say that Peter is …?" Maddie couldn't finish the sentence. She looked as if she was about to faint. Eleanor grabbed her by the upper arms and helped her to a chair. She whispered, "I'm so sorry, Maddie."

They watched as Maddie began to weep and rub her stomach. "I can't believe it. It can't be true. Peter can't be gone."

William finished taking care of Shireen. After which, she was assisted to a sofa where she could lie down and heal. Carly was moved to a first-floor bedroom where she could rest privately. William sat down in a chair next to the bed, holding her hand, watching and waiting for her to regain consciousness. Katie periodically came into the room to check on them. Each time, William would give her a glance, with a hopeful smile, and shake his head.

Maddie went out to the front yard to view Peter's body. Her tears ran down her cheeks as if someone turned on a faucet. Granger and Irwin began digging graves for Peter and the five lost dogs. Maddie went back into the house and sat alone, mourning quietly.

Zack and Drake sat on the front porch with big Betty, asking her questions. She wouldn't give many answers back. Zack asked, "Why would you do something like that. What on earth possessed you to go out there and murder innocent people in cold blood?"

Her response was, "It was all just fun and games. We was bored."

Zack got so angry he backhanded her across the face. "Fun and games? Someone lost their life in that lake!"

She asked, "So, are you just gonna to leave me tied up here on this here front porch? I'll freeze to death, you asshole!"

Zack restrained himself from slapping her again. Drake suggested, "I think we should leave her here. Let's go back in the house and check on Shireen and Carly."

As the skies became pitch black, Emily came into Carly's room and sat near her on the bed. William remained in his chair. Emily leaned up to Carly's ear and said, "It's time to wake up, mama. You've been asleep too long."

Carly's head rolled back and forth a bit but then stopped. William watched Emily as she laid next to Carly on the bed. He reminded her, "Be careful, baby. She has a lot of stitches. She's been through so much today."

Emily carefully put her arms around Carly. They watched as her head rolled around again. This time her eyes gradually opened. Emily said, "She's awake, daddy."

Carly looked at William and whispered, "William, I'm so cold. This room is so cold. Put some more wood on the fire."

Even though the room was actually warm, he obeyed what she asked him to do. He sat back down on the chair and took her hand again and said, "I love you, Carly. I know I don't say it enough, but I do love you."

She smiled a painful smile. "I know you do, William. I never had any doubt about it. And I love you more than you'll ever know. Did I ever tell you that you were the one?"

Her eyes squinted. William could see she was trying to mask her pain. Emily whispered, "I love you, mama."

Carly turned her head toward Emily and expressed, "Girlie, you have been the light in my life since the day I met you. No one could ever separate us because the love in my heart for you is an eternal love. It's like the love that I have for your daddy."

Emily rested her head on Carly's shoulder. "I know, mama. I know."

William and Emily waited for Carly to say more, but she didn't. Emily lifted her head and noticed her mother's eyes were still open but she wasn't breathing anymore. "Mama? Mama? Don't leave me, mama. I need you! Please!"

William hung his head in sorrow. He put his hands over his eyes to cover the fact he was crying. Emily realized she could say no more to bring her mother back. Instead, she leaned over, kissed her on the cheek and whispered, "Goodbye, mama," and put her head back down on her shoulder. They sat silently without alerting anyone else.

A time passed before Katie had come back into the room to see if Carly made any progress. It was then that she found out Carly had passed away. She went back into the living room to break the bad news to the others.

Pregnant Maddie, who was already grieving over Peter's murder, became almost hysterical all over again. She grabbed a flashlight, walked to the door and bundled up. She told the others that she was going to the front yard to view Peter's body one more time.

Zack reminded her to be careful out there alone. He sat on the sofa next to Shireen who was still exhausted from all that went on that day. She muttered, "Five of my babies, Peter and now Carly, all gone. Poor Maddie is so far into her pregnancy with Peter's baby and then this."

Drake mentioned, "We're going to have to keep a watchful eye on her, along with William and Emily, for a while. They're all in a very dark place right now."

Katie asked, "I guess no one's going to be eating dinner tonight?"

Heads bowed and others looked away. Eddie and Eleanor decided to retire earlier than the others that evening. Shireen followed a few minutes later. Katie opened a can of cling peaches and ate them out of the can. She explained, "I have to eat. I'm so hungry, I'm shaky."

Gwen and Irwin headed off to bed. Granger wasn't far behind. Katie, Drake and Zack sat in the living room. Their eyes were fixed on the crackling flames in the fireplace. Not much was said until Katie noticed, "Hey, did Maddie ever come back in the house?"

Drake said, "No, she didn't."

Zack looked at the clock and stated, "She's been gone for over an hour."

The three jumped to their feet and grabbed their coats. They ran out to the front porch and saw big Betty was gone. Her ropes were tossed all over the front yard. Zack called out to Maddie but got no response. Drake told Katie, "Get some flashlights. We're going to need them."

As they walked through the front yard, they observed Peter's body still laying there. Wrapped in a white sheet. They continued to walk towards the ominous lake.

They moved closer. They could hear faint voices talking in the distance. They began racing to the sound of the voices. Katie cried, "We can't lose Maddie and the baby too! We have to stop that woman, whatever it takes!"

As they reached the opposite side of the lake, they shone their flashlights toward the woods and saw Betty running through the trees. There was a gunshot. No one saw Maddie. Drake said, "I think we're too late."

There was another shot fired. They watched as Betty wove around the bushes and thick foliage. Katie spotted Maddie. The situation was exactly the opposite of what they thought it would be. Maddie was chasing Betty through the woods, wielding a shotgun. Betty was running for her life. She was most likely running faster than she ever had before. Maddie shouted wrathfully, "Come on, you fat pig, I can't get a clean shot!"

Betty turned to see how much distance was left between her and Maddie. Suddenly, another shot rang out and hit Betty in the shoulder. Maddie crazily shouted, "That bullet is for Shireen, fat ass bitch!"

Betty put her hand on the shoulder that was hit as she continued to wind through the forest and towards the lake. Another shot rang out. Drake, Katie or Zack didn't move or attempt to interfere with Maddie's revenge. Instead, Drake whispered, "Maddie needs to do this."

That shot hit Betty in the stomach. She looked down and saw blood discharging from her big belly. Maddie thundered, "And that one is for Carly!"

As Betty got to the edge of the lake, she realized she was too weak and couldn't run any further. Maddie arrived in the clearing and fired five more shots into Betty's arms and legs. Maddie hollered, "Those are for each of those innocent dogs you murdered!"

Betty was exhausted and bleeding. She fell to her knees and noticed the carcass of Johnny's body that had already been partially eaten by wild animals. Maddie came up from behind, grabbed her by her hair and announced, "And this is for Peter. I hope you rot in hell."

Maddie dunked her head into the icy lake water. Betty squirmed about, her arms and legs struggling to push her above the water line. Maddie didn't give up. She picked Betty's head up to give her some air, so she could dunk her under again, saying, "I'm not going to make this quick or easy for, Betty. You're going to suffer the same way that my Peter suffered."

The others watched as Maddie continued drowning the woman, then not drowning her, then drowning her again, and again and again until she felt satisfied and justified. She knew that she had accomplished what she came there to do.

Then, and only then, did she hold her head under the water for a long period of time. She did this until Betty eventually stopped moving. Maddie stood up and saw the others walking towards her. She said, "I know what you're going to say. You think I've lost my mind."

Katie put her arm around Maddie as Drake expressed, "Not at all, Maddie. We completely understand what you did and why you felt you had to do it. I think Peter and Carly would appreciate who you became in that moment. And who knew you could shoot like that?"

Katie scolded, "The only issue I have is that a woman as pregnant as you shouldn't be hunting hogs at this hour of the night." Katie laughed at herself again.

Maddie replied, "I promise. this'll be the last time I do something like that. I'm not insane. I'm just pissed off. And when I get pissed off, look out. That oversized bitch deserved a lot worse than she got from me."

The four took a slow walk back towards the house. As they passed Peter's corpse wrapped in white, Maddie asked, "Do you think we can have a funeral service for Peter and Carly?"

Drake said, "Of course, Maddie. Tomorrow. We'll take care of all that tomorrow. But tonight, we need to get some sleep."

The following afternoon a funeral was held. The twelve survivors said prayers, cried, mourned, broke down and hugged each other.

Drake and Irwin found stone slabs to use as headstones. Drake managed to radio Carolyn and relay the horrifying events that occurred.

Afterwards, everyone took several days to recuperate, rest and reflect on the magnitude of their losses. Each of them knew the devastating impact it would have on Emily and Maddie and the unborn child.

By day five, Shireen was well enough to

travel again. They loaded the wagons, readied the horses and regretfully watched Maddie, William and Emily bid one last goodbye to the ones they had to leave behind.

25

The covered wagons traveled a long distance through Georgia, almost a hundred miles, when they noticed the gorge was becoming a navigable valley and the mountains were low enough to cross without harm.

The temperatures had dropped even lower and the winds grew stronger as they headed further north. These were the coldest temperatures they'd had to deal with so far.

By nightfall, they pulled into Columbus and found a good-sized home to exist in while they were there. The house had several sound outbuildings to keep the horses contained during their stay.

After they all settled in, Drake immediately pulled out his map to plot their new route. He took Eddie to the side and said, "I think it's almost time to make our crossing. We've gone too far north as it is. The weather is just going to get worse as we go further up the country. If we don't try this and head south soon, we're going to start losing horses. If we lose our horses, we're in trouble. I think we should head east, passing the gorge and going over the mountains towards the Macon area. It's going to be another hundred miles but I'm sure we can make it through safely."

Eddie said, "Whatever we need to do, we'll do it, Drake. I agree that we won't survive if we go any further north. We have to do it soon. It's our only chance."

Katie joined them and mentioned, "It's only ten degrees outside, guys. We have to find a way to get back to where we were. I mean heading down south again."

Drake stated, "That's what we're trying to figure out now. We'll head out tomorrow, as early as possible and we go east."

Shireen passed by, struggling to pull a mattress across the room, feeling much better than she had previously. The wound was healing nicely. She let the others know, "I have the dogs set up in the garage, we have to keep the door open between the house and the garage overnight. I'm going to stay in there too."

The radio began buzzing with its usual loud static warning. Drake knew it was time to speak to Carolyn again. He found that the signal was weaker than normal. He could hardly hear her voice coming through. "Drake, it's Carolyn here. Drake, are you there? Drake?"

"I'm here, Carolyn. I'm here with Eddie and the others."

She asked, "How's everyone doing?"

He responded, "Everyone's freezing. This is the coldest I've ever seen it. How's the weather in your neck of the woods?"

Carolyn expressed, "It's been beautiful here. The highest temperatures during the day are in the upper fifties, and the lows are only dropping to the upper twenties. I've been seeing more sunshine each day. Plants are beginning to flourish here like they used to."

Drake stated, "That's wonderful."

"Yes, everything is green again and the ice has almost melted away completely. As a matter of fact, I went to the lake today to fish and I only had to wear a light jacket."

Eddie's face displayed a little envy. "I can't wait to be able to go fishing in nothing more than a light jacket."

Carolyn replied, "And I can't wait for you to join me at the lake. It'll be so much better when I have you all here with me."

Drake stated, "Tomorrow morning, we're going to head east, over the mountains. We have no other choice."

Carolyn asked, "Are you going to be able to get across? Down here the mountains are as high as the Rockies."

"It looks like we're at the foothills of the chain. The mountains are hardly even mountains here, but the roads and passes are most likely going to be completely iced over. I'm not saying it's going to be easy, but it is crucial."

Unexpectedly, the sound of static took over again. Carolyn's voice was gone. Eddie mentioned, "That was a terrible call. I could hardly understand what she was saying."

Drake laid the radio on the table and said, "That's because we're so far away from her. This was almost as bad as the signal we used to get when I was back in Houston."

Gwen, Irwin and Granger went down to the outbuildings to figure out ways of keeping the horses warm overnight. They were able to create small fire pits, in each of the two structures, and borders to keep the horses at bay.

Gwen announced, "I'm going to have to stay here overnight to keep the fires going. The horses don't have any land to graze on. If they don't find some soon, they'll starve. I can't lose any more of my horses."

Irwin volunteered, "I know, Gwen. We're only here for one night. But for now, I'll take care of the other building and keep the fire burning in there. Maybe we can get some help dragging some mattresses from the house."

Granger, overheard Gwen and Irwin's conversation. He took it upon himself to hook up a makeshift sled out of a few pieces of plywood. He borrowed several of the dogs from Shireen, hooked them up and went out into Columbus in a desperate search.

He eventually found an old, broken-down feed store outside the city. Gerber's Feed and Pet Supplies was stocked with hundreds of bales of forgotten hay. Granger found the bales that looked best. He carefully loaded them on the back of the sled and took them back to Gwen and Irwin with enough food to help sustain the horses. Gwen checked the bales and announced they were still good enough for the horses to eat.

Irwin and Granger set out again to bring a second round back. The Arabians and the Drafts enjoyed nibbling on the hay for hours. With a big smile on her face, Gwen thanked Granger, "You're certainly a resourceful young man. I never would have thought an old feed store would have lasted all these years but you were able to find one. You're a bright one, Granger."

In a bedroom, Maddie sat with Eleanor on the edge of the bed. Maddie was depressed and still upset over the loss of Peter. "I just don't know what I'm going to do without him. Very soon I'm going to have a baby to take care of, and eventually, the baby's going to ask me about Peter. I don't know what I'm going to say."

Eleanor said, "That's not going to be for a long time. You just have to tell your baby the truth. Celebrate who Peter was. He was a good man who loved music and loved you very deeply. I know the world we live in today is a cruel world and it's an unforgiving world that still contains creatures like Betty and Johnny Jones."

Maddie mentioned, "They informed the others that they had killed over twenty other people. And that crazy man, Hal, back in Diamondhead, went and killed several people before he wanted to kill us too. Irwin witnessed fourteen insane convicts committing suicide in a church. I'd say that's a lot of people. Maybe we're not as alone as we once thought we were."

Eleanor nodded, "It seems so, and as soon as others realize that Florida's climate is warmer than other climates, we might have hundreds of people showing up. Some could be good people and some might be like Hal or Betty and Johnny."

They felt the ground begin to shake for a moment. Maddie whispered, "Great, this is all we need now."

The movement ended quickly and didn't return as it had done in the past. Eleanor was happy to see this. "That's strange, we usually have a lot more shaking than that. All we can do is pray it stays that way."

Maddie hung her head and whimpered, "I miss him so much."

Eleanor comforted her. "I know you do, Maddie. If there was something that I could do to change things or take some of your grief away, you know I'd do it."

Maddie lowered her head and waited for a moment before she hinted, "There is one thing you can do for me."

"What's that?"

Maddie stated, "If the day ever comes, not today, not tomorrow, but if a day comes where I begin to forget about Peter, will you remind me I shouldn't do that?"

Eleanor gave a sad grin. "Oh honey, I don't think that day will ever come."

Sternly, Maddie asked, "Just promise me, if it does happen, will you make sure Peter's spirit and memory still goes on?"

Eleanor shook her head, seeing Maddie was dead serious. "Of course, I will. You know I will. That's what friends do."

"Thank you, Eleanor."

They sat there for a while, listening to the various sounds of the others heading to bed for the night. Maddie inquired, "Do you think you can stay in here with me tonight?"

Eleanor said, "Sure."

William laid on the living room sofa, staring at the points of the flames in the fireplace. Eddie laid on the opposite sofa watching William. Eddie called quietly, "William, you asleep? Hey, William, are you asleep?"

William whispered back, "No, I'm not. I haven't been sleeping very much lately, since it happened."

Eddie cited, "I noticed you were looking a little tired this week."

"I've tried to sleep but, every time I close my eyes, I see Carly standing there with all of that blood pouring out of her abdomen. I see her face all the time. I believe I still hear her voice calling me to the table for dinner."

Eddie rolled over and said, "It wasn't fair. You lost the woman you love but we need to think about Emily. Remember, she just lost the woman she called mother. And Maddie, she's going to need you to take care of her. She can't get through her pregnancy without your help. She needs a sound doctor, William."

Staring up at the ceiling, William admitted, "I know that I've been thinking of myself a lot, but it'll get better. I know what I have to do, for Emily and for Maddie."

Eddie probed, "What's that?"

William didn't give Eddie a response. He just turned his eyes back towards the fireplace and stared intently, blocking out everything else as the flames crackled.

26

The morning was icy and frigid. Drake saw that the thermometer only risen to a mere three degrees above zero. Everyone had bundled heavily and even stopped at stores on the way out of town to grab extra blankets to cover the horses and the dogs. They piled large comforters in each wagon and the drivers of each wagon were forced to wear ski masks and two pairs of gloves.

The caravan moved quickly at first as they exited Columbus and headed onto smaller, county roads instead of an interstate. Drake's wagon led them towards the insignificant basin that the gorge had become.

The wagons moved slowly as they crossed through the valley, avoiding as many icy trails as they could. Even though the valley was slower, it was easier and safer.

After an hour, they arrived at the base of the mountains. Gwen insisted that she should lead the team into the hills. She told Drake and Zack, "I know my horses well, just as Shireen knows her dogs. I can get us over this mountain if you just trust me."

Drake gave into her request and allowed her wagon to be the first wagon in the group. Moving sluggishly and cautiously, they travelled into the unsteady and untouched new mountains of middle Georgia. Gwen realized that her horses who usually moved ten to fifteen miles an hour were travelling at only seven miles an hour.

As they climbed higher, the temperatures dropped well below zero and the winds began to whip around the wagons. Shireen, Katie, Emily and Eleanor stayed wrapped up in comforters on the floors of the wagons with several dogs huddled under the blankets with them.

The snow on the mountain was deep and Gwen believed she was steering them in the right direction, not really knowing what the correct route would be, not knowing what surprises awaited them on the other side.

Drake saw that they were still going uphill after three hours. Sitting in the second wagon, he exclaimed, "We haven't reached the top yet! It has to be coming soon! Once we hit the top, I'm sure we'll be moving faster!"

Katie shouted back, "The top! If we even get

to the top! I don't know how much longer we can last in this cold!"

As they continued to climb higher, the covered wagons separated from each other slightly but, with the slippery paths before them, they couldn't stop to wait for the other wagons to gain momentum.

Wagon one was at least a hundred feet in front of wagon two. Wagon two was over fifty feet in front of wagon three. And wagon four, the slower wagon, was two hundred feet behind wagon three. Gwen just figured they'd all meet up again sooner or later.

No one even noticed when the fourth wagon began to slide on the frozen pass. Zack, Shireen and Emily felt a jolt, like a wheel had busted, and found the wagon was sliding sideways instead of forward. The cold horses whinnied, kicked a few times, and struggled to get their control back. Eventually, they were able to slow down and make the wagon stable again.

The horses were beginning to move even slower, perhaps five miles an hour at that point. The dogs were crying and howling at times. Four hours into the trip, Gwen noticed they had reached the top and were beginning to go downhill. She could see the pathway ahead that led to the valley below. It was much steeper and shorter than the side they had just climbed. She observed the paths were a little clearer and slicker too. She felt confident that the journey down would be successful and smooth. Her only concern was that she would encounter another gorge on the other side of the mountain.

Once they began to move down the other side of the mountain, the horses were able to regain some of their speed as they trotted over ten miles an hour for the duration. The temperatures were rising again but only into the single digits. Katie shouted, "We have to do something! It has to be soon! We're all freezing to death!"

Drake didn't know what he could possibly do to make things better. He, like Katie, was on the top of the mountain with very few supplies. He shouted back, "We're just going to have to tough it out and hope for the best!"

"I hate to say this, Drake, but I can honestly say this is the first time I ever thought that we're not going to make it."

Drake looked at Katie, knowing he was thinking the same thing. He shrugged and said, "If it's meant to be, it's meant to be."

In the fourth wagon, Shireen laid on the floor with Emily and the Huskies. The pups were crying out as Emily tried to pull them closer. Shireen hollered to Zack, "I think we should have planned this out a little better! We could have taken more time to get ready! This was all done way too sloppy!"

Zack agreed. "You're right. We could have planned more, but we had to get on the road sooner or later."

Shireen shouted, "And why did we have to move so quickly? Because Drake said we have to be in Florida by December! When did we name Drake the boss?"

Zack tried to calm her down. "No one said Drake was the boss of anything. He just wants to find us a better home, a warmer home, a warm place where we can settle down."

Shireen remarked, "I don't think you can see the truth, Zack. Drake wants to get to Florida to save one woman from being alone. That shouldn't be the reason we do the things we do. Sometimes, he doesn't think of us. He only sees Carolyn, and that's not right."

As the horses began to move at a steady pace, they eventually caught up with the other three wagons. Zack said, "I hear what you're saying, Shireen and maybe you're right. Maybe I need to talk to him about that."

Emily remained curled up under the blankets as Shireen stated, "No Zack, I think it's time that I have a talk with him. It's my problem. I think I can deal with it."

Zack shook his head. "No, how about we both talk to him? We're a couple now and we should face problems together."

Shireen liked this. She smiled, even though she was freezing and tired, and realized this was a great bonding moment for them.

The horses gradually made their way to the bottom of the mountain. Gwen and Irwin were elated when they saw there was no gorge and no valley, only flat roads again.

The skies were getting darker and they knew they had to find a place to rest and keep warm for the night.

Drake checked over his map and saw they had come out of the mountains further south than originally planned. He hollered to Gwen, "Let me lead the pack again! I see a place we can pull in for the night!"

Gwen reduced her wagon speed and let Drake get in front of the caravan again. Soon they saw Interstate 75 and signs for the city Warner Robins. The skies were black and they knew they had no other choice for now. As they pulled passed the city, Drake saw signs for the Robins Air Force Base and followed them.

The wagons pulled into a three-thousand-acre air force base. They stopped in front of a hangar and went inside. It was an enormous metal structure with several separate rooms. Only half of the building had to have been used to store the small airplanes.

Zack, Eddie and Granger went to the staff apartments and found mattresses that were hauled back to the hangar. Katie and Shireen used thick metal cans to build eight small contained fires within the building. Drake and the others went outside and hurriedly chopped down several trees for extra wood. The horses and the dogs were brought in and made comfortable.

The survivors lined the mattresses close together and the building slowly began to warm up. The day had exhausted them all. Maddie, Gwen, Irwin and Emily laid down and fell asleep quickly. The others sat around a large round conference table to discuss their next move.

Drake announced, "I've been studying the map and I think we should get out of here as quickly as possible. I wouldn't wait. Tomorrow morning sounds good."

Furiously, Shireen blurted, "After the day we've had, Drake? Of course, you want to move quickly, we don't want to keep your girlfriend in Florida waiting."

Katie was taken back by her rant. "What do you mean by that?"

Shireen replied, "I mean, that scene on the

mountain could have been painted very differently,
if it was thought out a little better. I just don't get it.
What's the big rush to get to Florida? I didn't know
we were punching a clock."

Katie turned to look at Drake. He stated,
"I'm just trying to get everyone to Florida, where
it's safe."

Shireen grumbled, "And in the process,
almost getting every one of us killed. Who said
Florida is a safe place anyway?"

"You've spoken to Carolyn. You heard her
stories of the area."

Zack interrupted, "Excuse me, Drake, but so
far Carolyn has told us she was attacked by a wild
animal and had to move out because Crystal River
had flooded. It doesn't sound any safer than some of
the places we've already been."

Drake asked Zack, "So then, you agree with
Shireen? You believe I'm leading you to Florida
only because Carolyn, there, and putting everyone
in unnecessary danger for Carolyn?"

Zack responded, "Why was it imperative for
us to leave so quickly? We weren't ready and you
could have got someone killed."

Katie jumped in. "I think you're both being
a little overdramatic, Zack. Everyone got through
the mountains just fine."

Eleanor put her hand up to speak. "I think

we could have worked out a better plan. There had to be an easier way."

Granger intervened, "There were a lot of things we could have done differently, but they may or may not have worked. The point is we all made it here safely. The horses are fine and the dogs are fine. Why's everybody complaining? This arguing is getting us nowhere."

Shireen asserted, "No one's complaining and no one's arguing Granger. We're just voicing our opinions. That's what people should do, or isn't that allowed at this table either."

Hastily, William stood up and became quite insistent, "I want this bickering to stop! We made it over the damned mountain, thanks to Gwen. But we need to stop making snap decisions like we've been doing. Carolyn will be in Citrus Hills when we get there, whether it's December or fucking July! She's not going anywhere. We need to stop traveling so late in the evening and we need longer periods of rest. Can't you see that the horses need that even more than we do?"

Everyone was shocked at William's speech he'd obviously been holding it inside for quite some time. Katie questioned, "So, what do you think we should do? What's the logical answer that everyone would be satisfied with?"

William replied, "Like any society, there's a

decision-making body. I say we create one who can do this."

They looked around at each other. Eddie said, "Okay, how do we go about doing this? Do we take a secret ballot vote?"

Zack blurted, "That's a good idea. When everyone gets up tomorrow, we'll have all twelve people vote for three leaders who will make the decisions and also be responsible for the choices they make. We'll keep this the same until we get to Florida."

Drake asked, "Why is it a twelve-person vote? Granger and Emily are too young. I think we should keep them out of it."

William said, "I agree with Zack. It should be all twelve of us. I believe that Granger and Emily are old enough to know right from wrong, and they have to suffer the same consequences as the rest of us if something happens."

Eleanor whispered, "William and Zack are right. I say we all vote."

Drake conceded to their demands. "Alright, tomorrow morning after breakfast, we'll have a discussion and then the vote."

The morning came as Drake and William explained they were going to vote by secret ballot for three team leaders. William reminded everyone, "And remember, you can't vote for yourself. The three with the most votes will be the new decision-making body until we reach Carolyn in Citrus Hills."

Everyone took their time and wrote down their votes, folded their papers in half and threw them in a hat. Emily drew the slips of paper and Maddie kept a running total for each. She read the first vote. "Drake! That's one for Drake."

Drake smiled and crossed his arms when he heard he had received the first vote. Emily read the second slip. "One for Zack."

Zack was happy to know that he was in the running. Emily pulled the third and fourth slips from the hat. "Shireen. William."

Eddie was wondering why no one had given him a vote yet. He crossed his arms, frowned and reclined back in his seat as Emily called out the fifth and sixth votes. "One more for Drake and one more for Shireen."

The survivors listened as Emily revealed that votes seven, eight and nine were for William, Shireen and Zack. As Emily pulled the final three slips from the hat, everyone waited in anticipation. "Drake, Eddie and William."

Irwin stood up and said, "This is how we voted. The new decision-making body of our tiny twelve person community will be Drake, Shireen and William."

Shireen was glad to know she was a person that everyone trusted. William was surprised that he was one of the three but decided that it was a good thing. Zack and Eddie were shocked to see they didn't receive as many votes as the others.

Once the meeting was over Katie, who had received no votes, stood up and said, "Okay, now make a decision. How long will we stay here and where are we going next?"

Drake immediately pulled out his map as Shireen and William congregated around for their first official meeting. Zack and Irwin watched them as they quietly whispered back and forth to each other, agreeing and disagreeing and finally coming up with a decision.

Once they were sure of their choice, Drake addressed everyone on the plan. "We decided to stay here for today only. There's a small city about ninety miles straight down the interstate. We'll be able to get there in only six or seven hours. I think, if we travel that far, we could start seeing a much warmer climate by tomorrow evening. I know that you're all tired and cold but, for the sake of these animals, we have to make this sacrifice and get out of the cold just one more time."

Everyone realized they had to do this. They were tired of being cold. Gwen was growing weary of seeing her horses having no energy from their lack of proper food and pastures to graze on. Zack announced, "Then it's all settled. We leave in the morning for Tifton and hopefully to a little warmer climate."

The following frigid morning they stopped the wagons at several stores to stock up on supplies as they left from Warner Robins.

27

Being back on an interstate was a smoother jaunt than the broken up secondary roads. All twelve survivors were drained from lack of sleep and exhausted from fighting the cold weather. As they traveled closer to Tifton, they did notice a change in the temperature.

They saw the thermometer rising from single digits to the mid-twenties in just one day. The wagons rode single file and parallel with the mountains, watching them grow higher and higher on their right side with each mile.

An extensive gorge was beginning to stretch out beside them, like they saw on the opposite side of the mountain, but this canyon was filled with water. This gorge had become a canal that went all the way to the Gulf of Mexico.

The day was uneventful, except when they saw several packs of wolves crossing the roads, before they happily pulled into Tifton. It was there they found an old farm several miles off the interstate.

They unhitched the wagons and put the horses in the pasture where a few patches of grass would help aid in their recovery. After a few hours, Gwen put them in the barn. The fires were started and most everyone retired for the evening, except William and Drake.

The two men sat in the living room chatting and reminiscing. Drake began, "We made some great time today. I think Shireen was right that the shorter trips and longer stays would help both us and the animals stay healthier and safer. I have to admit, she is a good woman with a smart head on her shoulders."

William added, "Anyone who cares as much as she does for her dogs has to be a genuinely good person inside. I can see that's who she is and I trust her judgement."

Drake, changing the subject, inquired, "How do you think Emily's doing so far? You know, is she having a hard time dealing with Carly's death and all?"

"She okay for now but she's still a little fragile. I can see the loss in her eyes every time I look at her. She may want to voice how she feels one day. She might want to let it all out and purge herself emotionally, but just not yet. I won't push her."

Drake said, "I observed she's an introverted young girl. Has she been like that since you first found her?"

William remarked, "Since I met her, since Carly met her, she's always been extremely quiet and she liked to keep most things to herself. She's never spoken anything about her family before the blast happened. We don't even know what she saw or how she survived."

"Kind of a mystery, wouldn't you say? I'd think she would want to tell someone about her losses, her struggles to get by."

Taking sips of his warm coffee between sentences, William commented, "She'll be alright and I hope she can wipe the memory of whatever happened to her out of her mind someday, or at least learn to deal with it emotionally. My only fear is that Carly's death will add to the trauma that she's already compiled inside herself."

Drake pondered, "Just maybe the birth of Maddie's baby will help. Emily would become a big sister to a newborn. That could possibly help her feel a sense of family the way she did with you and Carly."

"That's a good point, Drake. I think, once we get to Florida, settling in somewhere will be another way for Emily to become grounded again but it'll take some time. It'll create a sense of community. Eventually, we could find even more survivors out there, maybe some that are around Emily's age."

Drake stated, "I believe whole heartedly there's more people out there, many more people, and we have to find them or they have to come to us. With these mountains and now the canal alongside us, they'd most likely be people from the east coast of the country. Who even knows if we have a west coast anymore?"

William agreed, "That's true, just look how much the landscape has changed on our side of the world. I can't even begin to imagine what happened over there."

In the morning, Katie and Shireen were the first to rise and make the coffee. Shireen always needed that first cup of coffee to get her moving for the day.

As they stood around, waiting for the others to wake up, Katie remarked to Shireen, "I know the weather's still below freezing but I feel so much better now. God! What a difference ten or twenty degrees makes."

Shireen stated, "And from now on, the trips are going to be shorter and easier. There's no reason to break our backs getting to Florida. We don't have a set time to be there and Carolyn's going to be fine until we get there."

Katie held Snickers as she admitted, "You know, I was upset with your decisions at first, but now I see your point. It's not just us we have to look out for. We have the horses and all the dogs, like this little guy."

Snickers licked her cheek. The two women grinned at each other, realizing the friendship they felt for each other.

Drake and William decided to grab their poles and go fishing for their dinner at a nearby lake. Eddie and Zack set out to chop down a few trees in the front yard for extra firewood. Granger and Irwin hooked a few of the dogs to a sled and headed into town to take a gander around and pick up a few supplies.

Gwen went to the barn and set the horses free to roam around the pastures so they could feast on what little grass they could get to. She found this to be a perfect opportunity for her and Emily to clean out the stalls and fill their troughs with fresh well water.

Maddie and Eleanor decided to clean up the house. They knew, with the new rules, they would be at each temporary home for a few days.

As Drake and William cast their poles into the crystal-clear lake, Drake could hear the radio in his pocket making that buzzing noise that always preceded a transmission from Florida. He laid his fishing pole down on the shoreline as he took out the radio and waited to hear her voice. "Are you there, Drake?"

He gleefully responded, "I'm here, Carolyn. We stopped for a day or two. William and I are at a lake right now fishing for our dinner. It's kind of cool today, mid-twenties."

Carolyn laughed, "It's in the upper fifties here. Where are you?"

"We're in Tifton, Georgia. We got here last night."

She muttered, "Tifton? I never heard of it. What's it near?"

He explained, "It's about fifty miles north of Valdosta. Like I said before, we plan on staying for a day or two."

Carolyn's tone was sympathetic to all they'd just gone through. "That's good, Drake. You need to take a break and rest after travelling around those treacherous mountains. Do you know that tomorrow is going to be November 5th?"

William and Drake looked at each other not knowing the significance of the date that she had given them. Drake asked, "Why's November 5th so important?"

"It's my birthday, Drake. Tomorrow is my

birthday."

The two men wished her an early happy birthday and she thanked them. Drake noticed her voice was clear with no static interference. She observed the same thing on her end. Drake joked, "So, what do you have planned for your birthday? Going out to any parties?"

Carolyn laughed. "Well, I thought I'd start my day by sleeping in late. Then, I'd go to the lake a catch a fish or two for dinner. After dinner, I'll relax by the warm fire and have a glass of wine from a bottle I've been saving forever."

William listened as Drake did most of the talking. "That's sounds nice, Carolyn. It sounds like a nice quiet birthday."

There was a sudden change in the mood of the conversation. Her voice got low and sorrowful, "Yes, nice and quiet, like every other day for the last five years of this miserable existence. I didn't tell you that after I finish my wine by the fire, I'm going to kill myself. I have a crate full of sleeping pills that I collected from an old pharmacy in town. I'll take them before I turn in for the night and that will be that."

Drake and William gasped at her declaration of suicide. Drake blurted, "What are you talking about, Carolyn? This isn't the way it was supposed to end. You have to listen to me. You have to trust that we'll be there soon."

The men saw Shireen and Katie walking toward them to see if they caught anything yet. They overheard Carolyn on her transmission. Katie asked, "Did she just say that she was going to kill herself?"

Carolyn's voice came through loud and clear. "Hello, Katie. Yes, that's what I said I was going to do."

Shireen cried out, "Why? Why would you even think about carrying out something like that, Carolyn? It's such a selfish greedy act. You'll only be hurting us if you follow through with your plan. Please don't."

Carolyn responded with, "I just feel that the time is right. Tomorrow's my birthday. I've lost my husband and my children. All my other family and friends are dead. I've been here alone for five long years. I'm lonely and I'm tired."

William said, "But we're on the way. Before you know it, you'll have a whole new family to get to know. You shouldn't take your life. We all had to watch Carly die a slow and painful death, and she didn't want to die. Don't take for granted what God has given to you. Think of fourteen people who've risked everything to be with. You can't take your own life, Carolyn."

Hesitant, Carolyn whispered, "I'm very

sorry about Carly, and Peter too, but my mind is made up. Then, the twelve of you can go anywhere you want to go. You won't be bound to coming here to Citrus Hills and saving me from a pathetic life of boredom."

Drake stepped up and said, "We're only about two hundred miles from you. You can't do this, Carolyn. I won't allow it! You're already a part of our family whether you want to believe it or not. That's the simple truth. We've traveled hundreds of miles to be with you. I'd like to share something with you that I never told you before. I see nights when Katie and Shireen sit up worried about you, talking about you."

Carolyn's tone became less sorrowful and more curious. "Really, Drake? You say they worry about me?"

Shireen grabbed the radio and confirmed, "Of course we worry about you. We worry about you all the time, your safety, your loneliness, your health and so many other things. We wouldn't have made this journey if you weren't going to be at our final destination. You're important to us Carolyn. We haven't even met you yet but we consider you as important as any one of us here."

The conversation continued for almost thirty more minutes. Each one taking their turn at trying to talk Carolyn down from the ledge. Finally, Carolyn shouted, "Enough already! Enough! I won't do it. You convinced me."

Drake, in his own little quirky way, asked, "Are you sure you're not just saying that to shut us all up?"

Carolyn giggled at his quip. "No, Drake, I give you my solemn pledge that I won't do anything stupid, but you better hurry up. I guess I'm not as strong as I once thought I was, neither emotionally or mentally. Did you know that being alone can play tricks on one's mind at times?"

Drake responded, "I know that. Remember, I lived alone for three and a half years before I found Porsha. Everyone here has experienced that same loneliness. You've just had the bad fortune of living it out a little longer than the rest of us. I just want you to know that we understand where you're coming from."

The call ended and the four survivors stood around the shoreline of the lake discussing the problem. Katie reminded them, "You three are the decision-making body now. If you think we should get there faster, just say it."

Each one nodded their heads and then William said, "We should probably go tomorrow and head toward Valdosta. It might give Carolyn some comfort knowing we'll be at the Florida-Georgia border."

Drake looked at Shireen as she said, "I agree with William. Let's throw caution to the wind and get the hell out of here tomorrow. Besides, the further south we go, the warmer the temperatures will be, and I'm totally fed up with the cold. I'll tell the others."

Katie and Shireen strolled off to find the other survivors to inform them of the change in plans. Everyone was in agreement with the choice. Zack reasserted, "We have to get there and we have to get there fast."

Most of the supplies were loaded back into the wagon that evening. Gwen took care of the horses in the barn and Shireen fed the dogs and put them to bed. The twelve wanted to be as ready as they could be to leave as early as possible. The old farmhouse was warm and comfortable but no one seemed to get a good night's rest after hearing what Carolyn had shared with them that day.

28

Interstate-75 turned out to be a torn-up mess. It was harder to navigate than Interstate 10 had been. This road must have been hit harder by the earthquakes and storms than the other. As they rode past various small towns, they observed that the earthquake damage was much more significant on the east coast of the country.

The canal, alongside the mountain range, on their right had become even broader as they traveled deeper down through Georgia. The mountains grew taller and steeper also, but the climate was warming into the mid-thirties and daylight was lasting just a little bit longer.

Drake reminded everyone that their journey to Valdosta would only be a short four-hour trip. Then, they could spend the day there and head back down the interstate when the next morning rolled around.

Suddenly, as they moved along the interstate near a small town named Cecil, about twenty miles north of Valdosta, Eddie yelled, "Stop the wagons! Stop the wagons!"

Drake, Gwen and Zack pulled back on their reins and halted the horses. Drake and Zack got out of their wagons while the others waited. Eddie said as he pointed, "I saw something. It was over there alongside the highway."

Zack questioned, "What did you see? Was it a bear, wolves?"

Eddie clarified, "No, nothing like that. I saw children running over there."

Drake was puzzled. "You said that you saw children? How many children?"

Soon, everyone jumped out of the wagons

except for Emily and William. They could hear the what the others were saying from where they were seated.

Zack asked, "Are you sure you saw children and not something else running?"

Eddie thought about it for a minute as he tried to recall it in his head. "No, I'm positive I saw children running."

Eleanor pointed and said, "Look, over there! I see them too!"

Everyone turned their heads and saw a group of children running through an open field alongside the highway. Zack said, "Everyone stay here. I'm going after them."

Eddie ordered, "I'm going with you. Irwin, leave one of the wagons here and the rest of you should keep heading to Valdosta. We'll be right behind you."

The two ran off the interstate and into the field as fast as they could. The ground was slick but they were able to move without sliding. Zack was several yards in front of Eddie. He saw the band of children and followed them until he finally began shouting for them to stop. The children looked back and saw Eddie and Zack. They continued to run toward the town of Cecil.

Drake didn't like the idea of leaving the three men alone, but he listened and took the other three wagons down the interstate towards Valdosta. Irwin turned his wagon around and headed down the off ramp into the tiny town. He found the center of town and waited until he spotted someone, Zack, Eddie or any of the children.

Zack and Eddie continued on the same path as the children, getting closer and closer. The children finally stopped all at once, turned around and held up their guns.

Zack and Eddie stopped dead in their tracks. They saw six children. Two looked as if they were in their mid to late teens, two appeared to be about twelve or thirteen, and the other two couldn't have been any older than ten or eleven. The oldest was a boy, about sixteen. He called out, "What are you doing here in our city?"

Eddie responded, "Let's calm down. We just wanted to talk to you!"

The children glanced back and forth at each other, not knowing if they should trust the strangers. A fifteen-year-old girl, who looked as if she was seven or eight months pregnant, said, "How do we know if we can trust you, mister? We've never seen you before."

Eddie stepped past Zack, and just a little bit closer to the children, as he replied, "We don't have any weapons. We don't want to hurt you. Please, we just want to talk."

The oldest boy stepped forward and said, "I'm Brian."

Zack inquired, "How old are you?"

Brian answered, "I'm sixteen but our ages aren't that important?"

The fifteen-year-old girl stepped forward, still holding a revolver, and pointed at each of her associates as she introduced them. "My name is Alice and I'm fifteen years old. This is Olivia, fourteen, Marshall, twelve, Isabell, eleven, and our little Noah is ten. Is there anything else you'd like to know?"

Eddie saw Irwin walking in their direction. He politely said, "I'm Eddie, this is Zack and the man walking towards us is Irwin."

Little Noah saw Irwin and said, "Wow, he's really, really old."

Alice turned to the boy and shouted, "You better mind your manners, Noah!"

Eddie asked, "Are there other people here? Maybe a few adults?"

Brian stated, "No. There ain't no adults left in Cecil. It's just us."

Zack wanted clarification, "Wait a minute, you're telling me that only the six of you have been living here?"

Alice replied, "That's what we're telling you. We always have. We haven't seen an adult since it happened five years ago."

Eddie questioned, "You were able to survive all these years and the oldest one was only eleven when the blast hit? How is that possible? Noah would have only been five years old. Tell me, how can that be?"

Brian stated, "We take care of each other. We always have, since day one. I found Olivia and Isabell eating garbage to survive. A few months later we found Noah and then we found Alice and finally Marshall. Don't be fooled by our ages. We found a way to survive."

Irwin asked, "Where do you live?"

Olivia replied, "In a house. Where do you live?"

"Well, nowhere right now. Can you take us to your house?"

Alice muttered, "I still don't know if we can trust you, mister."

Brian intervened, "Come on, Alice, let's take them to the house. Besides, we have the guns, not them."

The six children walked them down a few desolate streets until they reached a large two-story red brick ranch home. The front yard was well kept and the house itself appeared to be in great shape. Everyone entered the residence. Brian waved his hand out and said, "This is our home. It's been our home for the last three years."

Zack observed that the house was spotless with a working well and septic system. They had an entire room filled with canned goods. "It's quite a nice set up you have here."

Twelve-year-old Marshall was excited to step forward to inform the strangers what his daily responsibilities included. He pointed out the back window and said, "I have a hen house. We have chickens and eggs all the time. I also have a small barn in back where I raise goats and pigs. They take up most of my day."

Eddie grinned, leaned down and said, "I'm very impressed."

Brian added, "We have a couple good lakes nearby for fishing. We even hunt deer and rabbit sometimes. That's what we were doing when you found us in the field."

Eddie commented, "And the six of you did this all by yourself."

Alice said, "We had to. All the adults we knew died off. I homeschool everybody. I got all the books from the Cecil Elementary and Middle Schools. That's what takes up most of my day. I have classes from nine in the morning until two in the afternoon, except on the weekend. Saturday is our day to play and have fun. Sunday, we hold a church service for an hour. Brian or Olivia usually do bible readings and then we sit around and talk about them. Pretty soon, I'll have my new baby to take care of."

Irwin inquired, "How long do you have until you give birth?"

"A couple weeks and I'll be a mama. I can't wait. Brian and I are planning on having a great big family, at least five or six children. I hope this one's a boy and I hope he turns out to be just like his dad, strong and good-looking."

Zack, Eddie and Irwin were stunned at the fact six children under eighteen were able to survive and actually prosper in the conditions they had been dealt. They viewed a beautifully kept home and a working farm with healthy livestock. They had achieved what Zack and the others could only hope to achieve once they got to Citrus Hills.

Alice asked, "Are you planning to stay in Cecil for the night?"

Eddie looked at the others for an answer. Zack and Irwin nodded their heads. Eddie replied, "We'd love to."

She explained warmly, "All the bedrooms are filled but the living room has two pull out sofas and a big fireplace. I'll make a big Sunday breakfast in the morning. I sure hope you guys like my bacon and eggs."

Eddie stated, "I wouldn't miss it."

The children, one by one, turned in for the night. The rules were that the youngest went to bed first, by nine o'clock. The middle children went to bed by ten. Then, Brian and Alice usually finished cleaning up and turned in by eleven.

Once everyone had retired for the evening, Zack, Eddie and Irwin sat up and talked amongst themselves.

Zack questioned, "Do we even ask them if they want to go with us to Florida? Would they give up this amazing life they spent so long building or do we just leave them here? Would you leave here if you were them?"

Irwin volunteered, "I don't think they'd go, even if we promised them the world. They started their very own community. And, by the looks of Alice's belly, the community's just going to get bigger and bigger."

Eddie remarked, "Seeing this tells me we can do the same thing once we get to Florida. We can build the same thing they have. It gives me a lot of hope."

Zack commented, "I want to ask them to go with us anyway. They'll probably refuse the offer, but it couldn't hurt to ask."

Irwin said, "I agree. We should at least give them the opportunity to say yes or no. They deserve that much."

Eddie grinned and stated, "Then it's settled. In the morning, we'll have a talk with them and see what they have to say."

Three of the wagons pulled into Valdosta. Shireen kept checking the interstate behind them to see if the others were catching up, but they didn't. The remaining nine survivors found a small home and settled in for the night. As they sat at the table eating dinner, Gwen asked, "What are we going to do if they're not here tomorrow? Do we just leave without them?"

Drake looked over at William for an answer. William replied, "Why don't we wait and cross that bridge when we get to it, Gwen."

Gwen asserted, "I just don't like the idea of leaving them in that strange little town with a group of children that we know nothing about. Children who could be dangerous."

Shireen implied, "Do you actually think a group of small children can do something bad to those three men?"

Gwen seemed embarrassed at her previous accusation. "No, I suppose you're right. But what if the children have adults with them. We have no idea how many people are actually in that place. I don't feel good about it."

Drake commented, "She's right. We just

saw a few kids. We don't know who else was waiting for them in town. It could have been a Johnny Jones or his wife, big Betty, or that crazy Hal Reynolds in Diamondhead."

Granger interrupted, "Cecil was only ninety minutes up the road. If they're not here by morning, a few of us can take a ride back."

William, finishing his meal, stated, "That's a good idea, Granger. I'm sure that Drake and Shireen will agree a plan like that."

Shireen commented, "Damn right, I agree. I not only agree but I want to go there myself to get my gunslinger."

Drake said, "I'll go with you. We can take a couple of the bigger dogs with us too, just in case it's not a good situation."

Gwen announced, "I'm going too."

Drake let out a long breath and remarked, "Gwen, you really don't have to do this. Shireen and I can handle it just fine."

"No, Drake, I'm going with you. I waited too long to find Irwin again and I'm not going to let anything screw it up this time."

Drake hastily gave in. "Okay, okay, Gwen, you can go with us."

Eventually, most everyone went to bed, leaving Drake, Shireen and William at the dining room table. William questioned, "Are you sure you want to do this? You three could be walking into a dangerous situation."

Shireen glared over at William and said, "Yes, we're sure. Besides, they may come back by morning and that'll be that."

In the morning, Alice and Olivia moved around the kitchen as quiet as mice. They tried hard not to wake their guests.

Zack was the first one to lift his head when he smelled the fragrance of bacon filling the air. He let the others sleep as he crept to the kitchen. Olivia said, "Good morning, Zack."

He made sure to whisper. "Good morning ladies. Something sure smells good in here. Are you the only two up so far?"

Alice replied, "Oh, heavens no. The boys have been out back for an hour taking care of the animals and Isabell is upstairs making up the beds. There's a system we follow here each and every morning. Well, every day, not just mornings. How do you like your eggs?"

Zack smiled, slapped his hands together and uttered, "You decide. I'm the guest here and I'm not picky when it comes to food. Any way you want to serve them, I'll eat them."

Alice giggled and stated, "Over easy is how you're going to get them."

Olivia asked, "Are you leaving Cecil today? Don't think I'm rude. I'm not trying to push you out the door. I just wanted to know."

"Yes, probably, our friend in Florida needs us to get there as soon as we can. But we do want to talk to the six of you before we go."

Alice questioned, "What would you like to talk about?"

Zack picked up a piece of bacon and took a bite before he said, "Why don't we wait until the six of you are all together."

"Sounds important."

They heard Irwin and Eddie waking up in the living room. Zack turned to Alice and said, "It is important, very important."

The three men sat at the table and had their breakfast. They waited for the others to return to the house. Alice alerted everyone, "The strangers would like to talk to us about something important. How's about we all gather in the living room?"

Zack paced the floor back and forth as he spoke. "I have an offer for the six of you … soon to be seven."

Brian grilled Zack. "An offer? What kind of offer?"

"We can clearly see how well you're doing here in Cecil, but we're on our way to Citrus Hills, in Florida, to find another survivor. Her name is

Carolyn King. We've been in radio contact with her for over two and a half years now. I want to know if you'd like to go with us."

The six children looked at each other and the strangers. No one knew what to say. They had never been asked if they wanted to live any place other than Cecil.

Eddie added, "This woman, Carolyn, said that the weather's even warmer there then it is here. Somedays, it reaches almost seventy degrees. So, there's lots of green grass and plants and no frost or snow."

Brian said, "You want us to leave our home and go with you to Florida? It's taken us three years to make this place the way we want it to be. We've worked very hard every day."

"But you could do it all again in a better climate."

Alice objected, "I don't like this, Brian. I have no intention of leaving my home and taking my baby hundreds of miles away. This is where we live. I'll have no part of it."

Olivia and Marshall agreed with Alice. Zack reminded them, "This was just an offer. No one is telling you that you have to leave, but eventually your supplies are going to run out. What will you do then?"

Alice said, "I guess we'll figure that out

when the time comes, but for now, we're staying right where we belong."

Zack sat down on the sofa next to Eddie and remarked, "It was only an idea we had to help you guys out. If you ever do decide to come to Florida, remember to look us up."

They suddenly heard the sound of horses and a wagon coming down the rocky street. Zack looked out the window and saw Shireen, Drake and Gwen. He jokingly announced, "It looks like the cavalry is here."

Brian peered out the window over Zack's shoulder and questioned, "Is this some kind of trap you set?"

Zack said, "No. Calm down. It's just some of our fellow travelers. They must have seen the smoke coming out of your chimney and our wagon parked outside."

They watched as the new group got out of the wagon with four of the dogs and walked up to the front door. Zack opened the door and invited them in. Isabell screamed, "Look at the doggies! I can't believe it!"

Isabell and Marshall knelt on the floor and began to pet and play with the Huskies. Brian introduced everyone.

Drake, Shireen and Gwen spent several hours getting to know the children better. They could see they were adamant about not uprooting their lives at the moment. Gwen and Shireen walked around the front street for a while trying to come up with solutions. They didn't want to just leave the children where they were. They came up with a plan but decided to talk it over with the four men first. When everyone was agreed they went back into the house to speak to Brian and Alice.

Eddie said, "Here's what we're going to do for you. Gwen wants to leave one of the wagons and three of the horses here. This way, if you change your mind and wish to join us, you'll have the means to do it."

Alice was overwhelmed. She said, "Thank you. I don't know what to say."

Eddie stopped her. "Wait a minute, Alice. There's more."

Shireen stepped forward and said, "Do you think the younger children would like to have some pet Huskies?"

Brian smiled. "You're just going to leave them here with us?"

"Why not? Zeus and Athena are great dogs. They love to play and they're very protective just in case anyone bad ever tries to harm you. These two will be extremely loyal."

Alice muttered, "That's so nice. I'm sure they'll love the Huskies. But why are you doing all this for us?"

Drake stated, "To show you we're not bad people. We just want the six of you to be safe and healthy whether it's in Georgia or Florida. Maybe someday you'll change your mind and join us. Until then, you'll have a new mode of transportation and some great dogs to watch over you."

The six children waved goodbye to the six strangers as they pulled their wagon down the road before heading out of Cecil and returning to Interstate 75.

As Drake pulled just one covered wagon into Valdosta that evening and they unloaded with two dogs instead of four, everyone wanted to know what happened. Eddie commented, "What happened is that we encountered some truly unbelievable and remarkable young children who thought like adults, learned like adults and worked like adults. They lived their entire lives like adults."

Maddie questioned, "And then you just left them there?"

Eddie stated, "It was their choice to make. Let's not forget that we live in a whole new world now. The rules have changed and we have no power over those children."

Gwen replied, "I say they're going to be just fine. I can feel it in my bones. I only wish we had our shit together as much as they do. I believe that someday, down the road, maybe in a couple years from now, they'll realize that they need to come to a warmer place. It didn't feel like we were saying goodbye. I'm sure we'll see them again."

29

The next morning, everyone packed up and hit the interstate again. As they moved at about fourteen miles an hour, they saw a big sign that read "Welcome to Florida/ The Sunshine State".

Everyone let out a sigh of relief, knowing they had arrived on the last leg of their long and terrifying journey.

The earth began to shake. Katie stood up in the moving wagon and looked up at the sky, as if she was having a one-on-one conversation with God. She shouted, "It's always something with you! This isn't what we need right now!"

As they continued on, the earth continued to shake more and more violently until it felt as if they were on the epicenter. The wagons were rocking forward, then to the right, then forward again, then to the left. They passed a sign for "White Springs" but didn't stop. They were determined to make it to their next destination, Lake City. The ground shook even more.

About twelve miles outside their planned

destination, Maddie grabbed Katie's hand and said, "I don't feel so well, Katie."

"What do you mean by that, Maddie?"

"I mean I really don't feel good."

Katie looked down at the floor of the wagon as Maddie pointed at the wetness around her feet and cried, "I think my water just broke."

Katie hollered, "Oh shit, guys! We have a little problem!"

Drake turned to see what the problem was. Katie shouted, "Her water just broke, Drake! She's in labor!"

The ground continued to shake as Drake attempted to speed the horses up a little but the movement beneath their feet was hindering their speed. They hesitated over and over.

Drake signaled to William of their situation. They slowed the wagons and Granger jumped into the fourth wagon, exchanging places with William. The ground began to shake violently again. William questioned, "How much longer do we have before we're in Lake City?"

Drake replied, "About ten miles!"

William had Maddie lie down in the wagon with more than a dozen comforters beneath her. He stated, "This isn't going to be easy! She's having contractions and they're coming closer together! We have to get to Lake City as fast as we can or she's going to give birth to this baby right here in the wagon!"

Maddie screamed out each time she felt a contraction happen. The ground continued to quiver but Drake was fighting to keep the horses moving. He was able to get them to trot a little quicker but they continued to hesitate each time that the earth quaked.

Katie sat on the wagon floor holding hands with Maddie. Maddie felt another contraction and screamed, "This really sucks! Oh, this really sucks! Are we there yet?"

Drake informed everyone, "About five more miles! We should be there in about fifteen minutes! Hold on!"

Maddie closed her eyes and waited as each mile seemed to take a hundred years. There was one more contraction. William hollered, "Like I said before, the contractions are coming too close! If we don't hurry up, she's going to be giving birth in this wagon!"

Drake could hear the static of his radio telling him that Carolyn was trying to make contact with him. The quake shook wildly. He heard the static buzzing but couldn't hold the radio and maneuver the frightened horses at the same time. Many miles to the right, he could see the canal was being stirred up and huge waves were crashing onto the sides of the mountains. Granger, covering his ears from the noise, shouted, "I've haven't seen a quake this big since right after the meteors hit us! Why's this happening now?"

Drake, watching the road closely as little cracks appeared that weren't there before, replied, "I don't know, Granger! Maybe it's the earth's way of shifting back into place! It's like a house when it's first built. It that takes time for the foundation to finally settle!"

As the unsteady ground began to quake again and again, they witnessed the wildlife; bears, deer, foxes and raccoons, fearfully running down the interstate and through the wooded areas for protection from the trembling. Shireen commented, "I've never seen the animals this shaken up! Even the dogs are uneasy!"

Zack hollered back, "The horses are doing the same thing! They don't know which way to go either!"

The quaking continued. Large gaps in and alongside the highway were created. The wagons tried to get to Lake City while trying to avoid the interstate's newest obstacles.

Once again, Drake could hear the radio buzzing at him. It was almost like a telephone ringing over and over. He muttered to himself, "Not now, Carolyn. Not now."

He saw what was left of the big green signs alongside the road that read, "Lake City-1 mile". He steered the wagons to the off ramp onto Highway 90 and raced into town.

Highway 90 soon became West Duval Street and eventually East Duval. He and the others searched the street for any safe structures, but there weren't any. Seeing that most of the town was in ruin, he made a left on North Marion Avenue and onto Lake Desoto Circle. It was there that he found a house with a barn and a few outbuildings. These structures seemed sound.

They parked the wagons in front while Drake and William went inside to check for safety. Once they gave the others clearance, Granger and Eddie hauled firewood. Zack and Drake assisted in getting Maddie out of the wagon. Eleanor, Katie and Shireen quickly cleaned up the inside to make a place for Maddie to have her baby. Irwin and Gwen brought in supplies. William prepared to help bring a new child into the world.

Maddie struggled with the contractions, yelping every few minutes, having a hard time keeping still. The earth continued to shake all around them. The others cleared the room and left William and Katie alone to deliver Maddie's baby. Maddie asked, "What's happening? Am I having the baby or not?"

Katie checked the cervix and alerted William, "It's at about eight centimeters. We still have time before the delivery."

Maddie screamed with each new pain. The earth quaked endlessly as they waited for her to reach ten centimeters. William muttered to Katie, "I wish I had something to give her to dull the pain. I have nothing."

Katie watched as the cervix got wider and Maddie belted out more screams. Noticing that the temperatures were climbing into the mid-forties, Zack and Drake stood in the front yard cleaning up as they heard Katie shouting, "I can see the head! She's crowning! Push!"

After Maddie let out a few more yelps and everyone heard William and Katie yelling, "Push, Maddie, push!"

This told Drake and Zack the baby was just about there. Soon, they heard a newborn crying and William announcing, "It's a boy!".

Shireen and Gwen came into the room and took the baby to clean it up before they placed him back in Maddie's arms. She held him and smiled, still out of breath and exhausted. She gave the new baby little kisses on the top of his head, whispering, "Hello, little man. Welcome to this new world. I'm your mommy."

Shireen transferred the baby to a small crib

they'd found in a local department store. Maddie looked at William and Katie and said, "Thank you for helping me deliver my baby boy."

William smiled and said, "He appears to be healthy and happy. Now, you need to get some rest, young lady. You've been through quite an exciting ordeal today."

Katie and William waited until Maddie fell into a peaceful sleep. They collapsed on the living room sofa and also fell asleep. Shireen and Gwen saw this and quietly stepped past them.

Gwen whispered, "Why don't we move the crib, just in case the little boy starts crying? Let's not wake them up."

The ground rattled again as Drake and Zack were walking down and around Lake Desoto. They stopped walking when they heard the buzz of the radio again. Drake reached in his pocket and held the radio near his mouth. "Carolyn, I'm sorry that I didn't respond to your last call but we had a little emergency here."

Carolyn inquired, "Are you talking about the earthquakes?"

Drake responded, "That was only part of it. You're feeling the tremors all the way down there in Citrus Hills? That's amazing. You're a hundred miles away from us."

"They started this morning. I don't think

I've ever felt them continue for such a long period of time. This is very unusual. What was the other part of your emergency?"

Drake laughed and shared the news. "On the way to Lake City, Maddie's baby decided it was time to come out. I guess all the rumbling sent her into early labor."

Excitedly, Carolyn questioned, "Did she have the baby yet?"

"She did. It's a healthy baby boy. She's at the house resting."

"Oh Drake, I can't wait to see him. Has she given him a name yet?"

Drake replied, "Not yet, but I'm sure she'll name him Peter."

Zack prompted Drake. "Tell her about what happened in Cecil."

She asked, "What happened in Cecil?"

Drake explained, "The strangest thing, we found a group of six children, between the ages of ten and sixteen years old, living and thriving on their own with no help from any adults. They school the younger children, attend church, raise livestock and chickens, hunt their own game, cook, clean and build everything all by themselves."

"Amazing. Are they with you now? Did you bring them along?"

Zack intervened, "They wouldn't come with

us. They told us they were quite content staying where they were, but we left them a wagon and a few horses just in case they changed their minds one day."

Drake said, "So you see, Carolyn, we're not alone. We continue to find other survivors in the world that are finding ways to make a brand-new life. Once we arrive in Citrus Hills, we can begin to build our community too. How's the weather there today?"

"Aside from the ground shaking violently, it's in the upper sixties and the sun is really coming through today. I can't believe you made it all the way to Lake City. That's just a hop, skip and a jump from me."

Zack informed her, "It's just a little over a hundred miles."

She announced, "I have to admit that I'm feeling better, more positive, knowing that everyone is that much closer. Those bad thoughts are slowly fading from my head."

There was a pause on her end. Zack asked, "Is there something else that you'd like to say to us, Carolyn?"

"It's nothing. I'm just being paranoid. It's silly really."

Zack asked, "What is it?"

She explained, "The woods behind the

house. There's been a lot of rustling around back there for the past few days. It must be a bear or something. It's nothing. Sometimes, being alone makes your mind play tricks on you."

Zack stated, "Well, you be careful leaving that house. Always carrying a gun with you just in case it is a bear."

Carolyn giggled, "I will, Zack."

Drake grinned and told her, "Well, it was good speaking with you but it's about time for us to sign off. We have some fish to catch for dinner tonight. You take care of yourself, Carolyn. I'll talk to you soon."

"Goodbye, Drake, Zack."

That evening at dinner, William announced, "I don't think we should move Maddie or the baby right away, especially with these aftershocks still happening."

Drake asked, "Then what do you propose we do, William?"

"I think I should stay behind with the mother and child, and Emily of course. The rest of you can go ahead of us. I don't see any real danger in front of us. Besides, it's only a few more days to Citrus Hills anyway."

Eddie looked around the room and asserted, "I don't like leaving you here with a weak woman and a defenseless baby. I think someone else should stay with you."

Granger raised his hand, "I'll stay with you William. The two of us can handle what needs to be handled. I can steer the wagon while you take care of Maddie."

William nodded his head and agreed, "That would work. Thanks for stepping up to the plate, Granger."

Eddie restated, "I still don't like leaving you here. I don't like it when we fragment into smaller groups."

William said, "We don't have much of a choice, Eddie. Maddie and the baby need at least a day of rest, then we'll be on our way."

30

In the mid-morning two covered wagons left Lake City on their way to Gainesville. One single wagon was left behind. William continued to make Maddie comfortable.

By early that afternoon, Maddie was up and walking around, though very slowly and carefully. Her maternal instincts were good and she began to take care of her baby on her own. Granger collected several pieces of firewood to keep the house warm and dry. He asked William, "When do you think we'll be able to go?"

"Maddie appears to be a resilient young woman. She and the baby are fine. I'd say we could leave no later than tomorrow morning. That'll only put us a day behind the others."

As the day progressed, William and Granger saw Maddie pull out her acoustic guitar to play and sing sweet lullabies to the baby. Granger remarked, "I haven't heard you play your guitar in a very long time, Maddie."

She explained, "Since I lost Peter, I know I haven't played. When he died, I thought my desire to create music died along with him, but I guess it didn't really die. It just went to sleep for a while, the same way Peter did."

A little confused by the conversation, he added, "Well, anyway, it sounds nice and the baby seems to like it."

Maddie glanced at her little boy and agreed, "He does like it. Doesn't he? I think he looks just like my sweet Peter. He has the same eyes, the same chin and same smile."

Granger looked closely and agreed. "There's no doubt that Peter was his daddy."

She picked up the guitar and began playing again. This time, she played a song her mother used to sing to her as a child.

Emily quietly crept into the room, sat next to Maddie on the sofa and listened to the music for the better part of the afternoon. Eventually, Emily and the baby fell asleep.

The other eight survivors made it to Gainesville by early evening. The quaking of the ground had slowly subsided and the weather was gorgeous. They pulled up to the old university and unloaded what they needed to.

Gwen put the horses in the auditorium after letting them graze on the plush grass first. Shireen ran the dogs down the street and in an open field. Drake walked around the old campus surprised by the way that so many of the buildings had held their integrity. His radio began buzzing. "Hello, Carolyn. How are you today?"

She quietly answered, "I'm doing quite well, Drake. Have you made it any farther south down the interstate yet?"

Drake stated, "I'm actually in Gainesville as we speak. I'm walking around the campus of the old university."

"You're kidding! You made it all the way Gainesville? That's so close!"

Drake remarked, "About sixty miles to Citrus Hills."

Excitedly, she probed, "When do you think you'll be here? Tomorrow, or maybe the day after that? When?"

Drake delicately attempted to explain the Maddie situation. "I think we may leave tomorrow but we have a slight problem. You see, after Maddie had the baby, William said she couldn't be moved for an extra day or two. So, he, Emily and Granger stayed in Lake City with one of the wagons and a few of the dogs."

"That only makes sense. You wouldn't want a new mother or child to be traveling in a wagon on these rocky roads."

Drake continued, "The problem is, that I don't know if the others are going to want to come to Citrus Hills without them. A trip like that would put over a hundred miles between us and them and, as you know, it's not just my decision anymore. It had to be decided by the board."

Carolyn's voice went from optimistic and thrilled to sad and reflective. "I understand. You have to do what's best for Maddie and the child. I have to admit, I'm not surprised. It's just one more in a long series of monkey wrenches we've had to deal with since this whole excursion to Florida had begun."

She knew he had no power over seven other people and she was glad to hear they were all so protective of Maddie and the baby. But she was still saddened at the fact that she'd have to spend even one more day alone, staring at the same empty walls in the same empty house.

Drake apologized, "I'm truly sorry, Carolyn. If I could change it, you know I would. I want to be there as badly as you want me there, but my hands are tied."

She shook it off and tried to change the subject. "No need for you to apologize, Drake. It's not your fault. By the way, did I mention to you that I thought I saw someone in the woods behind my house yesterday?"

Drake became alarmed, "No, you didn't happen to mention that."

She clarified, "I thought that I saw a man walking through the woods. I went out to check if my eyes were playing tricks on me and, sure enough, they were. When I got out to the backyard there was no one there."

Drake became concerned. "Still, Carolyn, keep your gun with you at all times. I'm not saying there was a man, but just to be sure."

"Yes, Drake. I've actually become a pretty good shot."

Drake said, "I suppose I'll talk to you again tomorrow."

Carolyn inquired, "I have a question. Once you get to Citrus Hills, how will you know how to find me?"

"Two ways. We'll look for the home with

smoke coming out of the chimney."

She commented, "That's smart except for one thing."

"What's that?"

"It's warm enough here during the day that I rarely burn a fire until I'm going to bed. What's the second way?"

"You'll give me the street and house number and I'll find it."

Carolyn laughed. "Funny, I never thought of that. It's 3929 North Page Avenue. I found a small subdivision of twenty-five or thirty homes. Most of them are still in excellent condition or only in need of minor repairs. It's obviously on the northern end of town. Located behind me are some dense woods and Forest Lake. Trust me, it's not that hard to find. You'll see."

Drake wrote the address in his journal and said, "Okay. You have a good night. I'll talk to you again tomorrow."

"Good night, Drake."

Drake made his way back to the others who had everything set up to stay the night. He sat down and asked, "I just heard from Carolyn. She wanted to know if we were planning on being in Citrus Hills tomorrow. Are we?"

Shireen said, "Don't you think we should wait for the others to catch up to us? Wouldn't that be the right thing to do?"

He lashed out, "I don't know what's the right thing to do anymore, Shireen! I try to make decisions and everyone questions them! Do we wait for a young girl and a baby who are in the capable hands of a very fine physician or do we get to Citrus Hills where there's a woman who's been trapped alone for five years and recently mentioned to us that she was contemplating committing suicide? I don't know, Shireen! Why don't you go on and make the decision for everybody!"

Katie, attempting to defuse the situation, commented, "Drake, all she did was ask a simple and logical question, something that we were all thinking about. I think you should take a break and calm down for a while."

Drake walked out of the room, leaving the other seven standing there wondering what they should do. Eddie said, "I think we should get to Citrus Hills. William knows where we're going. He'll be there in a few days."

Eleanor said, "I agree with Eddie."

Katie muttered, "I'm with them. We should find Carolyn. She the one who's been on her own this whole time."

Shireen protested, "I think you're wrong. We need to stay here and stay put in case William and Maddie might need our help."

Zack nodded his head and stated, "I like Shireen's choice."

Irwin and Gwen were in agreement with Zack and Shireen. They didn't want to leave anyone behind."

Katie said, "Then it's decided. The four of you can stay here in Gainesville and wait for the others to catch up. The rest of us will go onto Citrus Hills tomorrow and wait for you to get there. That should make you happy and it looks like everyone gets what they want."

Very little else was said that night. Everyone was either angry or embarrassed or frightened at the fact they were going to splinter into even smaller groups and that they could never seem to agree on the path they should take.

In Lake City, everyone turned in for the night. It was quiet and warm. Maddie slept on the sofa next to the crib. William and Emily were on a mattress they brought down from the upstairs and laid out on the living room floor. Granger curled up in his sleeping bag.

Slam! Slam! Slam! William sat up when he heard the clatter. He got up from the mattress and walked around the house checking for the source of the noise. He grabbed a shiny pistol from on top of the refrigerator.

Slam! Slam! Slam! There it was again. William walked to the back door and looked out to see if he could spot a bear or some other wild animal. Soon, he found Granger standing behind him asking, "What's all that racket? I heard it and came to see if you were okay."

William shrugged and whispered. "I don't know what it is. That's what I've been trying to find out."

Slam! Slam! Slam! They could hear Maddie and Emily waking up and calling to them. William came back into the living room. "I don't know what the noise is. Maybe there's a shutter loose on one of the windows upstairs."

Maddie stated, "But this house doesn't have shutters, William."

Slam! Slam! Slam! The baby started to cry out. Maddie picked him up and cuddled him in her arms. She mentioned, "I'm afraid. That noise will keep us awake all night unless we find out what it is and stop it."

William said, "I'll go outside to see if I can figure it out."

Emily ran to her father and cried, "Don't go out there, Daddy. What if it's a big bear or a coyote making those sounds."

Granger handed William a flashlight. Then he took another flashlight and a shotgun as they both exited the house.

Maddie sat terrified on the sofa with Emily and the baby.

As the men walked out of the front yard and into the street, they listened for the slamming noises again, but they were gone. William flipped his flashlight on as they walked carefully around the perimeter of the house. He shined the light into the backyard and saw nothing.

As he turned to walk back to the house, a light began to shine at him. Someone was shining a flashlight in his direction. He signaled Granger to join him. Soon, they saw a second light shining at them. Then a third. Granger mumbled, "I think we better get back inside the house."

William nodded his head and the two moved quickly into the house as they saw the lights getting closer and closer. Inside the house, Maddie could see how shaken up Granger and William were. She questioned, "What happened out there? What was making those noises?"

William nervously stated, "I don't know," as he handed her a loaded gun and said, "Use it if you have to."

The men began to barricade the doors and move tall pieces of furniture to cover the windows. Maddie questioned again, "What did you see out there? What is it? Is there a pack of wolves or a bear near the house?"

William explained, "I don't think it was a pack wolf, Maddie, since I know wolves don't carry flashlights."

She gasped. "William, you saw a person out there, someone with a flashlight?"

William corrected her. "No, there isn't just someone. We had at least three flashlights shining at us back there."

Maddie put the baby back in the crib and had Emily help her move small pieces of furniture to reinforce the larger objects. Emily looked at William and asked, "Daddy, are we going to die tonight?"

William stopped what he was doing and knelt down. He gazed into Emily's eyes and found himself speechless. He didn't know for sure if they were going to die that night or not.

31

Drake, Katie, Gwen and Irwin had their wagon packed up and ready to go that morning by seven o'clock. Shireen and Zack walked them out. Shireen said, "I hope you guys know why we're staying here in Gainesville."

Katie expressed, "Probably, for the same reason that we hope you understand why we're going to Citrus Hills."

Shireen snapped, "I get it, Katie. I get it. But we shouldn't part ways like this, with such hostile feelings towards each other. After all, you are my best friend in the world."

Drake turned to Shireen and stated, "I'm not feeling hostile, neither is Katie or the others. We just want this to be done, once and for all. We've been on the road for five long months. Some of us are tired and we want to go home."

Drake grabbed Shireen and hugged her. As he did this, he whispered in her ear, "Make sure you look out for them. I know you can."

Shireen smiled and kissed Drake on the cheek. "I will. You do the same. We won't be too far behind."

Moments later, the wagon was traveling out of Gainesville toward their final stop. Zack watched and waved as they disappeared from view. Shireen approached him and said, "I guess all we can do for now is wait."

Zack told her, "I'm going to put something on the street here. Something loud and colorful to let them know where we are."

"The art department is two buildings over. I'd bet you could find something loud and colorful in there."

"Good idea", he said before he kissed her on

the cheek and left for that building. She stood there watching the empty road, wondering when William and the others would arrive, wondering when Drake and his wagon would finally reach the end of their journey.

Several hours passed as Drake saw signs alongside the interstate for Micanopy and then for the city of Ocala. He turned off the interstate and onto Highway 200. He explained, "The map says it's going to be a straight shot from here."

He knew, at that point, they were roughly thirty miles from Citrus Hills and Carolyn King. His radio began with the buzzing noise. Gwen took over the reins of the wagons as Drake answered the call. He heard a scared, panicked voice whispering on the other end. "Drake, are you there? Drake, please answer me."

Drake replied, "I'm here, Carolyn. What's the matter?"

"Where are you?"

"We're about two hours away from you. Is everything alright? There's something about your voice that doesn't sound the way that it normally sounds."

She fearfully replied, "I saw him again. Oh God, I saw him again."

Drake questioned, "Carolyn, you saw who

again?"

"The man, the man in the woods. There was a man in the woods behind the house. I saw him this morning ... and I think he saw me."

Everyone riding in the wagon could hear the conversation. Katie asked, "Did he speak to you or try to approach you at all?"

"No, I think he spotted me and ran away again. I don't know who he is and I'm not sure why he's out there. All I know is that he's tall, very tall and dressed in black. I don't know if I could protect myself from him."

Drake ordered, "Carolyn, you get your gun and lock all your doors. Put some big pieces of furniture against them, cover the windows. We'll be there soon."

Gwen tried her best to get the horses to top speed. Katie told Carolyn to do her best to stay on the radio until they arrived. Drake asked, "Is he out there now?"

There was a moment when Carolyn walked over to the kitchen window and took a quick peek through the curtains. Nervously, she answered, "Oh dear God, he's out there again. He's just standing back there looking at the house. I don't know what he wants from me."

Drake questioned, "How far back are the woods from the house?"

"They start about three hundred feet from where the backyard ends. There's a lake to the right of them. Oh, Drake, I'm scared."

"I know you're afraid, Carolyn. You have every right to be scared. Just move furniture against the doors and windows. You have to shield yourself from him, just in case."

They could hear the sounds over the radio as Carolyn struggled to move larger objects toward the front and back doors.

In Gainesville, Zack and Eddie took a slow walk down the main thoroughfare through town, noticing how untouched most of the buildings and structures were. Eddie commented, "Man, whoever designed this university knew what they were doing. It sure has remained standing strong even after the meteors, the earthquakes and everything else that's happened."

Zack stopped walking. He looked off into the distance and down the road that led to Interstate 75. Eddie asked, "What's up, Zack? Why did you stop walking?"

Zack pointed down the road. "Look!"

Eddie glanced down the road and saw a tiny spec coming toward them. The spec got closer. "It looks like one of our wagons heading right for us, but which one?"

Zack squinted his eyes to see the distant wagon clearer. "I don't know. It could be Drake coming back, or maybe it's William."

As the wagon approached, Zack saw another wagon travelling a few hundred feet behind the first wagon. He was confused, "There's a second wagon behind the first. I don't understand this at all. How could there be two wagons?"

The wagons got closer and Zack said, "I think the first wagon is William's, but I don't know who's in the second one."

As moments moved by and the wagons got closer, Zack and Eddie walked into the middle of the street, waving their arms and shouting, "Over here! We're over here!"

The first wagon pulled up with William and Granger sitting in front. Shireen and Eleanor came out to see what was going on. William and Granger hopped off the wagon and then helped Emily with Maddie and the new baby. William hugged Eddie and Zack before he said, "Wait till you see who's coming behind us."

The second wagon pulled up. They could see it was the children from Cecil. Brian and Alice were sitting in front. Alice was holding a newborn baby girl in her arms. Zack asked, "How did this already happen?"

Brian explained, "After you left us, the

earthquakes started ripping through Cecil. We never saw quakes that big before. It destroyed most of the house, killed most of the livestock and sent Alice into early labor. We just decided, if we were ever going to move out of Cecil, now would be the best time to do it. If you went kind enough to leave the wagon and the horses there for us, we'd most likely all be dead right now."

The children got out of the wagon to stretch their legs, but no one unloaded anything. Shireen approached Alice and Maddie as they stood together holding their babies. "Congratulations to both new mothers. Have either of you given them names yet?"

Maddie smiled and said, "You know he's going to be named after Peter. Was there ever any doubt in your mind?"

Shireen turned to Alice and waited for a response from her. Alice bowed her head and asked, "Would it be wrong of me if I named her after my mother?"

"No, why would that be wrong? I'm sure it would be a great tribute to your mother if you did that, sweetie. What was her name?"

"Rosa. Rosa Marie."

Shireen conveyed, "That's a beautiful name. I simply love it. She looks like a Rosa."

Brian walked up to Alice and said, "I like

Rosa Marie too. Let's name her that."

Zack informed William, "We can help you unpack the wagons."

William said, "Don't bother, Zack. We're not staying. We got on the road in Lake City at six o'clock this morning to get here by ten or eleven so we could continue straight through to Citrus Hills. We just pulled into Gainesville for a break and to get something to eat. We had no idea you'd all still be here."

Eddie confessed, "We're not all here. Drake, Katie, Gwen and Irwin left a few hours ago and the rest of us stayed here, waiting for you."

William grinned. "I say we get back in the wagons and go. If we leave soon, we could be in Citrus Hills for an early dinner."

Eddie looked to Zack for guidance. Zack slapped Eddie on the back, smiled and said, "Let's pack up the wagon. We're going to finish this thing today."

Brian inquired, "Do you know how to get to Citrus Hills?"

Zack explained, "We've had it mapped out for weeks. All we have to do is continue down the interstate. When we get into Ocala, we take a right onto Route 200 then into Citrus Hills about two hours later. Once we get there, we have the address of the house."

Brian shrugged his shoulders and said, "Sounds easy enough."

"That's because it is easy, Brian. This day is going to be the easiest day that any of us have had in a long, long time.

Drake saw the signs that read "Ross Prairie State Park". He asked Katie to find Ross Prairie on the map. Her finger followed their route until she shouted, "I found it."

"About how far away does that put us from Carolyn?"

"I'd guess that she's only about fifteen or sixteen miles away."

He grumbled, "Dammit! That's still going to take us another hour!"

Gwen turned back and said, "I've got the horses moving as fast as they'll go. This road isn't too user friendly."

Carolyn's voice came back on the radio. "I think I've secured the house, Drake. Every piece of furniture that I could possibly move, was moved. I covered every window and door."

Drake asked, "Is he still out there? Can you still see out the window?"

The was a brief time when she walked to the window to peek through the tiny opening again. Drake could hear a shuffling noise on the radio. He was afraid that he might lose reception again, but it was Carolyn dropping her radio on the carpet. "I'm sorry Drake. It slipped from my hand."

Drake's heart was beating fast. "That's fine. Did you see him? Is he out there?"

She replied, "No, I couldn't see him behind the house at all."

He insisted, "Stay put and don't leave the house. We're almost there. It's only fifteen more miles. Hold on."

Carolyn nervously chuckled, "I don't have much of a choice now, do I?"

Suddenly, through the radio, Drake heard the sound of a window smashing. He asked, "What was that, Carolyn?"

He heard her voice, whispering, "I think he just broke one of the upstairs windows. I didn't think about the second floor."

Drake calmly and rationally told her. "Get to your gun, make sure the safety is off and point it in the direction of the stairs."

A moment later, she whispered, "Alright, Drake, it's done."

They waited anxiously but there were no other sounds. Carolyn said, "I don't hear anyone up there. No one's moving around."

"Just don't take your eyes off those stairs. Don't let your guard down."

The wagon passed a blue sign for Hernando. Katie quickly glanced at the map and shouted, "Five miles! Only five more miles!"

Drake heard nothing but silence on the other end of the radio. He knew she was scared and most likely trembling. There was a gunshot and the sound of Carolyn screaming. Drake shouted, "Carolyn, are you there?"

Everyone could hear the sound of a struggle taking place and then two more gunshots ringing out. "Are you there? Carolyn, answer me! Are you alright?"

More loud noises came from the radio, the sounds of furniture being moved and tossed around, another bullet being fired. Drake frantically asked, Katie, "How far do we have now? When do we get to Citrus Hills?"

Katie responded, "It should be right up the road, only a mile or two more."

Drake tried to communicate with her again, "Carolyn, are you there?"

Suddenly, an eerie and deep voice replied, "Carolyn's not here anymore. It appears she had a little accident."

Drake gasped. "Who the hell is this? Put Carolyn back on!"

The dark, raspy voice laughed and declared, "Unfortunately, your friend can't come to the phone right now, but if you leave your name and number, I'm sure she'll get back to you as soon as possible. And please have a wonderful day."

The crispness and clarity of the transmission became a buzzing static again. Drake saw Katie with a look of terror in her eyes. Gwen exclaimed, "We're in Citrus Hills! The problem now is that we have to find the address!"

Drake remembered as he pulled out his journal, "She said it was on the north side of town, in a very small subdivision of thirty homes. It was near a lake." He glanced down in the journal and stated, "The address of the house we're looking for is 3929 North Page Avenue!"

The wagon traveled up and down several streets, first North Croft, then North Fatima, until they found North Page Avenue. They made a right and followed it almost to the end. They saw the lake that Carolyn spoke of and then the address. Gwen stopped the wagon and everyone got out. Each one carried a loaded shotgun and walked with several of the larger dogs beside them.

Drake saw the front door of the house was left standing open. He ran inside to see the living room had been ransacked. No one was there. He ran to the upstairs while Katie checked the whole first floor. Her eyes scanned the rooms for any traces of blood. She didn't see any. Gwen and Irwin checked around the outside perimeter of the property with a few of the larger dogs.

Drake saw the broken window in one of the second-floor bedrooms. He saw no one was on that floor. He came back to the living room. Katie said, "The house is empty. I noticed there's no radio here either. He must have it with him."

Irwin, standing there with the dogs, hollered into the house, "We don't see anyone out here," as Gwen continued walking towards the woods alone, with gun drawn. Drake and Katie met Irwin at the front door. Drake said, "There's no one inside the house either. Where's Gwen?"

"She's around the back of the house."

There was a distant scream. Irwin shouted, "That was Gwen!"

Drake, Katie and Irwin ran around to the backyard but didn't see Gwen. Drake began moving towards the woods. The others followed, calling for the dogs to join them.

The dogs hurried to catch up with her. They stepped into the thick woods and glanced around at any sign of Gwen or Carolyn or the tall, dark man. Soon, Irwin found a gun lying on the ground. He cried out, "This was Gwen's gun. She must have dropped it."

Drake questioned, "But where's Gwen and Carolyn? And how did he get them out of sight so quickly?"

Katie mentioned, "Carolyn did say he was tall, very tall. Maybe this man's just that strong and fast that he was able to get them away from here before we could find him."

"But where would he have taken them? I don't know this area at all."

Katie answered, "I don't know, Drake. I wouldn't even begin to know where we should look. It's all new to me too."

Irwin asked, "Then, what do you think we should do?"

Drake said, "I think we should go back to the house and wait. Maybe he's holding them for some kind of ransom."

Irwin put his hand in front of Drake as he was turning to walk back. "Wait a minute. You just want to do nothing? You don't even want to look for them? Don't forget my Gwen is out there and I don't plan on losing her again."

Drake tried to reason with him. "Irwin, we don't know the area and we have no idea how well the dark man knows the area. This could be some kind of trap."

Again, Irwin waved his hand at Drake and Katie as he stomped off angrily deeper into the dense woods. "I don't need your help! I'll find her myself! Gwen!"

Katie shouted, "Irwin, please come back! You're being unreasonable! Come back before something happens to you too!"

Irwin ignored her plea as he moved even deeper into the forest. Katie turned to Drake and questioned, "What do we do?"

"We go back to the house and wait. If this man wants us, he has Carolyn's radio with him. I have a feeling we're going to be hearing from him real soon."

They went back to the house. Drake sat in the living room, took the radio from his pocket and set it on an end table. Katie sat down on the sofa staring at it. Drake saw Katie doing this and said, "For God's sake, you don't need to gawk at it. That won't make him contact us any faster."

They waited for thirty minutes before Katie stood up and said, "Let's get Irwin. He's been out there too long."

Drake said, "Hold on."

He grabbed a sheet of paper and a pen and wrote a long, detailed note. When he finished, he taped it to the front door and said, "Okay. Now I'm ready to find Irwin."

The three wagons pulled into town around five in the evening. They cruised up and down the streets until they found North Page.

When the pulled in front of the house, Zack and Eddie hopped out of the wagon and walked up to the front door. They saw the note, read it and ran back to the others.

Zack handed the note to Shireen. Soon, the wagons were slowly pulling away from the house but without Zack, Eddie, Shireen and many of the dogs. The wagons were eventually parked several blocks away from North Page.

William made sure that everyone stayed put, except for Granger and Brian, who each grabbed a firearm and filtered down the street that was parallel to North Page.

Zack, Eddie and Shireen headed behind the house and out towards the lake, each one was armed with a loaded shotgun.

No one spoke out loud. Instead, they used simple hand signals to direct when it was time to separate and move in separate directions.

A few minutes later, they spotted Granger and Brian several hundred yards away, moving in the opposite direction of them.

Everyone followed until they were on the other side of the lake and woods. Zack saw the street sign for East Keepsake Lane. It was the only street behind the woods that had any solid structures still standing.

Zack leaned into Shireen and said, "This has

to be the place. There're about ten houses on this street. They have to be in one of them. I can feel it in my gut."

They separated and soundlessly moved down the lane, behind the houses, listening for any noises coming from within. Creeping and using hand signals, each one kept an eye on the others. Most of the dogs followed closely and silently behind Shireen.

There was a light green house, then a pale tan house, then an off-white house. She moved down the lane like a nocturnal animal stalking its prey. As she carefully approached the back door of the gray house, she turned to see where the others had gone.

Suddenly, she felt the cold end of a revolver on the back of her head and heard a clicking noise. Zack and Eddie saw her standing there with the tall, dark man standing behind her. Zack shouted out, "Leave her alone!" as he ran desperately towards the gray house.

When Zack was only ten feet away from them, the dark man ordered him, "Don't come any closer or I'll kill her."

Zack stopped himself, while trying to catch his breath. The dogs remained sitting near Shireen, looking at the dark man, and growling. She asked calmly, "What do you want from us?"

The dark man didn't answer. He stood there watching Zack and Eddie, making sure they didn't try anything they might regret. Zack yelled, "Why are you doing this?" He was hoping that Granger and Brian would hear the commotion coming from behind the gray house.

Granger and Brian did hear them talking from the other side of the street. This was when they knew the gray house was the one.

They signaled to each other and stepped lightly to the front of the house. Granger jiggled the handle of the front door as quietly as he possibly could. The door opened and they entered, making no noise.

In the living room, they saw Irwin and Gwen tied up with rope and duct tape. They had obviously been beaten up. Gwen still had blood under her nose from where the dark man struck her and Irwin had bruises under his eyes.

Gwen was about to make a noise when Granger put his finger up to his mouth. Gwen stayed silent as Brian began to loosen the ropes from around their arms. They could hear Zack, Eddie and the dark man still shouting back and forth at each other.

Once Gwen and Irwin were freed from their restraints, Granger whispered, "Where's Drake and Katie and Carolyn?"

Irwin whispered back, "I think they're up on the second floor."

Granger told Irwin and Gwen to go back to the house on North Page and wait there with the others. They followed his instructions and exited quietly.

Brian headed upstairs where he found Drake in one bedroom and Katie and Carolyn in the other bedroom. Like Gwen and Irwin, they were all beaten up and tied to beds.

Granger soon followed up the stairs to help free his friends. They could still hear Zack and the dark man screaming at each other. Once they were freed, Katie and Carolyn headed back to North Page while Drake remained behind.

Granger asked, "Who is this guy? What does he want from us?"

Drake whispered, "He's insane. I mean he's completely off his rocker. He broke out of a mental institution when the meteors hit the earth. He told us he's been traveling the state killing anyone he meets … just because."

Granger questioned, "What do we do? He has a gun to Shireen's head."

Drake mentioned, "Oh, if I know Zack and Shireen, they already know how they're going to get out of this one."

Granger stated, "But he's standing right

outside the back door. Why don't we just take a shot at him?"

"Because he has a gun resting on the back of Shireen's head and a finger on the trigger. If we shoot him, his gun could go off and kill her. Let's just watch and wait for our opportunity to open up. I know Zack will somehow let us know."

Drake waved out the back window so Zack could see that they were all free. Zack's eyes turned back to the dark man. "Who are you anyway and where did you come from?"

The man replied, "I am no one. I have no identity to speak of. They took that away from me when they locked me away."

Zack blurted, "Locked away? Where were you locked away?"

"That doesn't matter where. It's none of your business anyway!"

Zack stated, "That' terrible, mister. I was just asking because no one should ever have to be locked away. What's your name again?"

Not paying attention, the man lowered his gun several inches as he spoke to Zack. Drake could see this from the living room as he stood only two feet behind the man with only a thin aluminum door separating them. The man told Zack, "I didn't give my name."

Zack asked, "And why are you all dressed

up in black?"

He laughed, "Because the devil always dresses in black."

Drake and Zack saw the gun lower another inch or two. Shireen could feel the back of the gun moving closer to her shoulder as she gazed down at the dogs. Zack asked, "And what happened when you finally got freed?"

The man grinned, "There were two nurses that survived the catastrophe also. They ran from me but eventually I caught up to them. I cut them from ear to ear. The most exciting part for me was that they knew it was coming. They knew it would be painful. They screamed like they were having sex." The man laughed manically.

Zack inquired, "And you killed both of them in cold blood?"

The end of the gun lowered a few more inches. "I killed them, then I had sex with them, then I ate them, in that order." The man put his head back and laughed again.

Zack lifted his gun quickly. Shireen dropped to the ground. Zack took a shot and hit the man in the hand. His gun dropped.

Drake took a shot from behind and hit the dark man in the side of the head. Suddenly, the dogs jumped on him as he fell to his knees.

Shireen raced as fast as she could across the

yard towards Zack. The dark man grabbed his gun again and aimed it at her back.

A shot rang out. Eddie fired a bullet into the man's chest. He dropped face down onto the lawn. Drake, Granger and Brian came out through the back door. Zack questioned Drake about the others. He told him they'd all be fine.

32

The thermometer had risen to near seventy degrees during the days. Six weeks passed, full of constant labor, day and night. Everyone pitched in to help.

The survivors had moved into six separate homes throughout the subdivision in Citrus Hills, all located on North Page Avenue.

Drake, Granger and Brian spent their days travelling around to nearby cities to find building materials and other supplies.

Their new planned community, which they eventually built a wall around to keep unwanted predators out, consisted of twenty-seven sound homes, vegetable gardens, two lakefronts, working wells and septic systems. The entire vision was designed by Eddie.

As the weeks passed and everyone got to know each other better. Several of the survivors began construction of a barn in the center of the unused land, an old golf course. Eventually, the golf course was turned into a pasture to keep Gwen and Irwin's ranch of horses.

Drake and Eddie began construction on a greenhouse where they could grow citrus and other plants that wouldn't be able to flourish the cooler weather.

The survivors expanded their community with a small schoolhouse that doubled as a church on Sundays. They created a working farm from animals they found wandering in the wild. Soon, the farm consisted of cows, pigs, chickens and goats. Brian, Alice and the rest of the children took care of the livestock.

Drake and Katie got to know Carolyn better, promising her Christmas would not be spent alone ever again. Carolyn was gratified when Drake handed her Maximillian, the Miniature Schnauzer. Her first words to him were, "Hello, Mr. Max, I'm going to be your new mommy."

William and Emily began to get closer to Carolyn too. That Christmas Eve everyone gathered together in a huge hall near the golf course. A tall tree was cut down and decorated. The traditional Christmas hymns were sung and homemade gifts were exchanged. They celebrated and gathered at a long table with a hearty meal that was prepared by

Katie, Alice and Eleanor.

Soon, Alice was pregnant again while she was still nursing little Rosa, with many more babies to follow. The community began to grow quickly when Katie, Shireen and Eleanor announced they were also expecting. Soon, William turned one of the unused homes into a hospital.

Eddie and Drake started working on the old golf carts from the country club. They were able to find dozens of batteries and, soon, the residents of Citrus Hills were driving the carts around the streets of their community.

The earthquakes continued to shake the ground on a regular basis and they still lived with a fear that things could change in the flash of an eye. The acid rain seemed to vanish and develop into normal precipitation again. The days were filled with over seven hours of sunshine and the evenings were quiet and cool.

It was a beautiful April morning in Florida when Drake talked Zack into going for a ride to the west coast of the state. They invited Katie and Shireen along.

The foursome rode out of their protected community and to the coast. They arrived at the new beaches that were located only ten miles away, where Crystal River used to be.

Drake and Zack decided to see if it was safe to go in the water. The two women sat on the beach watching the men go in. As they swam around, they saw a great deal of marine life that had survived the mini-ice age.

Eventually, Drake and Zack got out of the water and sat down on the sand next to Katie and Shireen. Shireen turned to Zack and remarked, "It's a whole new world for us. Do you like it better than the old one, Mr. Gunslinger?"

Zack chuckled and nodded his head. "This one is much better, Dog Lady."

Drake smiled and said, "It's like that island I always wanted to go to when I wanted to get rid of the world."

Katie mentioned, "The other day Emily asked me how I could like this uncertain world better than the world we came from. I told her the old world was just as uncertain, if not more. We had natural disasters then, but we also had pollution, wars, drugs, murders, crooked politicians running our governments and so many other things. This world is just between us and mother nature. And this world will gradually grow into the old world in a few thousand years. I'm just glad I won't be here to see it again."

Shireen nodded, "It's funny. My entire life I found it easier to relate to my dogs and cats and birds than I related to humans. When everything happened and I met all of you, that changed. I could actually talk to people and care about people the same way I care about my dogs. I say goodbye to the old world, good riddance."

Zack gazed at Shireen and joked, "Yeah, I thought you were a little crazy when I first met you. Actually, I still do."

Shireen giggled and returned with, "Back at you, big guy."

He continued, "But you eventually became the one. The one I couldn't find in San Antonio, no matter how hard I tried. This meteor shower was meant to be and we were all meant to meet and be together, forever."

Drake stood up and looked out over the gulf, towards the tall mountains. He took in a long deep breath and closed his eyes. "No, this is it guys. We spent a lot of time on those interstates. We lost some of our comrades much too soon. I'm not lying when I say I still miss my friendship with Porsha. She was the one I started this entire journey with. Then, our young Granger lost sweet Naomi who was like a mother to him. Tony was a great guy. I remember the look on his face when he tried to save Naomi and Debra from that gorge and realized he was going to die too. He had a look of panic and, at the same time, he had an air of acceptance and

peace. Then, I believe the worst days were when we
had to watch William and Emily suffer as Carly
slowly slipped away, with Maddie having lost Peter
just the night before. And as we got here, we nearly
lost Carolyn too. We had to set all their souls free to
arrive here safely. Maybe that was God's plan for us
all along. They were never meant to come here to
Citrus Hills. They were only there to facilitate us
and guide us on our way. We have all of them to
thank for our safe passage and I'll never forget any
of them."

Katie announced, "I do thank them every
day when I kneel down and pray. They'll always be
in our hearts. I just wish we could do more, so no
one ever forgets them."

Drake pulled his journal from his top pocket.
"I can do more. I can keep writing it all down and
make sure we read it from time to time. They were
six angels sent to us but everyone here showed such
bravery and strength. I'm going to create a book we
can share to remember how we got to Citrus Hills
and what we sacrificed along the way."

Zack kissed Shireen on the cheek, put his
arm around her and they stared out at the orange
sunset. Drake shoved his journal back in his pocket
and snuggled up to Katie. He looked at her and said,
"I love you, Katie."

Made in the USA
Middletown, DE
09 January 2022

58234544R00248